ECHO OF THE
SILENCE

ALI TAREQUE

Arrow Books

Director of Marketing: Amy Moore
Executive Editor: Mary Wilson

Cover Designer: Sabyasachi Hazra

Published by Arrow Books
2967 Dundas St. W Suite 675
Toronto ON M6P 1Z2
Canada
Arrow Books
P.O. Box 446
Alief TX 77411

Echo of the Silence
ISBN 979-8-9884094-1-0
Library of Congress Cataloging-in-Publication Data

Echo of the Silence by Ali Tareque
Library of Congress Control Number: 2023913660
Printed in the United States of America.

ECHO OF THE SILENCE

To my late father *Md Abdul Halim*
who could exalt from a world worlds apart

Contents

I

A PROLOGUE FOR PENELOPE

Penelope peeks into the box of a dozen bare, wooden pencils on her desk. Her daily ritual of caressing them—and maybe the stagnated smog from the overcast marital weather in her room—gives a distinct hue to the shafts, which don't look like real wood. In the colorless embossing, each pencil claims to be of different hardness. Or softness. Penelope sharpened them and left them in the acrylic box to mingle with each other. She has only ever put three into work. In return for their service, they have earned extra room to jiggle along their length. To jiggle, and to get noisy by knocking on the transparent walls side to side. Not that Penelope is at any liberty at this moment to let those three actually get noisy and breach the midnight sleep that Jacobi has taken for granted. Three decades of sharing a room—and a bed most of that time—crystallizes some expectations and makes questioning them no longer an option.

Two of Penelope's active wooden writing charges are #2s, and the other is a #3. She has no particular reason for using one over another on any given day. But every day, before writing, she shuffles through all twelve with her fingers and settles on one of these three.

It has been just a year since she started writing with pencils, since she attended a writers' conference in the city. A prominent author, as prominent as Penelope herself but younger by at least two decades, presented the audience a dozen "good" reasons to use pencils over pens. Or computers. Exactly twelve reasons, no more, no less. He probably came up with the number "twelve" before coming up with the twelve reasons. Some of them were probably just fillers, but Penelope did not find them easy to weed out. She found none of them particularly convincing. To add to the futility of this rather contrived habit, not a single one of her previous books has been written in pencil. She has twenty-something published books now, lined shoulder-to-shoulder under the hutch of her writing desk, arranged in no particular order. It has been a year since her last book came out and spawned a lukewarm response relative to the earlier few. It has been just about a year that she has failed to finish, or even significantly start, another. Even her promise to Madison, her agent, of a date for a first draft in a few weeks sounds no less a travesty than her newly adopted pencil ritual.

There was a peculiar force with which that other author campaigned for pencils. It could have just been a little side speech in an attempt to insulate himself from his impending midlife writer's blues. Despite his rather charming graying sideburns, he couldn't have been much more than forty. Or it could have just been an innocent con to score some brownie points as a presenter. But he spoke with a gumption that led her to purchase this assortment of pencils. The impetus was to purchase them, not use them.

Later, she discovered a thirteenth reason, the only one she cared about, and formed a little speech of her own: "When I shuffle through them, I get strength, a drive. They lie there, ready to produce words at my command. Three of them in the war zone and the rest waiting in the reserve ranks, not fought with but not uninitiated, either. I need the reserves no less than the ones on active duty. They will always be there, for me to know that I will never be out of words. If I ever get tired of my words, I can just throw the box away."

Rehashing her little speech in her head, Penelope grumbles. This pretentious idea of garnering strength from pencils, which she sells to her audiences as a discovery, was her own invention. There was really nothing to discover, however, and nothing in fact was discovered. Still, it's a ritual she follows only so that she can gain, and sustain, a similar kind of "gumption" as the author who advocated for the use of pencils when it is her turn to stand at the lectern.

But was that it? How is it, then, that she distinctly remembers the 3rd of his twelve reasons to use pencil, that he mentioned to have quoted from the owner of a famous pencil manufacturer? Something to the effect of leaving a pencil in a drawer, and when you are very old, and you want to give something to your great-grandchild, you pull out that pencil, which still works. This old hutch of her desk hides a Dixon Ticonderoga that she has carried for a shade over forty years. It wasn't a gift, but its owner left this only, albeit incidental, memento before disappearing from her life.

Today, fingering through her three used pencils, Penelope feels spent. She pushes the box away and curls her fingers into a fist. The center of her palm hurts. For a moment, she wants to risk piercing her palm with those pitiless fingernails. She opens her hand to examine her nails, neatly painted red. The red shines in the light from her lamp, and Penelope smiles. It is not her nails' fault that she painted them red. She again shuffles through her box of "soldiers," trying to repress the restlessness that makes her knuckles shiver. She picks up a new pencil and shuts the box with a loud click that sounds more decisive than angry. That spawns a soft ruffle from the bed, where Jacobi is asleep.

She places the tip of the pencil on the writing pad and waits for distraction to give way. Instead, however, she reads the imprint on the pad left by her writing on the previous page. Her eyes wander to the body of the pencil, which carries a few embossed letters.

Why am I chasing words in negative spaces?

Penelope pushes the chair away from her desk and stands. Jacobi lies curled under the comforter in silent slumber. She does not call it sleep—it is too quiet for that. She opens the small door on the shelf on the upper right of the hutch and produces a pack of Virginia Slims and a lighter, stowed away under a single paperback. She drops them in her gown's pocket and, keeping an eye at Jacobi, shuts the little door. It makes its usual squeak at the end, but Jacobi does not move.

Penelope picks up her shawl from the floor, wraps herself, and walks out to the balcony. She looks up for a moon that she knows she will not find. The tiny bit of sky suffocatingly sandwiched by the surrounding buildings was half-occupied by the branch of a tree. The narrow strip of sky merely offers her a few dim dots of stars. She burns through half the cigarette and throws it in a spiraling glow of red through the dark nook of the tree. She returns to her desk to find the fresh recruit standing at attention.

"Jennifer," scribbles Penelope, if only to drown out the shadow words of her previous page.

* * *

A small lady springs up, carrying a bulging stomach, which has already borne four children, one of them a miscarriage. She seeks comfort in her green flip-flops, her big toes split from the smaller ones and trying to get back together. Her golden hair, bound into a bun, makes her round face even rounder. A few strands of stray hair sway in the wind from the revolving fan on the floor and float in front of her face, which is thickly covered in makeup. The breeze spreads the heavy smell of her perfume and reminds her that this is a flower shop, after all. Her edgy red lipstick fails to conceal the softness of her lips. Her nose wrinkles on both sides when she tries to make a word or two sound funny as she talks to the half a dozen of her charges. She tries to smile at the attempt at humor from a soft-spoken elderly employee, but her heavily lined eyes get misty and reveal that she has not gotten the joke.

* * *

Penelope does not use erasers, a tip she picked up at the same writers' conference. Everything you write attains a life, and given a chance to live, it can come back to you. You don't know who comes, and when, but when one does, you may appreciate that it did. Or something similarly tacky like that. Penelope crosses out Jennifer's name with a neat single strike, and the green slippers clatter away over the sticky floor, but a whiff of the petite flower shop manager's perfume wafts through those eight letters and lingers in Penelope's room, suffocating her. She looks away to catch some breath, but realizes she will have to come back to the page, to the line right beneath those eight letters, the portal to the smothering memory of that perfume. Jennifer is not altogether an unreal person. No characters are. She has memories of all of them, some of which bring a jovial mood, some sad, and some yet other emotions. This one, to which she ascribes the appellation Jennifer, elicits a rather morbid and depressive timbre in her mental fabric. Not everything that one lets live necessarily leaves one alone, after all. Penelope wants to break her year-old habitude and erase those eight letters to seal that portal and push it out of her mind. But she cannot gather the energy to look for an old eraser that still might be hiding in ignominy somewhere in the maze on her desk.

She clenches her teeth and writes on the next line: "Sarah."

* * *

The girl in her early twenties does not have much of a bottom. And it shows, even though, or maybe because, she wears a pair of baggy jeans. Do they still sell those pleated pants that were everywhere a few years back? Her smile is sweet, and the way she walks, stooping a little like someone convalescing from a prolonged sickness, makes her look very vulnerable. Her eyes are pensive. Her hands are thin and pale, and her fingers look kind with their reddish knuckles. Her sneakers clod along big and heavy under her gaunt body, almost offering an excuse for her slow gait. This morning she was late again at the burger joint The pitiful frailty of her body does not dissuade her manager. Not more than a little, anyway.

But her watery eyes, her sweet and feeble voice, have endeared her to the younger assistant manager, who, at every chance, tries to do small favors for her. He lets her take more than her fair share of left-over foods for her two daughters and her mom, who watches them. The young man's boyish eyes make Sarah want to kiss his forehead, but she senses they are so eager to misconstrue her intention that she fears to even return his smiles. She has seen so much in her not-so-long life, of which he will not want to know most, if any. But she takes care to wear lipstick and spends an extra few seconds checking her hair on the sun visor mirror in her car whenever he is on the roster with her. It is a small favor in return for blowing a waft of fresh air that touches her dark, putrid, humongous cave of a life.

* * *

Penelope now *does* look for an eraser. The top of her desk is a battle-field, and it protects her from her little offense. Her shoulders sag in frustration. She bends over the page and intently strikes three times through the five letters on the second line.

"Julie." Penelope writes each of the letters with distinct pauses be-tween them.

She looks up at the two names she has crossed out and smiles. She cannot do this all night. Even though that would be going against what she advises in her lectures, "Keep trying until you get the right word, even if it takes you the whole night." But she barely has the whole night to do this. Jacobi will soon turn over to his right side to reach for her receding bumps. She doesn't mind that he won't find them. But his grumble will break into the little bit of quiet she has patiently crafted for this night. Not too many nights before the date, she had promised Madison. Is it the twenty-third today? Five weeks to go? Six? And she is still playing with names.

She traces her pencil on the five letters on the third line and digs into the period at the end. "Julie."

* * *

Julie rubs behind her left ear with her index finger and lets a smile spread on her face. The wrinkles beside her eyes deepen. John patiently awaits her response. His wild beard and thick glasses do not give him away, but Julie knows that, behind his carefully maintained inscrutability, he smiles at her indecisiveness. His tall body stands even taller in his over-sized leather jacket. Her neck hurts from looking up at his shaggy face, which seems to almost hang from the ceiling.

"Honey, you go ahead and pick the place," she mumbles as she dances her pen between her index and middle finger.

"But it's your turn." He doesn't even try to be subtle in his playfulness. She was too engrossed in writing, and he knows that she can't quite focus on what he says.

"I know." She lifts the pen and plows it through her curls. "But I can't think of any. Why don't you just pick some place and let me know before you step out?"

She waits to detect movement in his face. He doesn't budge.

"Or if you give me a few more minutes, I might come up with something."

"It's okay, baby," he says as he puts his cap on. "I had Greenz in mind. You like their warm pear and pecan salad, don't you?"

"Oh, that's a great choice. You are such a sweetheart."

"And I hope that young waiter is back from school." John's voice is deadpan. "And his heartbreak for you is mended by now."

"Oh honey, don't start that."

"No, I will let you be."

John stoops over for a kiss, to which Julie instinctively offers her right cheek.

"Call me," he says over his shoulder as he heads for the door.

Julie anxiously awaits the security beeps that will confirm John's exit, as if her thoughts will somehow manage to swim over to him. She lets Hank, the young waiter, walk in front of her in his impeccably white shirt and slick black apron, but does not let him speak until the ice-crunching sound of John's heavy steps fade away from the porch.

Julie drops a sigh in the air and her pen on the pad and goes to the kitchen to fill up her mug. The coffee tastes bitter; it has been in the pot for a while. She stirs in half a spoon of sugar. Through the miniblind over the kitchen sink, it's sunny outside, and glare from the ice on the neighbor's roof flashes on her face from across the street.

Hank tried to hit on her both times they were at Greenz, last summer. Actually, hitting would be an overstatement. He was shy as a squirrel. John and Julie meet for lunch every Tuesday, taking turns picking the place. Julie was the first to pick Greenz. That day, she arrived a few minutes before John, and had a little chat with Hank. His smooth, almost shiny cheeks on his gaunt face made his big eyes look defenseless, and he could barely look at her. He asked what she wanted to drink and if she wanted anything else before her guest arrived.

"Just water, please."

"Ice?"

Julie looked past him for a moment in her usual distraction. Then, suddenly conscious, she smiled and blushed, for reasons she could not figure out. "Yes, please."

Julie sensed that her smile set something rolling. She could swear Hank lingered for an extra second before leaving. When he returned with her water, he appeared ready for something that he had probably even rehearsed for.

"Your water ..."

Something definitely was present in those two words. Julie looked up inquiringly.

Hank looked back, though the extra effort took quite a toll on his face. "You smile beautifully," he sputtered with an almost robotic finality.

By that time, Julie had changed her mind and wanted an iced tea. But the theatrical demand in Hank's voice for his swift departure was so pressing that she had to forgo the request.

"Oh! Thank you!" she said.

John showed up soon, and for the rest of their time at Greenz, Hank never looked at her again.

The following week, John had a playful smirk on his face as he stated his choice: "What about Greenz?"

"Again? Didn't we go there last week?" Julie didn't sound too sure. "Or was it the week before?"

"No, it was last week. But maybe someone is waiting for his sweetheart. Don't you think so, honey?"

"No one is waiting for anyone. Cut it out, John."

"Are you blushing?"

"I am not!"

"You want me to make you blush?" John narrowed his eyes.

"Don't do that now."

"Why, are you scared?"

"Stop it, John, will you?"

She blushed, and both of them knew that she was not blushing for the reason they were talking about, and both of them knew that John would not acknowledge that, and both of them knew that Julie would have to get physical to stop him.

She stood and pushed John on the chest with both hands as she said, "Stop it. Stop it. Stop it now."

John laughed and held Julie in his arms, and dropped onto the bed with her. They made love. That made John a little late to work that morning, but he did not mind being late once in a while. As the owner of the boutique architect firm in midtown, he knew that his handful of charges did not mind a relaxed morning once in a while sans their top boss.

Later that day at Greenz, when John went to the restroom—which could very well have been simply a playful gesture—Hank came over with the look of a fawn caught in the middle of an open glade. He mumbled that he was going out of town to college the following week and wouldn't be back until next summer.

"It was nice meeting you." It sounded like he was going to follow up with a "please come again," but instead he looked down. After a moment passed, and then another, he looked into her eyes.

"Is he your husband?"

"Why do you ask?"

"Can I talk to you?" Hank couldn't hide the tremor in his voice, even if he had tried.

"What do you mean?"

"Can I have your number?" He paused and flushed massively. "Or I can give you my number, if you prefer."

Before Julie could let her preference be known, John returned and tried to assess the state of affairs. The waiter looked like a freshly budding leaf on a shaken rose bush, but Julie simply looked amused. John concluded that his game, if there was one, was a success, and, as if to put a proper end to the fun, he asked for the check.

When Hank returned with the receipt and bade them good-bye, he looked more composed.

"It was nice to see you," John said earnestly. "Hope to see you soon again."

"Actually I am going to college ... out of town ... next week. It was a pleasure serving you, sir."

"Oh, is that true?" John made himself sound slightly disappointed. "Don't worry. We'll be around." He smiled.

* * *

Penelope drops the pencil, tries to kill a yawn, and sips from her mug. The stale coffee is also now cold; the little bit of sugar she added is too weak to fight both offenses. She tiptoes around the bed to face Jacobi. His fat cheek has dug into his hand. He snores softly, and from his open mouth a tiny rivulet trickles onto his wrist, and from there to the pillow. She returns to her desk less discreetly than she left it.

* * *

"What are you writing?" John asks Julie, as he comes home from work. He isn't really all that curious about Julie's writing, but once in a while his sense of spousal duty strikes. Julie never lacks enthusiasm to talk about her work though.

Until today, that is.

"It's ... it's about a young student," she stutters, before correcting herself, "Well, not that young." She does not explain how young the student is not, and looks at John to see how much damage she has managed to prevent. But John is already in the bathroom now, washing his hands and face, the door half opened.

"Shouldn't you get some sleep?" John half-heartedly asks as he gets in the bed. "Want a back massage? You must be very tired, all this writing."

Julie does not feel like making love now, but it's a nice opportunity to put a period on the subject. What could have been a "Honey, I'll be there in a bit" becomes her jumping up from the chair.

When all is over and, after a few minutes on the bed with Julie's left foot heavily covering John's right foot, the regularity of John's breathing offers the unbreachable assurance of a prolonged lull, and Julie slides out of bed. Her writing pad is burning on the desk. She picks up her pen and writes about a young man. A young man she names Henry.

* * *

Henry hid behind a peach tree that stood alone in the middle of the field, its loneliness compensated by an expanse of overgrown branches and dense, lush leaves. Henry was so intently merged with the tree that he could be just another branch. One that was more branch than the others. One that wanted to be a part of the tree, but ended up over-doing it. The tree itself, not in need of any such pretension, remained content, or even indifferent, with its mundane reality.

Everything arboreal about Henry was exaggerated. His overgrown beard and hair assumed the look of shrubs creeping over his emaciated, hairless torso. Through the thick of the intruding vegetation, his chest burnt in the sun and acquired the brown tinge of a branch. The large and deep chaps on his skin resembled tree bark from a distance. His worn clothes, which only covered his arms and his loin, were green with moss and flapped in the wind with the same abandon as the other leaves. His Adam's apple bifurcated the flow of his beard. His burning eyes, which bore the lust and hunger of a thousand years, could give him away. But his sheer will to keep himself unseen had overgrown his brows and shaded his eyes.

He needed this transformation, because this was the only tree in the vicinity of the pond where he could lurk to quench his voyeurism. The field was on the grounds of a castle. He learned to elude the eyes of the guards, but he needed more anonymity to escape the auspices of the bathers in the pond. The playful nymphets could sneak into him in a hundred different ways, and the slightest hint was enough to give him away.

Among them, there was one who had the keenest of senses. A priest's daughter, who had the most beautiful hands. But she also had the most beautiful waist and most beautiful nape and the most vulnerable lips. Her eyes were contemplative and serenely happy. He never saw her breasts, because her hands or hair were always in the way. Henry wondered if she always knew he was there, behind the tree. She never glanced this way, not even in passing.

One morning, the girls at the pond raced to the tree. A lonesome peach on a branch had ripened and glowed like a sun, red and orange, against a sky, lush and green. The girls bet each other about reaching the tree and plucking the fruit. The winner was to take over for one of the other girls scheduled to serve the overlord that night. They rushed through the meadow. Their skin had been made tender under the water, and the thick grass blades were rough on their soles. They yelped and gasped. But they laughed, too. They laughed more than they ran. Their fresh, wet skin glittered against the sky, and the droplets from their long swinging hair raised a rainbow in the backdrop; their giggles rang through the air and their bare breasts bobbed merrily against the sun.

The priest's daughter did not join them. She stood, waist deep in the water, and gathering all her hair over her right shoulder, she covered the side of her breast, looked sideways toward the mischievous girls, and let play a coyness in her eyes that felt almost redundant.

Henry knew the other girls would not recognize him even if they were to unwittingly touch him. He extended his arm, plucked the prize peach, and hid it under his loincloth. The girls were too occupied wading through the morning air and glittering in the morning sun. They reached the tree breathless and fell to the earth, crumbling among the roots. They had a winner, but there was no peach to pluck.

"Where did it go?"

"I told you there was no peach on the tree."

"You did not!"

"And you! Don't tell me you haven't plucked it already? You might own the race, but you cannot have the peach all to yourself."

"I didn't! Why would I do that?"

They fought with their guiltless unreasonableness, pushed and yelled at each other, then started to laugh again. Walking back toward the pond, their cooled, bare bodies shivered and, when one of them realized that she could run, she ran, the others followed suit.

The priest's daughter was swimming near the middle of the pond. They shouted at her and splashed into the water. She waved in an invitation to join her, but no one was bold enough to go that far from shore. The pond was big and deep, true, but more foreboding were the legends of demons lurking in the middle. Only the priest's daughter could brave those feared fables.

Henry knew where the priest lived, and where his daughter's room was. That night, after the moon sank behind the woods, he stopped by her window. His heartbeats made the trees throb under the thick mesh of stars. He left the peach on the ledge where she sat every day to enjoy the sunset.

The following night, the peach was still on the ledge, untouched. Henry rubbed his mossy hands until a thin layer of green dust accumulated beside the fruit. The next night, the peach was still there, but the dust had been disturbed, forming an impression of her thighs. Every night from then on, Henry left the green crumbs from his hands, only to find the peach sitting forlorn, and the impression of her thighs on the ledge, until the peach started to rot and its sweet smell turned putrid. When its skin cracked and it commenced its slow implosion, Henry took it. It glopped in his hand and melted around his fingers, but above his head, the moon had taken over its peachy roundness, shining against the dark sky. Henry put the wasted peach on the bank of the pond where the bathers gathered every morning, and waded toward the middle, where only one demon waited.

He did not know how to swim.

II

THE STORY OF JULIE

The minute hand on the wall clock gingerly pushes toward twelve, as the hour hand hovers around two in stocky uncertainty. John's alarm clock draws a sharp picture of the present in glowing red: 2:03. Julie has to consult both to imbue a sense of balance in time.

Late reading of time in the morning frustrates her. It helps to have another account of time that reduces that measure even by a few minutes.

She gets up from the chair and stops by the window. Through the parallel slits of the blinds, the world outside is gray. She inserts her fingers between two of the panels and widens the opening. It is empty outside. She lingers for a few seconds until things form in the void: a black sky, and a street below it. Across the street, a house materializes, and then two others appear on both sides. This grows into a full row. On this side of the double glass windowpane, the nascent outdoors seems quiet, and she can hear John's soft snoring. It is not quite a snore, but the heavy and rhythmic sound of breathing. She looks at him. He has curled a bit more. His tall body has contracted to such baby-like smallness that Julie wants to comb her fingers through the locks on his neck. But she doesn't risk her solitude.

She walks in soft steps around the bed in front of John, seeking a spot to sit. John has this habit of shifting toward the side of the bed when he sleeps. Sometimes, his knees or hands hang over the edge. But he never falls. Now there is a gap between his folded knees and bent head, but not enough to squeeze into. She considers whether taking her robe off would help.

She undoes the belt and spreads her robe over him. She imagines herself a giant albino bat, white wings wide open, and feels like a nymph given to adolescent whims. John's breath now howls through the circle made by his chest, stomach and lap, creating a whirl in the small closure. Julie's flimsy bat wings flutter, and the little hairs on her body stand up. Julie pushes aside the robe and squeezes in the opening of the sleeping gusts. This smothers the storm just as a small spring gushes and spreads somewhere in that concourse.

* * *

Penelope sits up and tries to come to terms with her breath. A sensation that she hasn't experienced for quite a few years has suddenly started to claim its erogenous grasp on her body. When her breath syncs with that of dozing Jacobi's, she flips back through the pages she just wrote. A faint query tries to swim up and surface through the defense that Penelope's mind has set up with words—the words that conjure her stories. To push that query back into the depths of her quandary, she marshals her mind into editing.

She strikes out a few words; elsewhere she squeezes new ones in between lines. At one place she chips in two whole sentences, carrying over several lines into the margin, and then she draws circles around them to keep them from mixing up with other corrections. They hang precariously in that feeble sack, and a few longish words here and there poke at the flimsy wall, threatening to tear through their coerced existence. She feels safer. But only for a moment. She can feel that query pressing its adamant head and threatening to breach her long-held bastion.

She flips back through her pages again to scour for another bout of distraction. But this time, all she can see is that miserable question peeking back at her.

Julie. Julie. Who is Julie? What is she doing here?

Why can't she write her own story? Why does she need Julie? Isn't it her own story? The one of Henry's? Or is it?

Doesn't matter. It doesn't matter whose story it is. It's too intense, and Penelope cannot gaze back at them and see them as they are.

Forty years is a long time. All these years, she has sailed a route that, despite its twists and tortuousness, has led her to a certain archipelago that precludes exposing herself to these emotions. Julie is her protection from that exposure. But Penelope cannot be sure if she can carry on much longer. It has started to weigh on her and tax her mind. For a moment, she contemplates tearing up those pages and taking over the story herself. She grabs them between her thumbs and index fingers and starts pulling.

But something stops her half-way. Her mouth curls in bitterness. It's a life that has advanced a little too much. It's a character, a protagonist, her own creation. But more than that, it's a person that she has been denying herself for way too long. She can no longer pluck it from its existence. She can play with it, take it to places, offer it a fate, but she has led it to a destination from where it's too painful to be done with.

Julie needs to stay.

Penelope smooths the tears at the tops of those pages and writes, "Julie writes ..."

* * *

Henry sat on a stone bench in a park, his bronze skin peeking through dusty white clothes. He wanted to rest in silence, but the wind was too high and fluttered his robe as if to swoop him up and fly him through the branches of the trees that were dancing in the impending gale.

A girl of seventeen or so sat with a man on a nearby bench, a straw bassinet at their feet. From the bassinet came sporadic cries that reached Henry even through the wind. If the girl's companion was not her husband, he had to be the father. Each time the little creature cried, the man stooped over. To wiggle his finger into the tiny folds of the neck, Henry thought.

"She likes you," the mother cooed.

"Of course she likes me!"

"Yes, she likes her father."

The man laughed, then slouched on the bench. He looked tired. Very tired. Leaning his head on the backrest, he closed his eyes, and within seconds, dozed off. The girl moved to make room between them and lifted the basket onto the bench. The baby started to whimper. It must have been the wind. The little thing did sound comfortable wrapped in the plush blankets, but still, she was only a baby, and the day was getting chilly. Henry wanted to suggest she not keep the baby outdoors for too long.

As if reading his mind, she turned and, as her eyes hovered on him, the wind receded to a breeze. But then a gust made its way between them.

The girl brightened up with a smile and looked away. She had a smile that was agonizingly beautiful.

As Henry bathed in the pulchritude of the image of her face, he discerned something intriguing in that smile. If the capricious wind of the restless evening carried a hint of invitation in that smile, there was something else that was quite intimate—too intimate, in fact, for a stranger like him. The pain that the beauty of her face evoked in him—a longing that sustained for only a fleeting moment—belied the extent of suffering it caused. Henry unstuck his eyes and let them veer toward the basket, which jerked in short spurts perhaps as the baby kicked its wall. He then looked at the pitiful face of the young father, who had sunk farther into sleep, his mouth agape.

Henry stayed put, but this was not a complete retreat. Her smile had breached his reserve; he looked back at her. She was small, a little chubby. Her bosom was in good proportion with the rest of her body, but it was no doubt gorged with milk. Her small hands were well-shaped, and her fingers, joined together in the cold, had taken the roundness of a de-thorned cactus leaf. Her nape was gorgeous in her little postpartum plumpness, but her shoulders were too short to decline elegantly. Maybe she was just cold, and she tried to brace herself. His heart filled with pity. He wanted to hold her hands and kiss her shoulders.

A gust of wind made her shiver.

She looked back again. And smiled again, a smile about a secret that only two people shared. Yet only the girl played a part in their shared act; Henry merely caught gawking and having thoughts about touching her. His embarrassment was only to the world that excluded himself and the girl. But somehow she found a way to live in that world at the same time, and he was embarrassed to get caught in her eyes, too, so he failed to smile back. The girl, who shared with him their secret, seemed to enjoy his travail.

By the time Henry brought himself to smile back, she had already turned away. Her long braid swung in the air, and something hard at its end struck the backrest, raising a clank that jolted the dad from his slumber. He slowly got up and stretched. The girl stood, too. She looked even smaller on her feet. The dad, a head taller, seemed to notice Henry only in passing. He lifted the basket and led the little family away from where Henry sat. The wind picked up, the tall trees swaying wildly against the dying light. Long branches whipped and whistled through the air. Under the wailing trees, the girl's long skirt and shawl fluttered, causing her to appear ruffled like a sparrow. She stopped for a second to gather herself and looked back at Henry one final time. She did not smile, as if that were not necessary. The bridge was built, and the creek had been crossed. Through squinted eyes, which struggled against the smarting gusts, she looked at him with calmness, and concern. Any bar that could have kept him from following her was now drowned.

He maintained his distance. The girl never looked back; she knew her stalker would not relinquish her. Her nonchalance was stronger than the ensuing storm, and it caused his heart to brood. He was afraid of losing her. He followed them like a ghost-ridden soul. After a long walk through the endless rows of trees and then through the streets deserted to the howling wind, they stopped in front of a large house. In the burgeoning dusk, they stood for a moment, and the man tried to kiss her on her mouth. She turned her head and let the kiss land on her cheek. Lightning struck a tree somewhere, and thunder followed, accompanying the sting in Henry's heart. When he recuperated from that sharp bite of jealousy, he realized that the girl had turned her head not only to evade the kiss, but now she was looking directly at him. Even from this distance, he spotted the eerie calmness in her eyes that had dragged him this far along.

The father handed the bassinet over to her and, opening a small inset door on the stately gate, disappeared inside. The door clanged shut loudly against the metal frame. Henry waited for the girl to look back at him, but instead, she turned left, and through the rapidly descending darkness, scuttled as fast as she could, clutching the basket close to her stomach, until she disappeared.

Darkness grew by the second. Henry darted toward the big house. Before lunging into the dark alley on the left of the imperious home, Henry stopped for a moment and looked at the house. A few large drops of water pelted his face and shoulders. He spotted the father of the baby on a balcony on the second floor. He held a woman in an embrace that kept her richly ornate dress from flapping in the gale. He tried to kiss her mouth, her face, and her neck and pried his hand into her chest until it got lost beneath her blouse. The lady tried to stave off his intrusion but did not let go of his embrace.

Henry stood as if in a trance. A few more drops splashed around him, and the evening suddenly halted. Wind swirled for a last time and died on the ground, and the rain started pouring. At that moment, the woman caught sight of Henry. She flushed and slowly but resolutely pushed the young man away. The young man followed her gaze.

Henry slipped into the dark alley, now soaked by the relentless raindrops. The lane led him to an endless number of other lanes, each one gloomier than the one he just exited. A few houses let bleak squares of yellow light seep through their measly windows, but they were so dim that they thinned and dispersed in the rain before reaching the ground.

The sudden turns and unpredictable lengths of the lanes did not let his movement settle into a pattern. The lack of geometric monotony kept him going. But there was also this flitting smell that the rain kept washing down.

Henry followed the smell of milk that exuded from the baby's mouth. He discerned another smell that, as he walked along, was particular to the mother and that evoked a blend of colors and shapes: the smoothness of her pale skin, the roundness of her petite body, the dullness of her unkempt hair, and the stark vivacity of her smile that had been at the same time coquettish and kind. He followed that smell down lanes that grew darker and narrower. The houses' walls were drenched and they drained thin plains of water from the gutters that welled up.

Rodents appeared. At first, they made their presence known in furtive rushes along the walls, and then with bolder darts across the lanes. The occasional squares of yellow light now deserted the night altogether. Henry's feet splashed through rainwater that now streamed from one side to the other. Still, the smell never went away. Suddenly the rain let up, just as he reached the end of the labyrinth. He found a "T," and a wave of wind brushed over his face from his right. He turned, and the lane ended after a few short steps, leading him to an open field.

The air was fresh, the wind cool and wet. He took a deep breath. The smell that he had sought was replaced by that of wet earth. He turned to have a look inside the maze behind him. Wind was sucked in the pitch dark vortex. There was no point going back. He could not have outrun the wind that drove away the smell he had been chasing.

Henry was lost. He had been lost for a while, but he was also running away from that realization. The artless gray of the dark expanse that laid in front of him smacked him in the face in the form of a gust of fresh wind. He looked at the sky for orientation. The rain was over, but the sky was still covered in clouds. He came out of the alley and stepped into the open field. The grasses were higher and tougher than they appeared. It took him quite an effort to venture a few steps in. When he turned back, he could suddenly see the Castle tower soaring behind the city houses toward his left. He could not make out which direction that was, but decided to walk toward it. He had never been to the Castle, but headed toward the safety of its collective familiarity.

He continued along the city border. On his left, tall, wild grass kept the swampy land out of sight. On his right, stocky and angry-looking houses stood shoulder-to-shoulder to conjure up a defense that repulsed and attracted him at the same time. Wind whooshed in and out of the intermittent alley-mouths, making the whole skid row look like a huge monster lying prone in a cool slumber. Henry walked on the line, crossing occasional backwoods pushing into the purlieu, fermenting dumps, thick and steamy pools from the city sewer outlets.

The walk to the Castle was long. Stars popped as the sky cleared, and Henry now knew how to find his way. But he did not stop his march for the Castle. Neither did he give up on the stars. He looked at them and tried to connect a few dots. He tried to think of the relationship between the young mother and the young man. He was not her husband. A thought budded that the young man was not the child's father, either, despite what the girl had said. He did not know why, but as he closed in on the Castle, Henry became further convinced of that. The city frontier started to clear out. The houses became sparser, and grassland took over the suburban interruptions.

As the Castle rose against the horizon at a quicker pace, Henry wondered about the baby's father. He did not want to see the mother anymore. First, he tried to remember a face that he had seen a long time ago, one that he always remembered whenever he thought about the Castle. He could never find a connection between the face and the Castle, but it always happened. Henry knew the irrelevance of this random recollection to the father he was looking for, but he had to start from somewhere.

In any case, there was nothing intrinsic to that face that commanded his attention for long. So, he discarded it and tried to recall another face. Then another. He browsed through all the faces he had ever seen from all the places he had ever been and tried to think of who could be the father. As if he were looking for a mark on a face that would tell him without a sliver of doubt that that was indeed the baby's father.

It was hopeless, and Henry knew it. But this irrepressible urge to know the answer jostled him through the myriad of faces. He rushed through all the images over and over again. He could not keep them out of his head, and they started to move around at such a frantic pace that his head spun, causing him to stumble and fall. He hurt his knees and his elbows, but the fall cleared his head.

As he staggered back to his feet, in front of him the large gray castle loomed against the backdrop of the clear sky, escorted by Orion on its left and Cassiopeia on its right.

III

A QUEST FOR A FATHER

Henry's odyssey to find the baby's father started at daybreak. The sun shone brightly and soon dried up the moisture left by the night's downpour. The puddles on the roads shrank into mud, and mud hardened into cakes that dried so fast they cracked with soft pops all over the streets, sounding like a hive full of buzzing honeybees from a distance. The fine dust from the tiny explosions rose up with the air warmed and lightened by the heat, got baked in the sun and found places in the throats, eyes and nostrils of pedestrians, squeezing out moisture from their mouths and burning the backs of their noses. Henry plodded through that morning haze, his effort to search for the father equal to the quest for a sip of cool water.

He walked along the whole length of the castle by its outer wall and reached a marketplace. Inside, it was so saturated with noise that it felt as if all the sound from the torturous outside was rounded up within its boundary. Shoppers and storekeepers raised their voices to drown the shouts of others in their relentless bid to be heard; the others did the same. They bawled at the top of their voices. They waved their hands frantically. They toiled, they labored, and they perspired. The heat of the day mingled their evaporated sweat with the dust that got kicked up from the earthen aisles and brewed a thick concoction that connected each individual with all the others. It was the temptation for this poisoned soup of fraternization that sucked Henry inside the marketplace more than anything else. Anything else except for his quest.

He trudged through the rowdy miasma. In front of some stores, the customers looked up to the storekeepers, who held their fort behind the safety of high benches, advertising their goods and haggling for prices. In stores where no shoppers crowded, sellers pressed their thighs against the benches to stoop over and shout about their wares in a high pitch.

Henry stopped in front of a cloth store. The storekeeper's voice was already hoarse, the rest of the day still looming. He offered Henry a smile that bore no intention to read Henry's face.

"What would you like to see, sir?" He waved his hand like a magician as if he was going to produce, from the thin air, whatever Henry wanted.

Henry looked about the shelves behind the keeper, and his eyes caught sight of a roll of emerald-colored cloth on the top shelf.

"How much is that cloth? That green one?"

The storekeeper hurriedly started to lift the roll of cloth from the shelf.

"Don't bother taking it down. Just tell me the price."

"No, sir! You got to see this ... the best silk you will find in the whole market. And you need to touch it to really know what I am talking about."

He produced a narrow rickety tool from behind his high bench and set it below the shelf. When he stepped on it, staggering on his one foot, Henry left the store. Henry wanted to ask him questions, but the storekeeper had no answer to offer. The storekeeper was in a spell that he needed to be in to sell his goods. He could not afford to break that spell. Henry needed nothing of that.

He passed through the rows of jewelers, through the grocers, the fishmongers, the meat market and the produce stalls. He was tempted to stop and ask questions. But it would only have served the purpose of the asked, not him, the asker. As he tore himself away from the market-place and hit the dusty roads again, he decided that there was no point in asking. One could only ask questions for the answers one could expect in return. One needed to know the answer to know whom to ask, and where to. By then, one already knew the answer, and there was no reason for asking anymore. Asking questions was either fruitless or meaningless, unyielding or inconsequential.

At the end of the road burnished by the heat, the city floated on its own mirage and, when Henry made it there, his skin was caked with dirt. A bathhouse on the outskirts beckoned. He needed a wash, but he was also looking for a face. In that hour of late morning, the steam rooms were full of old men. The flapping skin of their chests and bellies and necks hung from their body. They breathed in the steam with their eyes closed and yelped as their nostrils burnt in the heat. Their modesty was at the mercy of towels precariously dangling around flabby waists. Their cheeks look craggy, even the ones that were shaved. Their lower lips swelled and hung obscenely in a stupor in their effort to reduce the sting of hot inhalation.

Henry asked them about their offspring. Their dreamy eyes came to life and they talked about their children and their grandchildren with great interest, and to great extent. Some started with a child who was not their first. Some started with a grandchild. The rest followed an order, starting with their firsts. All of them had favorites. They went on telling, and then weaving, stories that yarned around their offspring, and then moved to other stories, of their lives, and then of the lives of others. Slowly, their accounts lost relevance with the children. On some occasions, some story would find its way back to its genesis, and the narrator would attempt to abandon their serendipitous voyages, but not without a great sigh that could only be associated with heart-wrenching farewell.

Those comebacks would not last long, and soon the old men fell prey to other streams of tales. At some point, they would lose track of where they had started and why they had started, and would meander along a path that felt dark, strewn with the rocks and thorns of old-age miseries. They lost the ardor with which they started, and their voices became forceful, then lugubrious, but still dragged over that path with the same force, if not pace, bruising and wounding along the way.

Henry felt the darkness ooze out of their tales and seep inside him. He looked through that gloom as deep as he could, searching for a path that could lead to his answer. But those few and far between flickers of light were too far away. Besides, that anecdotal gloom sapped his energy to proceed. Before he drowned in that grim, wet and dripping labyrinth of ruminations, he tore himself out of the steam room, away from the bath house.

But as he left those steamy ablutionary taverns, the flock of old people brought forth a realization that these were merely his own future self, stranded in a murk of rudderless pursuit to find significance in their own offspring. This truth haunted him like a picture burnt into one's awake mind.

To shake it off, Henry went to prayer halls in search of quietude, sitting on the cool stone floor, where his ankles hurt as he sat with his legs criss-crossed, but his bottom and back cooled against the wall.

He then went to schools and riversides, town offices and whore-houses and all the other corners of the city. When he exhausted all the places, he decided to go out of the city.

* * *

In the fourteen years that he traveled, his intent prevented him from growing old. When he returned, a different city awaited. He had always been a stranger in his own city, which had distanced itself from him, rowing along the current of life. Henry had swum against the flow, and now found his anachronistic travail working in his own favor. He encountered faces that were strange to him and offered the freshness of unfamiliarity. He found places that had been through so much change that he could afford the pleasure of discovering them anew.

The path he took along the river on his way home narrowed, gradually lost its shoulder, and then completely died, leaving him pre-maturely on the bank. The river had shifted and eaten into the riverside market, and with that, the market also shifted. The fish sellers had been near the river. As the river closed in, they were squeezed for space. But beyond the fish stalls stood sheds for rice, onion and potato. They were made of brick, and these owners were the least willing to give room to the fish sellers. They were not to share their space with fish that already reeked as it was. Instead, the fish sellers resituated their stalls to the other side of the market, and squeezed themselves within the thin sliver of land between the market and the street. Wind could not reach from the river passed the whole width of the market to blow away the stink of leftover unsold fishes, and the piles of rotting fish innards.

On the other side of the street stood rows of dilapidated buildings, which the owners rented out for lodging. Their proximity to the market and the river meant that their rooms were in good demand. But as the stench from the enclosed fish market invaded the apartments, they lost tenants.

A feeble conclave of the old landlords went to the fish sellers and asked them to move away from the street. The fish sellers protested that they had no better place to go, and advised the landlords to talk to the store owners' association. The association leaders directed the geriatric clique to the rice, potato and spice sellers. They, in turn, showed the little group the door of the town office, where the remainder of the old landlords lost their way in the dusky maze of hallways, and in the ranks of clerks and their assistants.

Drained, when they stepped out of the building, they were approached by a person, who, despite his corpulence, walked briskly enough to catch up with them from behind. He panted, looked at them sideways and made an act of trying to hide the insignia on his chest with his plump hand. In a whispering voice that smacked of a professional casualness, he introduced himself as a mere Good Samaritan. In exchange for a small amount of money that "could be negotiated later on," he offered a service that would save their rheumatic legs from shuffling along the long corridors of legalities. They accepted it.

The fish sellers only had a few large baskets in their tiny sheds in which to keep the fish. When they closed for the day, they took only their knives and other utensils home.

One morning, a few days after the landlords struck the deal with the portly officer, those large fish baskets and sheds were found broken and scattered. Scores of dead fish lay on the ground in a flood of slimy water.

There is no telling whether a similar kind of deal had been made on the other side, but the following night, the houses on the opposite side of the road came down burning.

When Henry walked along the river, all that was left were the charred foundations and half-burned pillars and crossbeams. Any unscathed lumber had long been carted away. A group of children played hide and seek, and another played pretend-family inside the blackened minimality of the ruins. Henry tried to locate his home in the rubble, but his memory was old, and the fire had erased and rearranged the boundaries beyond repair and beyond trace.

Jostling out onto the street, Henry found his connections with the city in utter disarray. The images of places he thought he knew swarmed and pushed each other behind the curtain of his fading memory. After that brawl among his memories subsided, only two places survived: the castle, and the house of the young man whom the child's mother had addressed as the father. He wanted to see the baby, and he knew of only one place to start from, to reach her. He set out for that house.

The undertaking was difficult. The city had changed so much; so had his memory. As he pushed himself along the estranged streets, occasional old signs would appear familiar: odd old houses that survived the perils of demolition and rebuilding, improvement and makeover, and made it through with the color and trims of their old times intact, sticking out from the backdrop of change in life and change in the memory. Odd concrete road signs broken at the legs, lying on the ground, reading old names in old ways of inscription, telling stories of old times. A tree at the corner of a field, whose crooked branches had interwoven into the shape of a coital position. Now it had overgrown its youth and morphed into a gnarl that was dark, the youthful sensuality replaced by the abstruse confusion of an aged wisdom.

There was a fountain in front of the city center. They had paved new walkways and planted trees along the street in the front. The old wooden walls were replaced with bricks. The fountain was left alone. In fact, it had been repaired. Henry could not remember the fountain working before, just the tip of the small pipe sticking out from the center, no water. The round basin with a decorated rim used to be covered in rotten leaves and garbage thrown by passersby. Once in a while, Henry would clean up the mess with his hands and try to peep into the pipe. It was dark, and the layer of green moss that covered the inside of the pipe made it impenetrable.

Henry used to wonder how the fountain looked when operational and would contrive the most fanciful patterns of streams that no town architect could ever come up with, nor any physicist could have justified being possible. In his fantasy, the water climbed up the sky, making a thin glistening column that reached the clouds, never to come down. Sometimes it spiraled upward and gyrated, its tip ending in spray. He fancied the mist coming down on the hot shoppers in the summer. Other times, he would picture the water columns splitting into three, five or seven tiny streams, going up and flattening like flower petals trembling in a breeze before coming down to cover the whole edge of the basin.

But his dreams were even stranger. In them, the fountain could change its shape, size and color and would come to life. In one dream, he was chased by water in a thick stream. He tried to run away, but the farther he went, the thicker the stream became until it covered him and he felt like he were drowning. Then, suddenly, he turned back, and catching the little breath he was left with, he ran toward the fountain. When he reached the basin, the stream was again small and thin, and it shot toward his groin. It was warm. He woke up to find his bed wet.

In another dream, there was a basin full of sparkling water, the bottom of it marble-white, so large that he could wade along the brim. The sky was bright and blue, the small waves in the basin shimmering in the sun. He kicked water in the air when the basin started to grow. It grew until it was huge, and its brim stood so high that he could not reach it. The water rose and rose until it went over his head. He tried to swim, but his arms were heavy. He wanted to jump to get his head above the water so he could breathe, but his feet were pegged to the bottom. Then the light dwindled from above, the blue sky turned gray, and he started slipping toward the center. The water grew darker and colder. He tried to stop and run toward the edge, but the more he tried, the faster he slipped. When he realized that he could not prevent his fall, he looked for the pipe in the center so that he could climb up on it. But when he reached it, instead of the pipe, he found a hole, with water swirling down it. He tried to stop himself by placing his feet on either side of the hole. But the swirl pulled him with increasing power until his knees buckled.

He did not make it to the abyss. He woke up. There was always something that saved him from falling down a precipice or drowning in a pit.

Every morning, after his dreams, Henry would walk by the fountain and find its gray, listless, pitifully small basin with rotten leaves and bird shit in it, and the tiny, dirty pipe in the middle depressing. He wrote petitions pleading to fix the fountain. He did not know where to send them, so he attached then to the base of the fountain.

They never worked. Until now.

Today, in front of the city center that he hardly recognized, the spring was working. A few dead leaves floated on the water and a tiny, almost sickly, stream came out of the pipe. In the afternoon breeze, it made an uneven cone that could not even reach his height before falling back. The water plane it made was not smooth, and each little gust of wind broke it up. Henry did not know whether he better liked it working or would rather have had it dismantled along with the renovations, leaving his fantasies unscathed. He resumed his walk, leaving the fountain water fighting the weak wind.

The sun followed him through all the turns and bends of the streets. When he finally reached the front of the big house, Henry was tired. His weariness was more for the thought of facing the daunting task of mitigating his prolonged absence than due to his long and arduous voyage. That he came back to this place after such a long time, from where he never really drifted away, had distanced him from others, whose worlds did not stay tethered to the same place. Even if they did, that would have been in different dimensions, which did not matter to him.

The balcony was empty. Emptier than the mere absence of two souls. It was as if, when he was away, nothing took place there that could keep up with the time and fill the emptiness that it entailed.

But it was probably not as empty, after all. After staring in that general direction for some time, as the light around the place became a little mellow, Henry felt that something, something very familiar, had taken place there, just a while ago. He did not know what it was, but he wanted to have a grasp on that fleeting sensation. He sat on the sidewalk and waited. And looked. This same birdhouse hung from the ceiling, and the same garden chairs were on the west side. From the door hung the same velvet curtain, now moving slowly in the breeze. The embroidery in gold and silver threads sparkled in the sun. The fabric looked lighter than he remembered, more scarlet than crimson. It could have been the sun.

The sun! Henry suddenly realized what made him feel strange about the moment. The dying light of late afternoon. Light quickly fading, the shadow of the house falling on the lane on its right. Only now he noticed that lane, through which the young mother had disappeared. Once the evening darkness matched that of the afternoon fourteen years ago, the house looked the same, too. Henry's heartbeat quickened with anticipation, and blood rushed by his ears. He stood and waited with an eagerness that had survived all these years.

Just when he felt the time was right, the curtain split, and two people came through it. A man and a lady. They cuddled, and the man kissed the lady. The lady tried to move away. He rubbed his mouth on her ears and her cheeks and her throat and her nape. She held him in a weak embrace. Clutching his shirt, she tried feebly to push him away. This was the young man whom the child's mother had addressed as the father. He had grown old. So did the lady. But this was not the same woman Henry had seen earlier. She looked familiar, but Henry could not place her. She was so small that the man had to stoop to reach her shoulders. Her body had a lovable roundness. When the light dwindled further and Henry felt that she was going to look his way, she did. And only then did he realize that she was indeed the young mother, her roundness and shortness accentuated with age but she still possessing that same smile. She spotted Henry and looked surprised, but only in the way when someone finds a resemblance in a stranger to someone she knows.

* * *

Henry sat far enough not to be noticed by the man, but near enough for the woman to notice. All these years of his travel taught him how to wait, and how to masquerade. His whole voyage was a test for waiting. And he had learned to act, to cover up his intent, so that he could reach the people whose answers he sought. He sat there waiting for something to happen. He did not know what would happen. But he did not care. He knew something would happen. It was just a matter of time.

After a long time—how long he did not know, because that was the reason he could wait so long, not knowing. He took over the spot of a hydrant on the sidewalk and dogs relieved at his feet, birds dropped on his head and shoulders, ants made trails through his limbs and green mosses extended their abode through his ankles, above his knees—until one day the mother walked toward him. As she appeared through the small inset door, crossed the street and approached him with a slow gait, he knew it would be a long time before she reached him. He knew better than anyone else how a few moments could loom longer than years. But he was not troubled. He had learned to wait.

His scalp perspired under the winter sun, and sweat crept down his neck. The morning silence banged into his ear and provided no respite from his agonizing intent. A wisp of wind pushed toward him but halted in the middle of the street, letting a few leaves hang in midair.

When the leaves came down with an unbearable slowness, the wind broke and dispersed across the street.

When she at last reached him, she stopped and looked around. He sought the smell he had followed in the dark of the labyrinth that night, which reminded him of her pale skin and plump petiteness, her dull hair and heavenly smile. He savored the air saturated by her nearness. When his daze cleared, he discerned other smells wafting from her. Her bodily fissures revealed smelly lives. The chapped back of her feet, the zits on her back, the folds on her crotch and the cracks on her parched nipples, all had joined to overwhelm the past that he had carried over twenty-eight years. Henry strove to save it, and she let go a hint of a smile. The smell of her smile had survived all those years, around her tongue, between the closeness of her teeth and in the wetness behind her lips. She stood there for a long moment and then, gathering the frill of her skirt, slowly squatted beside him. Her stomach squeezed against her thighs, and she panted. When her breath came to terms, she put one of her hands on Henry's hair, which flowed down his neck and back.

"What do you want?"

Henry waited.

"Why are you back?"

There was nothing to rush for Henry.

"If you thought you were her father, you are wrong."

It started to slip away from him. In all the twenty-eight years he had thought of it, this had never occurred to him. Now that she had mentioned it, he wanted to protest, to proclaim that she was just deceiving herself, and him. He never thought he was the father, but now that she had denounced it, it was revealed as the only possible truth. He wanted to protest, but he had learned to hold back, too. Protest was futile. Whatever was protestable was not worthy of protest. Truth was pointless. Unquestionability was everything. She had questioned the truth, and had made it lose its substance.

Henry had learned to wait, to disappear in the backdrop of mundane temporality. But there was no meaning in waiting if waiting was done for its own sake. There was no meaning in disappearing if it was only for the sake of the backdrop. It started to slip away from Henry. The ant trails were disturbed; they broke from their line and rushed into his ears and nose and all his orifices. The soft carpet of moss on his legs became wet with dark yellow liquid, which turned red. Lice, the size of cockroaches, came out from his long hair and beard and bit into the wide gashes of his parched skin.

Henry slipped away.

IV

THE GREEN FESTIVAL

Julie digs into the top drawer of her dresser and pulls out a swimsuit. The large red and yellow flowers on the white spandex smell of her college memories. She won a few intramural contests in this suit and enjoyed a few cheerful afternoons with friends in pools. But against the backdrop of her more in-fashion collection of black and gray tracksuits and sweatshirts, the almost puerile pleats near the base of its straps make it look too feminine, almost mawkish. She pauses for a moment and scampers through the effacing passage of time that connects those few years, and struggles to mitigate the two ends. Instead, she finds her two selves splitting and standing at each end, facing and despairing at the apathy of each other's immutability.

Once the two anachronic twins rejoin, she looks at the face in the mirror and catches a glimpse of a smile before it hides. She shoves the white suit in the back of the drawer and in the back of her memory. Then she rummages through the dark heap of clothes to bring out another one. An emerald green one. She places it on her chest and fancies herself walking alongside the pool. The drab piece of apparel makes her slender frame feel safe.

* * *

Julie rests her elbows on the pool's edge and tries to catch her breath. As the water drips out of the front of her goggles, a tall, strapping man in a pair of white trunks materializes at the other end of the pool. He sets off with an awkward motion, splashing water all around. Julie watches for a few seconds as the man's strong arms plunge into the water in inept motion before reappearing from his sides. Then she starts off for a few more laps. Somewhere past the middle of the pool, she passes the man. Large waves heave her body, and large boisterous water drops pelt her back. She passes him once more, closer to the end of the lane, after which she catches up with him and overtakes him. When she stops again to rest, the tall man joins her. He stands beside her and pants hard.

"Am I ... doing something ... wrong?" he says, his words interrupted by the spurts of his breathing.

Julie raises her goggles from her eyes to her forehead and looks at his face. Under a week's worth of red beard, his face features a meekness that belies his strong body. But somewhere in the depths of his brown eyes, she spots a smile that glints, as if to laugh about his own helplessness. He does not appear as meek anymore. His yellowish teeth look oddly kind through his lips, still parted from his effort to bring his breath to terms.

"You see, I can hardly do a couple of laps." He now brings his smile out from his eyes and spreads over and around the reddish, wet stubs on his cheeks. "May sound odd, but I never swam until a few months ago. Some water phobia, I guess. Just managed to get over it. Not sure what it is, but I can say you have a very good form."

"See, freestyle ... it's really hard to do more than four laps in a row," she says as she he turns toward him, to which he reciprocates. "I can barely do more than six laps at a time."

"I see."

Julie senses a drop of water gathering at the tip of a tendril beside her left ear. It unsticks itself and runs down her cheek, collecting other beads of water on its way to the tip of her chin, which she has lifted to look into the tall man's eyes. From there, the drop slithers down the precipice and rushes down Julie's throat. His eyes follow the flitting drop. After it reaches her valley and before it gets soaked up in the emerald fabric, his eyes stray toward her highlands. Julie catches herself standing on the wrong side of that passage of her youth from the morning, flushing like a young girl. The man gains his composure with such grace that she finds her embarrassment laughable, and she laughs it off.

"But you can use one of those pool buoys between your thighs," she says, pointing to wire bins near the wall. "That way you won't tire yourself out as fast. Also, your arms will get more exercise, and when you get used to it, you can go without. Let me show you."

She gets out of the pool. As she walks to the bin, water gets squeezed out of her suit and streams down the whole length of her legs, leaving a trail on the floor. She stands on the ball of her right foot, her left foot back in a lunge, and picks up a foam dumbbell from one of the bins. She sits on the edge of the pool, her legs hanging and feet dipping into the water.

"You put this between your thighs and move your arms like this," she says. "Raise your head to the side to breathe after every three strokes, or four, whatever works for you."

His broad frame advances to her, radiating a strength that almost feels helpless in his effort to listen to her words. As she talks, his eyes veer to the ripples crushing on her legs.

She suddenly feels bare and senses a cool wind wrapping that bareness, and half-shuts her eyes to enjoy that embrace. The warmth of the water creeps through her feet and lures her into the pool.

"Let me show you."

She spreads her thighs, places the foam dumbbell and slides under the warm water.

John follows.

* * *

It was a festival. They called it The Green Festival. No one knew why it was called this. Perhaps its inception predated the last traces of the collective curiosity of the villagers to know its origin. Or the speculations around the origin of its name that those villagers crafted, and the rumors they let spawn, mingled with other myths and legends, to create such a chronicular commotion that no one knew why it was called The Green Festival.

The women did wear green. Emerald green. Only the women, not the men. The men wore white. This led to a loose consensus among the women, and a smidgen of covert discomfort among the men, that the festival had commenced exclusively for women. And, like most un-substantiated beliefs, it self-promoted its own conviction. But the men attended the festival more than the women did, almost as if they had a point to prove. As for the women, their concession was mitigated by the realization that it could hardly be a festival for them, were it not for the men.

The two forces—female certitude and male discomfiture—the two unlikely counterparts frolicked and scuffled and nestled, and bred oodles of activities for men. They raced along the length of the valley and came back spent and empty handed, their faces smeared in smiles of ignorance. They joined in the contest to throw sacks of grain to reach the future they could not see. They hurled their lances and shot arrows that skewered no one's heart. They ran and jumped into air that took them across no abyss. They wrestled, they boxed, they tugged, only in the futile attempt to saturate the air with their feeble breath and the languid stench of their sweat. But the wind from the sea was strong, and blew relentlessly to sweep away their attempts to stamp marks in the valley air.

The women cooked food. They embroidered clothes and draperies, crafted pottery, and carved jewelry. They arranged their artifacts on tables in different stalls to make themselves more conspicuous to the jostling crowd. They also engaged in a few sports, but the only game in which they competed with men was the swimming contest, the festival's kingpin.

The festival took place on a plain between the foot of the mountain and the lagoon that led to the sea. In the middle of night, when the kids were sent home or were laid down sleeping on the mats behind the stalls and all other activities were smothered under the weight of the night, they dared each other to swim in the lagoon and into the sea, as far as they could.

There had always been an equal number of male and female contestants. No record existed to indicate which side had won more often. Rumor abounded, predominantly among the women, that they were the uncontested winners, because many times one of them had gone so far out to sea that she never made it back to land. Making it back was not a prerequisite to win; the only deciding factor was the extent one braved to venture. But that was largely the women's side of the story; nothing was ever substantiated, no annals kept.

There was one person, though, who balanced the ominous proof and frustrating disproof. He was the wealthiest and most handsome man in the village. Some called him Cupid; some, Hades. But most called him Narcissus. His favorite pastime was drinking with his solemn procession, on the wrong side of midnight, flaunting his exploits with the beautiful girls from the village. The stories that trickled down from that exclusive binge were so imbued with bombastic inebriety and ornate with such improbable pomposity that they went around as fables, which everyone liked to share and not without their own contributions.

One such story claimed that every year, some time before the festival, Narcissus would cherry-pick a beautiful girl from the village. As he did to innumerable others, he would seduce her and devour her youth to the point of exhaustion. When he acquired a fatal command over his enamored prey, he would threaten to desert her. To all her tearful entreaties he would respond by daring her to win the swimming contest, after which he would receive her as his bride—only, of course, if she made it back to land. No one ever returned. Every year, the story went, they had gone so far into the deep of their love that they exhausted themselves too completely to redeem it.

Men were not inclined to vouch for the male cowardice that this story entailed. So, it lived on as a rumor that was alleged to be spawned and promoted by the women merely to feed their petty sense of pride.

This year, the word was that Narcissus had chosen Echo, a deceased priest's daughter and a beauty unprecedented in the village, as the pawn for his bet. Even though it was just a rumor, the whole village had been so consumed by her beauty that the news brought a mist of sadness into the air. Their evening activities fell short of leading the festival to the hour of their midnight rite. Only the clown went on making fun of himself and of the people. Even his shrill voice started to sound affected, and as if he himself was struck by that realization, he fell silent and gathered his chimes and frills at the foot of the bell tower, as though time oozed thicker there than elsewhere.

When the moon finally neared the solstice, the contestants stood ankle-deep in the lagoon waiting for the bell to toll. Henry followed Echo this whole evening, but never got closer to her than he was now. Only ten steps away, he looked at her. Her bare shoulders shone in the full moon, her eyes were closed, and her hair braided and gathered on her head like a crown. Her scarlet lips trembled in the cool air as if longing to plunge into the warm lagoon. Henry could not have known if Narcissus had bid her to marry, but it was for all to see that Echo was his latest prey, and now she appeared to be in a trance. It did not matter to Henry. He had waited for this moment for six months.

Six full moons ago, Henry first saw her at the house of a courtier. Echo had accompanied her mother. Her mother, a widow of a priest, battered and embittered by the hardships of life, had brought a petition of some sort to the official for a stipend. Echo had stood behind her mother, her head stooped and her eyes deciphering the baroque motifs of the lush rug beneath her feet. Henry stood there, stupefied by her beauty, and the official gave in to the same beauty and accepted the widow's appeal with a promise to lend the weight of his words to proper offices. The elderly courtier had asked the widow to pay him a visit later to let him know how things went for her, and specifically mentioned not to forget to bring her lovely daughter with her. Henry knew that that was not meant to be a visit merely for receiving gratitude from the widow for his favor, rather a covert way of setting up a rendezvous with the widow's daughter. Neither was it the first time the widow had exploited her daughter's beauty to purchase necessities. Some of those exploitations had much deeper implications for Henry's own life, but he would not know this for a long time.

Henry did not care. Or, he did, but could do nothing about it. Ever since then, he waited for this moment. He crafted schemes to converge the long days of his yearning winter and pining spring to this night of summer solstice.

In a few minutes, he would be swimming alongside her and get to the furthest point into the sea so that he could be alone with her. And perhaps touch her. The lagoon was quiet. Any small wave raised in the sea were thwarted at the mouth of the lagoon, and if any part of the sea sneaked inside, it only showed in the slow rocking motion of the water around their ankles. The water was so clear one could see the minnows mocking their own shadows on the sand. On nights like tonight, the water reflected the moonlight, as if smeared by a layer of cream on the surface. Late in the night, when the moon prepared to set on the other side of the village, the layer between water and sky would disappear altogether.

The moon hovered. Echo opened her eyes, lifted her feet from the wet sand. She wiggled them in the water to wash the sand off. The ripples carried crescent strips of moonlight on their crests and spread until they reached Henry. He stooped over to touch that light with his hand, and then the bell rang, tearing through the dolor of the evening. The contestants waded through the water. Henry forgot to join them as his eyes followed Echo to see her in the full view in the moonlight. When waist-deep in the water, she threw her arms out and floated on her stomach. Henry watched her body glide on the sparkling silver. Her arms appeared from beside her thighs and rowed through the soft blue air of the night. Water sloshed over her hip and waist from left to right, right to left. Soon, she reached so far that he could barely hear her arms splashing, and only then he remembered to jump in.

He must catch up with her! Not only to touch her; he also had to save her from Narcissus's hirelings, if what he had learned of the rumors was to be believed.

Echo swam like a fish. No match for her, Henry threw his arms in the water as if he was moonstruck and he soon lost his breath before he could gnaw much into his distance from her. He lay on his back and pushed his feet to get his breath back. The moon flushed on his face and struck him blind with its beauty. The sky, her modesty unprotected by the tiniest bits of cloud, draped on all sides like sparkling black velvet. Suddenly, the land and water out of sight, he was as if transcended into the sky. The soft splashes from the sea sounded as if they emanated from far below, as if from a distant storm. But he did not have much time to waste. As he flipped back on his stomach, the sky crashed down over the sea, and the storm became meek splashing on the serene lagoon.

Henry saw that Echo loomed much closer than he feared. She was floating on her back, having her share of the black night's moon, or maybe just saving her energy for the impossible distance she had dared to cross to unite with Narcissus.

Henry took a long breath, slid under the water, and swam as fast as possible without creating much turbulence on the surface. Gradually her wiggling legs came in view through the crystal blue. He sped up and got close enough for his face to feel the undulation her feet raised in the water. He quietly raised his head and maintained that distance. She swam ahead, steady like an arrow. Henry followed, swaying left and right to get the sight of her profile. He could carry on like this the whole night. But a noise reached him, and the surface, which had been nothing but a steady sequence of parabolic waves so far, manifested a different pattern.

He raised his head and looked around. A boat floated just ahead. One of the judge boats, Henry thought. They set off five judge boats to keep track of the contestants who made it into the sea. There were two more boats to his far left and far right, whose lights dwindled fast. They must have, by now, passed the initial threshold. That itself was a long way. Henry thought Echo was going to turn around. But she did not. She went on. The other two boats veered away until they disappeared beyond the horizon. The swimmers, whom those boats had been lead-ing, probably had given up and were returning to shore.

Echo kept swimming. The moon crept down quietly behind their backs and the water ahead of him cleared. She flipped onto her back and kicked her feet. Henry hoped she would tire and turn around soon. Before he lost his chance, he wanted to touch her. The sole judge boat in sight maintained the indifferent distance from them; this was his only chance. He sped up to close in with Echo, but the judge boat slowed and started to close in, too. As it came nearer, something about it did not look right. It was not a judge boat after all. The small dory had only two people on board. Henry recognized them as Narcissus's henchmen.

The stories about Narcissus and his hirelings are true after all, Henry thought. They would lift her up on the boat, rape her, kill her, and dump her in the water, if the other part of the rumor was to be trusted. They probably saw Henry closing in and decided that they had had enough of waiting. Henry knew they would not spare the life of a witness.

He slowed down to create a gap between them. When the boat closed in on Echo, he dipped and went as far down as he could, where they could not see him. He looked up. The water's surface created an ethereal shadow play against the backdrop of the moon. The corn-shaped silhouette of the boat paced toward Echo, and Echo tried to swim away. But her limbs were tired, and the gap between the two shadows diminished.

Henry positioned himself beneath the boat and started toward the surface, wiggling his body to gather speed. The boat closed in with Echo. Henry went to one side of the boat, from where he could now see two hands reaching down to grab Echo. Henry hit the side of the boat hard with his shoulder. When he raised his head, he heard two splashes on the other side, a small one followed by a bigger one, and the boat swung left and right, empty.

"Come on quickly, get on the boat," Henry yelled over the com-motion that had made Echo stop and turn back.

"Who are you?" With her head bobbing up and down in the dis-turbed water, Echo sounded more bewildered than scared.

"No time for questions. You are in great danger. Get on the boat, and I'll take you to safety." He assessed the escalating situation and said, "I am holding the other side of the boat down, so you can get up from this side."

When he reached the other side, one of the men swam toward him. Henry swam around and propped his back against the starboard side and held it with his hands. He brought one of his feet up and kicked the man's face.

By the time Henry and Echo got on board, the other attacker was quickly approaching. Henry looked for the oar, only to find it floating on the water behind the approaching man. Henry yanked at one of the foredeck planks to use it as an weapon. It squeaked against the nails and loosened a bit, but did not break. By that time, the attacker closed in and was holding onto the edge. Henry punched his face. Something crunched under his fist, but the man still held fast. Henry threw another punch with all his might. Something snapped, and his ring finger exploded with pain, but he succeeded in unbuckling the man's grip.

Henry came back to the loosened plank and, with his left hand, pulled it from the deck. The person whom he had kicked in the face made a feeble attempt to approach the boat. Henry lifted the plank threateningly in the air. Nails glinted in the moonlight. The man retreated. Henry then tried to paddle the boat away from the men using the broken plank as an oar and, with the first push, his broken finger spread a lightning pain all over his body. He shrieked, his knees buckled and he crumbled on the deck.

"What happened?" Echo said as she looked at his wound, which dripped blood on the deck. "Give me the plank."

Echo took the makeshift oar from Henry, pushed him aside and started paddling herself. Henry lay on his back, gripping the wrist of his injured hand with the other hand. Despite the debilitating pain, his pleasure to be so near Echo overwhelmed him. She sat in front of him, and the moon shone on her wet body. She pulled the makeshift oar alternatively on either side, and her muscles danced and waved through her chest, stomach, waist, and thighs. Her legs stretched and her feet pressed against the sidewalls. She breathed hard in her effort to exert force, with her lips apart and her breasts moving up and down. Henry rested his eyes on her. A trail of blood trickled down from his finger to his thigh, and he trembled.

When they were at a safe distance from the attackers, Echo quickly crawled over to Henry. She straddled him and bent over him, producing a small knife from around her waist.

"Who are you?" Echo hissed as she pressed the blade against Henry's throat, her nostrils flared and eyes glinting with fierce vengeance. "You've been following me since morning. Why?"

Henry savored the touch of her body, her warm breath on his face, and he felt dizzy. He couldn't understand her rage, but it only magnified the beauty of her eyes. Drops of lagoon water dripped from her tendrils and caressed his shoulders as they slid down. As Henry smiled with contentment before losing consciousness, the fury in Echo's face started to grow blurry.

V

THE LOSS OF ECHO

When Henry opened his eyes and the mist of his awakening cleared, the sky was lighter over the stern. The sun had pushed aside the black velvet night and drowned it. But it cast no shadow on the deck. He was the sole body aboard, lying along the length of the boat, his right arm dangling in the hole that he had inflicted upon it to procure a make-shift mobility device the previous night.

Echo was gone. Henry raised his head and spotted the broken plank propped against the bow. A healthy strip of land bobbed up and down between the sky and it's reflection on the water. Land was near. He withdrew his arm from the dark cleft to push the deck with his hands, and a blinding pain passed through his body. His throbbing finger sent monstrous waves of pain along the sea and, for a moment, the sun appeared to be shutting its shop early. Once those waves subsided and the light resumed, Henry raised his wounded hand and found it neatly wrapped in a green piece of cloth. His weariness was helped by the few hours of sleep, but he was feverish and weak.

The boat was anchored at water no deeper than the height of two men. He pulled the anchor and took up the plank. Paddling was not easy with one of his hands incapacitated and his body trembling in fever. The calmness of the sea and the distant quietude of the village saved him the rush. The morning tide helped him ashore before the sun started to bite into his brine-coated shoulders.

Back in the city, Henry found the streets empty and the warm air steeped with a peaceful quietude like every morning following the day of the festival. But all the way to his house, Henry shivered, and his pulse beat in his ears like a drum. He reached home only to plunge headlong into a feverish dementia.

* * *

After days full of nightmares and dreams, one morning Henry woke to find himself on his bed in a fetal position, the tiny room saturated with a festering stink from his finger. When he unwrapped the bandage and washed the dried blood and pus, the finger sported a bulge around its base and a crown on one side. He washed the piece of cloth, but the red mark on the cloth would not go away. He let it dry on the window ledge and decided to take a walk in the sun.

Stepping outside, he found that the first piece of news that flew in the air was about the wedding between Echo and Narcissus. In fact, that was the only news around. So, Narcissus was a man of his word, after all? Or had he finally worn out his lascivious life and decided to anchor it at a port?

It was a port where many men in the village had wished to anchor. The morning was wet with dew that held on to the frail melancholy of a collective loss. He walked past street corners, tea stalls and market-places imbued with buzzing crowds, each large enough to carry the sadness, yet small enough to sustain its solemnity. But, as the day advanced, the moist heaviness thinned, and the clumped-up dolor in the chattering was gradually replaced with a jovial warmth, as if in anticipation of the impending wedding gala.

Henry stopped by a busy tea stall where the keeper had settled two monstrous kettles on an earthen stove. One had its lid open. It was full of milk, heated to become a thick, reddish-yellow liquid, with half of its surface covered with a dancing layer of congealed cream, the other half pushed open by the boiling milk. The second kettle was covered, and the dark brown cheese cloth tied to its spout meant that it was full of steeped tea. The keeper was busily filling trays of thick and stocky porcelain teacups with ladles of tea and splashes of boiling milk.

Henry took a small chair in the corner with a cup with a broken handle as the other customers busily chatted. His cup was too hot, and with no handle to hold on to, he left it on the saucer to cool. It had never passed in his mind to win Echo; only that he had his longings, and they happened to revolve around her. Now that the reality of his loss materialized, his body revolted. His body had longed for hers and had stayed put in the hope of a future that did not have a form. Its days and nights chipped into that relentless granite of dark mountain to gnaw into it and dig through it a tunnel that always hoped for an end, to see the light and smell the scent on the other side, even a distant other side. Now that it suddenly ceased to be, that jagged wall of granite mountain came crashing down on him. And his body revolted. His fingers wrapped around the small miserable cup and pressed on it. The blackened roughness of the broken handle and the heat of the scratchy china bit into his palm. The brown liquid under the smoking surface trembled until it spilled on his hand.

Henry stormed up from his chair. He walked along the streets aimlessly, day after day, until the repetitions of avenues brought the smothering of familiarity, so much so that he had to drag his body as if he were wading through a thick soup of contemplative closure. He then deserted the streets and went to the sea. He walked along the beach. He walked so far that the sands started to dry up and congeal into rocks, first the size of pebbles, then the size of his head. Eventually the rocks grew so big that one day he found himself stuck on the precipice of a mountain, his skin scraped bloody by kindless edges and parched by hot surfaces. Beneath the precipice, dark waves crashed into the rocky walls, spraying whites of cruel foam. When he got back home, he undertook a vow of celibacy.

His pledge for abstention helped him survive Echo's loss. It was a ritual that kept him involved the whole day and night, without having to do anything. It turned the pain in his heart into a pleasure, one that had no pointy corners or sharp edges to scrape his heart. It filled him with such bliss that it overflowed on everyone around him wherever he went.

But it could not go on forever. That pleasure slowly steeped the whole village, and soon there was not a place left that he could go without being smothered by the frothy miasma of his own joy, fermented by the weight and heat of its own redundancy. His bliss, or what he thought was his bliss, stemmed from his effort to forget her. All he did was try to get around that. But there were only so many ways around it. And none of it took him past that process of oblivion. He had to let his loss face him to get over it. He wanted to see other women.

But now the days had shortened and nights grew colder. The last leaves had long since fallen. Women gathered less frequently in the cold streets. When they did, the bright colors of their autumn dresses were shrouded in the gloomy gray of thick wool. But there was something more in the way of his venture. The women in the village collaborated to conjure an eye for him. And of him. It reflected his own sight, which had been rendered translucent by his sufferings and longings. When he looked at them, he saw his self-reproach in their eyes, an admonition for breaching his unavowed fidelity with Echo. Those monstrous and self-deprecating eyes grew larger and larger until they soaked in all the sneers that accumulated in the darkness of the collective, sinister night. At last it forced him away from the eyes of the village.

He walked where houses were few and far between and streets transformed into earthen walkways, covered and shadowed by trees and shrubs. He would walk down from those rutted pathways and push his way through thorny bushes and muddy creeks.

One day, after a walk so long that his mind was distracted from his furtive way of going, out of his engrossment by the weariness of long days and nights, he ran out of roads and found himself standing in an unexplored pocket of the village. He was alerted by the quaint houses and unfamiliar signs from the people. But something foreign about the place stopped him from turning back. The small houses feebly stood on their worn-out posts, but exuded a peculiar neatness from their gaudily painted walls and floridly decorated screens in front of open doors and windows.

A darkly pleasant demeanor about the place staved off his urge to dive back into the backwoods. The door screens waved at him warmly, and Henry took a step forward. The sun had started to stoop beyond the copse that he had just left, and the last warmth of the day from the dusty roads called him forth. Henry took a few more steps. A woman stood in front of a house. Her dress was scanty for the cool afternoon, but not without a lot of care invested in it. Before he knew how to react, she spotted him standing precariously on the edge of the elevated road, and turned her head in such surprise that her long earrings could be heard jangling.

For a moment he wanted to retreat. But when, through the eyes of that woman, he first sensed the absence of admonition in his own mind, he was appeased. With all her make-up and bawdy attire, her eyes were enticing and her smile was alluring, but their artless affectation glowed with such innocence that Henry was drawn in.

Still, his body was not ready to break the thick torpor of its prolonged recluse. His seclusion was born out of his intent to avoid encounters with minds. But it also kept him from getting to a body.

This was a distinct kind of connection with other people, Henry surmised, that kept him away from women. He had become inclined to introspective dialogue with others, in which he used words that had context only in the depth of his own consciousness. So, even though in his own mind he offered himself reciprocation from others, it was never to be in reality. As such, all his attempts at talking to others were destined for disaster, and that failure was more complete with the women. Because their eyes were always more voluble than the men's. The paucity of words in the eyes of the men at least offered him comfort that came from the distance it posed.

In the women's eyes, the warmth of that distance was absent. Even though they tried to insulate themselves under the falsity of their expressions and clothes, and the craftiness of their words, and the eluding sensuousness in their gestures, their eyes always betrayed. That bareness had been more difficult for him to cope with.

Today, however, there was something different about the woman in tawdry clothes. Her eyes were barer than those of women from other places. It came to him as a surprise that there could still be another layer of guise that could be shed. Henry smiled, and she looked startled. The last peel of her defense came off, and so did the playfulness in her smile. What was left was so vulnerable and pristine that it looked unlikely she herself could have recognized it as a smile.

He waved his hand and, before he could turn, more women out in front of the other neighboring houses came into his view, and even though it was getting colder, the number of skimpily clad women grew.

Henry headed back to his house, but had decided to come back. To this woman.

* * *

Sitting in bed the next morning, Henry thought about his preparation. He had no idea how to visit such a woman. Whether he was to take a gift for her. If taking flowers would look passé. What the proper attire would be. He thought only a little about what would be a good time for the visit. His mind was fixated on late afternoon, because that was the only time he had been there. For him, the place was the combination many factors: the mellowness of the time, the warmth of the dusty road, the coldness of the air, and colorful houses with his woman in skimpy red standing in front of it. All of these were necessary components of the whole. Because there was no knowing, any absence of some part of all these factors might have failed to beckon Henry back from a path that promised no destination.

Henry dressed in his finest and set off on the long trek. He followed his shadow, which was dark and stocky at the beginning. By the time he closed in on his destination, his penumbral lead had become soft and pliable. Henry sidetracked into a marketplace and went from store to store in pursuit of a perfect gift. A proper gift—perfectly proper.

So far, he only thought about flowers, believing that one gave flowers to someone with whom one had—or potentially could have—a loving relationship. Even though he had seen his woman only from afar, the way he could send his gesture to her was the closest intimacy he had shared with any woman in a long time. But then it occurred to him that there were probably a slew of other people with whom she shared more intimacy and that she might find it very commonplace to receive flowers.

So, the idea of flowers as gift was relegated to the end of his priority list. He looked for dresses. Some looked bawdy, some too demure, some fit only for older women, others too puerile. He ceased his pursuit when he realized that he did not even know her size. He then thought about books. The only books he could consider in his state of mind were ones of the romantic kind. All others felt completely irrelevant, as if they were for people from a different world. But, at the same time, the romantic ones struck him as too melodramatic against the backdrop of this burgeoning relationship.

Henry considered carved shells and colorful rocks, crystal statuettes and ivory figurines, esoteric paintings and amorous sculptures. But the search was futile. The image he conjured of her room was fleeting, like clouds in a windy sky. It morphed even as he pictured a niche, or a table-top, or a bit of uncluttered space on the wall. The locus of his imagination waltzed along and evoked transmutation on all the attributes of the room he wanted to come to terms with. The color, the smell, the light, the furniture, and their overall setting. Even the number of walls in the room changed, and, with that, changed their color, and their opacity.

It was hopeless. He decided to forgo the pain of mitigating two abstractions—the elusive projection on his woman's countenance and his own bearing on her—as equally ephemeral. He searched through things that bore more mundane connections: crockery, small furniture, linens. But nothing donned a palpable smile on her face, for him.

Then, a pet shop found him trudging down a corner of the market-place and drew him in with its motley noise. Inside, it seethed with calls, colors and smells of birds and animals from distant lands. When his eyes joined his other senses, adapting to the bleak candles covered in dusty oil paper, he spotted a pair of black Siamese kittens in the back of the store. They crouched in a small basket and looked at him with the imploring turquoise eyes of human babies. Elsewhere, a tiny, fuzzy puppy stood on its hind legs, its little tongue sticking out and its paws on thin wire of the cage. And there was a large colorful bird that looked like a macaw, but sang a sad song in the language of a faraway land. When he thought about it, trying to fit another life in the uncertain and unsettled expanse between him and his woman felt bizarre, indeed.

He went from store to store to see what they had to offer until he exhausted them all. After that, he revisited them and went round and round until it was dark, when all of a sudden a chilling whistle from the night watchman marked closing time. He found himself stranded in the middle of the courtyard, which started to fill with the sound of shutters falling and the smell of smoking wicks from the blown-out candles, his hands full of flamboyant rejections of all the gift ideas presented to him. As he left, a thought bobbled up in a corner of his mind that he had been running all evening, only because he was not ready to visit her. But he was too tired to pay attention to that thought, and at the same time too tired to push it aside.

The next afternoon he set himself a cutoff time for his search. If he could not settle with any proper gift by then, he decided, he would simply get a bouquet of roses. But that did not work, either. The flower shop closed before his planned time, much earlier than the rest of the market.

The following day, he went directly to the flower shop. But it did not have the bouquet he had decided on purchasing.

The morning after that, he found that all his running around had rendered his attire unpresentable. His shirt was dirty and wrinkled, the hem of his breeches sweaty and muddy. He set on cleaning them.

On the fifth day, the smell of his newly washed clothes made him cheerful, and in the market he felt he could bring himself to properly appreciate one of the bouquets. But he had spent too much time on cleaning and ironing, and by the time he reached the woman's neighborhood with a handful of red roses, the street looked much different than it did the first time. It was dark already. The neighborhood was full of people strolling down the streets and gathering in front of houses. Candles covered in shades on exterior walls kept the housefronts lit, but could not push the darkness far away. The shades were colorful and dark. Dark blue, dark purple, but mostly dark red. When he approached the houses, his roses changed color to become dark and mysterious. Even the leaves and petals seemed to have morphed, their thorny edges curled into dark smiles.

As he reached the woman's house, his woes were exacerbated. In place of his woman, four other women stood, striking an image of four baroquely ornate pillars of an antiquated mausoleum. She was not there. They smiled at him, but their smiles were dark against the background of red light. As he wondered whether to ask them about his woman, one among them, dressed in a black blouse and scarlet skirt, stepped up, raising a clatter from her stilettos, and stopped in front of him. Her smile smelled of wine and cheap perfume.

"Whom has my good man brought those pretty flowers for?" Her breath warmed the air between them, but her smile did not bridge her eyes with her lips. She clasped the bouquet and his hands into hers and brought herself closer to his chest.

She fluttered her eyelashes and said, "For me, sweetheart?"

Her long fingernails scraped his wrist, and he yielded the flowers from the shudder her closeness had raised in his body. She took his resignation as an assent and bumped her chest on his, and, for a minuscule moment, a blink of a smile occurred between her eyes and her lips. When that bridge was broken again, Henry scrutinized her face. He spotted wrinkles on her cheeks tucked under layers of makeup, and her tired eyes smelled of a middle-aged woman. He pitied her and wanted to hug her. But the cold of the night had started to flank and push into the feeble orbs of the candle flames, and his arms felt weak. Besides, she was already leading him inside the house, her nails digging into his forearm through the frail defense of his shirt sleeve.

Henry stole a fleeting look at the three stranded women, whose tired eyes followed Henry and his date for an idle moment before withering and languishing like fireflies in a spider web. Something struck him. Something that did not represent the whole composition the troika of sirens had struck in the backdrop of the scarlet halo of their candles, with the perplexity of their seductive attires and the disquiet of their darkly contrasting makeup. Instead, this lurked somewhere in that lurid formation and kept flitting away from his grasp. But he could not linger. He was led through door, the screen pushed aside, and landed inside a small room.

Before Henry could make out anything of the inside, what struck him was his unfamiliarity with the place. Unfamiliarity of a world that this house contained. A world that not only he, before now, never thought of entering, but also had maintained a conviction to not enter ever. And his denouncement of this world let brew, in the backdrop of his mind, a distance, a detachment rather, that had been so complete, it made its unfamiliarity more than unfamiliarity. It bewildered him, as he was torn away from his world that offered him the assurance of familiarity, and plunged into another world for which his quiver held no weapon.

Through the glasses of apprehension he found each wall was painted a different color: red, violet, blue and black. As if to let his mind flee the almost sinister languor of its bearing, the four colors reminded him of the four women of the house, not that he correctly remembered the color themes of their clothes.

Beneath the blue wall opposite to the front door stood a narrow, low-lying bed, neatly made with a shiny blue sheet and two square pillows with tassels at both ends. With no headboard or footboard, it could have just been a wide-cushioned bench. A blue chill emanated from that bed and made him perspire. His knees felt weak, and he wanted to sit on it.

A small, square table in the middle of the room tilted on one shorter leg. A flower vase, unfittingly large for the tiny room, stood on it. But when his hostess dropped the bouquet on the table, the bouquet compared even bigger than the vase. On both sides of the right opposite corner huddled two doors, one closed and the other leading to another room. The walls in that other room were also painted in different colors and had doors. Henry could make out the yellow and blue in the other room. So, the walls of this house are painted in more than four colors. Maybe, there was, after all, no significance of the different colors on the walls?

Disillusionment—that re-disjoin from the world outside this house —did not sit well with him. He needed connection to keep things bearable. So, he resumed his color-coding. He thought the black wall was painted for his host. As he tried to concentrate, the other three women standing outside slowly materialized in his mind. He wanted to think that they had stood in the same sequence as the colors of the room went from wall to wall. Clockwise. No, counter-clockwise. Or some order, any order. Out of that order, the simplicity of the wall paints started to become transposed into their corresponding women and the mist of his perplexity started to clear. But before long, that clearing up became spotty, and swirls of confusion started to appear from the daze. Maybe, in his mind, he had merely re-permutated their picture outside to juxtapose with the colors of these walls. Maybe they had not even worn any of these colors.

And what about his woman from the other day? No wall painted for her in the room, was it? And where was she now, anyway? Visiting an aunt? On the other side of town? Maybe she was sick. Or maybe she was in that other room, or another beyond it. Taking a nap. What was there beyond this closed door? Maybe she was there. With another guest. Someone who had come before he did, and she had grabbed her guest's hand with her long nails dug into his shirt sleeve and led him into that room. Henry became restless; his palms felt cold. But he also felt good. He felt good because he was experiencing something familiar. It was not a different world, after all. None of the walls bore green, but he smelled the warm smell of his own jealousy. And felt more at ease.

He focused on his hostess, who busily walked around the room and picked up small chores from the bareness of it, like smoothing a crinkle on the bedsheet, picking up some litter on the floor. She stopped in front of a small, square mirror, framed in dark wood, on the violet wall. It tilted a little too much at the top, and did not accommodate the height of the residents, because even she had to bend her knees to look at her face.

"Doesn't someone else live in this house?" he asked. "Besides the four of you?"

She moved her head in different directions, making faces at the mirror. She paused and looked at him for the first time with the honesty of a smile-free face.

"No one lives here."

No one lives here! Right! The house did not even seem to be furnished for that purpose. They only received their guests in this house. Henry was more comfortable now. This was not a world to land in after all, just a rendezvous. A sojourn. The colors had no meaning, and he needed no meaning anymore, either. The squareness of the tiny rickety table, the sag of the framed mirror on the wall, none of this had any attachment to anyone. The vase stood in the middle of the table with an overbearing largeness, and it felt necessary to be in this room just to offer the room a mote of quirkiness. His bouquet was still bigger, and there was no way it would have fit into that vase. It looked pretty on the table just as it was. Inside the room, not only the colors of the flowers had revived, but they also were accentuated by the variegated glows from all the walls.

Just when he started to get used to his oversized bouquet, his hostess pulled out a pair of scissors, deftly snipped the flower stems, and made them fit in the vase. The bouquet lost its largeness, and in its place on the table surface, a bunch of snipped stems of different lengths lay randomly on the table.

She stepped out of the room and returned with a tumbler full of water.

"Do you know where the other lady lives?"

"Which other lady are you talking about?" she said as she poured the water carefully into the vase.

"She was here the other day."

"What other day?"

"Last Friday. Afternoon."

"I have no idea who you are talking about."

She set the empty tumbler on the table and looked at him with a vague frown, which she then quickly flooded with an abundance of smile.

"Sweetheart," she said. "I don't remember who was here yesterday. And you are talking about last Friday?"

She twisted to the right and bent a little backward to have a last look of her own face in the mirror, and, as if happy with what she saw, lightened her tone: "And what is so special about the other lady?"

"No, nothing. Just someone I happened to see."

"And you fell in love at first sight?"

She turned full-faced to him and looked relaxed as she said, "Are you here for love, honey?"

She played with the last two words with a flair for seduction. She stepped out of her heels and started toward him slowly. She was surprisingly short without her shoes. Her gait changed, too. Her feet were plump and moist from wearing tight shoes. Her hips swayed in the rhythm of a slow dance. A trace of a coquettish smile surfaced from the wrinkles beside her eyes, floated over her rouged cheeks, and swelled around her lips like a river reaching its mouth. Through her smile, her wet tongue laughed like a baby. When she stopped in front of him, her chest against his stomach, he caught a glimpse of her belly through her large, drooping breasts. She looked up at him, and he found the color on her lips smudged, small hairs peeking out from her nostrils and her eyes reading the greatness of distance in his eyes.

"Are you not taking me?" Her smile diminished, and a storm of confusion started to form.

Henry plunged into the comfort of that storm and implored, "Lady, would you please try to remember who was here last Friday afternoon? Please? It was just before sunset. She was in golden red. But the golden could have been from the dying sun. Because her face and her arms and legs looked golden, too. Do you at least know who she was?"

The smile disappeared as rage took over. She took a couple of scorching steps back, and stood with her feet sticking together.

"What do I care who was here?" she howled. "If you don't want to have business, why are you wasting my time? I might have landed a profitable client by now."

She pondered her statement a bit, then looked away, her cheeks burning in indignation.

"Or who knows what might have happened?" she said. "Those damn girls haven't caught a single damn fish yet."

She paused, as if taking account of the previous week, then said, "You can find your way if you don't have any business with me."

Henry turned.

"And you can take your flowers back. Damn, I cut those stems. Oh well, wasn't my fault."

"I don't need them," Henry said as he went to the door.

"Wait! I don't know who you could be talking about. There were three of us here last Friday afternoon. Did you say she wore red?"

"Don't worry about it. It's all right."

Henry stepped out of the house. The cooling air carried and blew onto him a laughter that the other three girls shared. He knew right away what had struck him as strange when he had first seen the group. One of the laughing ladies was the woman from his previous visit. He stopped and tried to find his *woman* in her. Today, she was in a violet blouse, and her eyes were surrounded by dark violet shade. The corner of her fresh lips trembled in a confused smile at his stare. She did not look much different than she did the other day anymore. But somehow there was still a very acute difference, and it was not this person that he had come for.

He continued on his way.

VI

❧

THE HOUSE OF ARTEMIS

After their fourth encounter in the pool, John flanked Julie's wet, petite body with an honest laugh of frustration.

"Your swimming schedule barely follows a pattern, does it?" he said.

Julie looked up, her eyes fogged in an audit of the past, which could have been anywhere from six to eighteen months. Or maybe even two years. In that time she had cut her long hair, but that could have provided no context for him, as her gray, silicone swim cap rendered that timeline irrelevant. Then her newer swimsuits had been more succinct, maybe to tone down the extent of her foray into her thirties.

In between, she encountered this chance-met pool-goer how many times? *Since when had he been stalking me, anyway?* Stalking! That came out a bit unfair. Julie tried to focus and read his face, and in his gentle eyes she spotted a swirl of confusion arising from her delay in responding.

"Yeah, I just work it in around everything else," she said with a smile. "And there is too much of everything else."

She just wanted to buy a few seconds to gather herself. But she had lost her train of thought. Besides, his now-hopeful eyes stubbornly stood in the midst of her attempt to gather the threads she wanted to string together. Her poor little seconds steeped through her fingers, dropped in the pool water and quietly dissolved.

"What about yourself? You are very particular about your swimming, aren't you?" she said.

"You can say that. Only that I have been working it around just one thing," he said, the ridges of his smile softening. "Or, should I say, around one person."

Did he really say that? Julie was suddenly wearied by the daunt of responding to a situation that could determine a new chapter of life. She looked weakly into his eyes to find, and borrow, an answer.

* * *

Penelope drops her pencil. It lands on the edge of her writing pad and rolls toward the bottom of her desk calendar. She waits for a yawn that does not arrive, and reaches for the pencil. But instead of picking up her wooden soldier, she pulls the calendar closer. The top page features an extreme close-up of a pink dandelion taken from below, towering, and brushing over the five rows of tiny numbers on the right side. The days of the months have been annotated more frequently with every passing year. The unmarked ones do not offer much breathing space, either. She has to fill those days with miles of scribbles, then retrace them. But one blue circle looms only two days away; every time she looks at it, her sexagenarian heart races.

A conference is scheduled to commence at a local hotel. Among the guest speakers will be an acquaintance from days long gone. Someone who left her unannounced, on an unremarkable day within their youthful mirth. An acquaintance who could not have become a friend. Because he had started to smile a smile that he smiled only when she was around, and smiled only with her. At least, that's what she thought. Her days had advanced like a net that sifted all the laughter and fun, all the bliss and happiness of life, converging toward a halo consisting of only two people. There was no promise to weigh down that light. No rendezvous in which to throw cinders, or to stoke their fire. There was no fire—just light. Their meetings were by chance. Chances that were assured by the way their lives steered them to encounters. Their stares struck in each other's eyes glints of happiness that they wanted to keep un-reined for as long as they could. The sparks off their chance touches were yet to kindle fires. But the wind was too bright and sonorous to require fire. Then, suddenly, one of them ceased to be. He just disappeared.

That disappearance was so un-assuring and so unconfirming that she did not know whether, or when, to turn her back on that shared halo of merriment. Whether to shut her window from the wind of melody they had set free in the air. But time did not cease to flow through her darkness, and when her confusion dwindled on its own, she passed through puzzlement, pain, anger, mourning, detachment and apathy, and then, after what felt like years of rowing down the slowing stream of a maturing river, she dared to look back toward the distant bank with the fond sweetness of a dead legend left behind long ago.

So, when Penelope learned about this guest at the impending conference, she was surprised by the way her mind, and her body, responded.

It has been quite a struggle to stay on course to deliver what she has promised her agent. She turns the calendar around, and the phosphorus-white back of the small time-keeper gapes back at her. Penelope wonders if it is suppressing a smirk. She pushes it away and turns her attention back to the page she just finished.

"Or, should I say, around one person." The sentence that she just wrote stares at Penelope. Did she just write that? It attempts an undoing of Penelope.

Why did he never say anything like that to her? Forty years ago? A realization comes over Peneleope, one which appears equally strange. In the last few days, while working on her assignment, she has peeked into the thoughts surrounding her bereavement forty years ago. This awareness has been shaping slowly, but resolutely: that there was something she might have done, albeit inadvertently, that led him to disappear. Did he have any doubts about her bearing on him? She never used words to communicate her feelings for him. But was that even necessary? Didn't she communicate with her whole existence? With her smiles, her tone and enunciation, her stares, and with her whole being when close to him? How was it possible that the unbearable serenity she rejoiced in while in his vicinity couldn't bridge the mortal distance and scream to the whole of his existence to pronounce that which remained unpronounced?

And then there is this new phase to which she now has been elevated. She can't blame herself anymore. She did more than enough of that for the longest time, maintaining an excruciating guilt that she couldn't ascribe to any particular action of hers, or inaction. But not anymore. How come he couldn't say something to the effect of, 'Or, should I say, around one person.'?"

Something that simple. Or even simpler than that. He never said anything. Not with words. But she could tell from all the things he did, the way he laughed with her, the enunciation of his words, and his whole being, that he brought the same unbearable serenity, and all. So, he didn't really need to speak out—at least, not for Penelope. Because she herself never had any doubt. But if he had any doubt, why didn't he tell her something? If he did, she could have blown the doubt away. And none of the rest would have happened.

Or maybe not? There was one thing about him that she couldn't quite understand. He never gave her the stare that signaled his getting lost in love. There were moments that he could have grabbed her and offered the look that contained all those meanings. But he never did. The few times when the opportunity arose, he broke the spell, fumbled a few words to work through them. He was too shy, or too scared, to seize the moments.

Moments. Those few precious moments. He didn't capture them and thus they were lost. Afterward, a vast multitude of disfavored moments were added and accrued, and the road laid by them now extends through the dizzying length of decades.

Looking down that long, insolent road, exasperation forms in Penelope. A rage. An angst for not taking some matters in her own hands. Penelope plows her fingers through her mostly grayed hair and presses her fingertips stiffly onto her scalp. When the flare of the rage quietens sufficiently to let her thoughts somewhat settle, she picks up the pencil —with an intent to take things in her own hands.

* * *

That was the last time they would meet at the fitness pool. That day, Julie triumphed that daunt of responding to John's candid confession of stalking her. She retorted favorably, and a courtship ensued. A string of rendezvous, none at the pool, was followed by an engagement phase, a not-so-conspicuous wedding, and then Julie's moving and settling in at John's house.

Years passed.

A chance encounter with a college-going, gaunt young man with dark, curly locks infused an enlivening and surreptitious wind into her mind that was barely content with the mirthless and mere settling that was her marriage. In response to an urge to yield to that puerile touch of romance, whose chance of realization looked only remotely plausible, Julie started writing about a young student, who was, well, not that young.

A pining Hank came back from college emboldened beyond Julie's expectations. The flurry of his actions, measured and multitudinous, briskly led her to a point where she could not pen the story of that young student any further. Fulfillment is the demise of fantasy, after all. Writing for Julie was a foray into the fantastic. When that was killed, her penmanship had to cease. Julie had to cease.

* * *

But the story could not rest in peace. Penelope takes over, and proceeds with the story about a young man named Henry.

* * *

Henry fetched a small wooden box from under his bed. He took out a tiny roll of green cloth and unfurled it. The stain of his blood in the middle was like a dark and mute archipelago. The frayed edges tried to curl in his grip. Henry tried to make out the smell of her touch. He had not washed it after taking it off his finger. It still smelled of salt and iron. He sat there until the burning in his fingertips spread over his palms and into his chest, his lips and his eyes. By the time he returned it to the little box, he had decided to go back to the House.

Henry waited until the following Friday, and when he reached the House, the last light of the day had left. He knocked and was told that his woman was with a customer. They showed him the small chair beside the door, but he preferred to stand outside. There, he had the company of two other women, one of them the lady who had taken him in last Friday. She appeared not to recognize him. People walked by like a procession of drunken phantoms. Some hurled obscenities at the women, who hit back with more profanity, all in good humor and not without laughter that only the drunkenness of night could make happen. When passers-by commented on Henry, and they frequently did, the women joined in and laughed at him.

The weak circles of light from the candles on the ground trembled with their laughter, and so did the embroidered screens on the door, until a middle-aged man staggered out. Henry's woman followed the man to the door, stopping short on the threshold. She looked different than the other two times he had seen her, but, by now, he had become used to the loss of consistency; in fact, the constancy of her change made him feel rather at home. From this almost implausible, voyeurish distance of their first frontal encounter, Henry tried to steal a look at her fingers holding the door screens, the arch of her bare right foot pressed on the raised threshold, and the pitiful sweetness of her face smudged by violently disrupted make-up.

"You want to come in?" She sounded uninterested and looked weary, her hair disheveled and her clothes disarrayed, but her voice rang sweet and melodic—almost puerile. She scraped out a sliver of a smile and let the screens go as she gathered her hair with her hands and tied it into a bun.

Henry followed her inside and said, "Can I talk to you?"

"Talk? What you mean?"

She stopped in the middle of the room and turned around, saying, "You are not a cop, are you?"

"No, no, I am nothing like that."

"You sure don't look like one. What you want to talk about?"

"I ... I saw you the Friday of the week before last. You remember—I waved at you?"

"They all wave. And they all hurl profanities." She put her hands on her waist. "What's so special about you?"

"Nothing," he said.

But she would not relent without a better answer, so he said, "Okay, I did not say anything. I just waved."

"So, that makes you Prince Charming?"

"No. I didn't mean anything like that. Forget about it."

Her face softened as she buried a pitiful smile.

"So, can I talk to you?" he said.

"What is this matter of talking? Of course not!"

She took a step toward him with her shoulders and head jutted back, as if to make him retreat.

"If you have no business, I don't want to waste my time talking to you," she said.

"I will pay you for your time."

"For just talking?" The space between them mellowed, and her hands loosened from her waist. "Okay, I don't mind that."

"Thanks."

"For what?"

"Nothing."

"Good. Have a seat. I'll be back in a moment."

She whirled of her skirt and her hair among the diffused colors of the walls and went into the other room.

Henry looked at the rickety chair beside the door, which had an indefinite color, and sat on it. It bore him with a surprising solidity, raising no creaks of uncertainty, setting off no retreat of discomfiture. The room did not seem outlandish anymore; familiarity had quietly sprouted in the silence. The bright walls did not seem overbearing. The large vase teetered at the edge of the table, bearing new flowers. Not fresh, just not the ones he had brought the week before.

Henry wanted to think of what to talk to her about. He could have asked her her name. Then what? Maybe he could ask her about her life. But how? About what? He knew nothing of her that could offer him a head start. But maybe there was not absolutely nothing. They had their lives, after all. There could be things that overlapped in both of their lives. He loved the sea, and could talk about it. But the sea was at the far end of the city. Maybe she was not interested in the sea. They could talk about the Green Festival. People from this neighborhood were not allowed at the festival, but some were hired to perform in the dance shows, which were held in closed-door huts. Young boys tried to peep through cracks in the tightly knit straw walls at the lustrously and scantily clad dancers. Henry had never been inside, but had heard the amorous music seeping out. Did she ever dance in the festival? Henry wished he had been at one of those shows.

A muffled tinkling came from the room she was in. Henry strained, but all he could hear was a half-intoxicated exchange of words from outside the house. He returned his attention to the room. The flower vase stood on the other side of the table, its base almost extending beyond the table's edge, as if pushed aside to make room for something else. But the vase was alone.

Henry's hands involuntarily set off to pull it toward the center of the table. But the rest of his body responded with reluctance. There was still this apathy in him to everything in the House that he decided to ignore. He did not need to rise to reach the table, which was almost within touching distance. All he needed to do was bend forward a little. But his palms tingled even at the thought. The glassware suddenly loomed large, and he saw how dirty it was, its walls smeared with white, salty residue, its bottom strewn with rotten leaves. He could smell them, and he shivered on his little chair. Something, some other door maybe, banged shut behind the closed door, and the vase trembled. Had it moved even closer to the edge? The floor sloped slightly toward that direction, and the glassware threatened to fall and crush the ennui of the evening. Henry shifted to the edge of his chair and bent forward.

As he held the base of the vase, the door swung open and hit the wall with a bang. Henry was startled and almost dropped the vase on the floor. But he quickly extended his left hand to stop it from falling. He placed it in the middle of the table, he hurriedly stood. She wore a long, heavily pleated, bright yellow skirt with red laces and sequins, and a short blouse.

"What are you doing?" she said unmindfully.

She had done her hair during her little break; her lips glistened red, and her eyes sparkled in shades of sapphire. She went to the little, square mirror and busied her hands adjusting her clothes and smoothing her makeup.

"I was just ..." Henry had to look around to remember what he had been up to and found the empty glassware. "This was almost falling off."

"Come in." She threw a glance at Henry and, digging up a rash bit of smile, turned around and walked into the other bedroom.

Henry followed her, but he could barely go past the middle of the room. A bed occupied most of the floor, and a dresser with a foggy mirror on the other side made a faint effort to balance the weight of the space. This bed was wide, unlike the one in the front room, and nicely made, with plenty of pillows of different sizes heaped in a random fashion. The thick, ornate bed posts bore the luster of their most recent varnish and almost reached the ceiling, from which a cheap chandelier hung with only a few of the candles burning.

"Sit."

The only place to sit was on the bed. She had already taken up that space, propping her back against a couple of pillows, her left knee bent upward and her right leg folded underneath it. Her feet were colored in vermilion and topped by a pair of golden anklets.

"Sit," she said again and, as if to make room, grabbed her knee with both her hands and pulled it toward her chest. It was a tiny room. To get to the bed, he would have to squeeze around the corner of the bed and dresser. The top of the chest was empty, except for a wooden hairbrush lying on its back. Its bristles did not have a single strand of hair entangled in them. The mercury on the mirror had started to peel off from the edges. Behind it, the wall was painted white with coarse, uneven strokes. Who did it? Must be someone from this house?

"What, you've come to talk to the wall?"

Henry turned his head. She sat straight, her long neck outstretched. Her hands lay still on her lap, her legs steadily held to their position. Her eyes slipped past him to the hazy mirror, and she twitched and moved her facial muscles as if to perfect the blemishes her hands had left while she made up her face. Her lack of focus emboldened him to have a look at her. Between her puckering and twitching, he found her lips to be full. Her eyes were a bit too close to each other, but they were deep, and her eyelashes were long. There was a small spot on each of her cheeks. They were placed with such perfect symmetry that she suddenly looked dumb, even if only for a moment. As if on cue, she conjured up a one-sided smile to break the tension of that evenness and raised her right hand to take a measure of her hair. While at that, she looked to her left, which gave Henry a chance to wander from her face to her neck and her chest. A large spot on her right ribs peeked below her short blouse. It looked like a scar, and a very fresh one, too.

"What happened there?"

"Where?" She followed his eyes and took her arm down. The scar ducked under her blouse.

"That bruise."

She raised her elbow. "This one? Why, it bothers you? I can put out the light," she said, seemingly enjoying his embarrassment. "Or get myself a shawl if you want. You just wanted to talk anyway, right?"

"No, it does not bother me. I was just wondering how you got hurt."

"Okay, here is the deal. You can talk all you want. But no personal questions. Will that do? And what's up with standing there? Why don't you sit?"

Henry looked around for a last time to make sure there really was no chair.

"What, you looking for a chair? Listen, no one comes here to sit in a chair." She sounded pert and started to shake her right knee. "Darn, no one comes here just to sit, anyway. So, you gotta sit here on the bed."

The left side of the bed was adjacent to the wall, and the footboard was too high, so the only place to sit was near her outstretched right foot. He looked at the floor and, squeezing himself through the bed and the dresser, sat on the bed.

She held her knee again, and the scar peeked through. It looked worse up close, healed and all.

She followed his stare and said, "You want to touch?"

Henry looked away in embarrassment.

"No, it's okay. Come here. Give me your hand. Actually I will feel good if you do."

She bent over and pulling him close to her, placed his hand on the scar. Henry wanted to think about things he wanted to talk to her about. But the smell of her skin seeped into his body and danced through his arteries. He managed to steal a look at her face. She looked happy. She did not let his hand go, and now she started to caress it.

"So soft," she said, stopping at his ring finger and feeling around its base. "What happened?"

"It's nothing."

She waited a few moments, then smiled and said, "You want to see more of my scars? I have some on my back."

Henry's hand was burning, and he was drowning in the smell of her breath. He could not say anything. She let his hand go and unhooked her blouse from behind, holding on to the front with her chin. She turned her back to Henry. They were actually not scars, but large wounds that were still healing.

His eyes became moist. He caressed them with his hand, and when a tear fell from his eye, he brought his mouth tenderly down onto her neck.

"What is your name?" he asked, his voice muffled by the buttery skin and the lump in his throat.

"I have some scars on my chest, if you want to kiss them."

Henry raised his face to hers.

"What?" she said. "You want to, or not?"

She waited a few seconds and then took her blouse off. Henry clasped her hands and stopped them.

"No. Put it back on."

"All right. You wanted to talk," she said, her face stern. "But first, put this on me."

"What is your name?"

"No personal questions, I said."

"They call you by some name?"

"Okay, if that is it, you can call me Psyche."

"Psyche?"

"Does that work for you?"

"Yes, it does. Psyche, have you ever been to the Green Festival?"

"Sure, why not? What about it?"

"Oh, nothing."

"Oh yeah, we are not allowed there. But we have our way."

"You mean you dance there?"

"Dance? Of course we dance. Like everyone else."

"No, I mean if you dance in the shows?"

"Oh, the dance shows. Some do. I never did. I was already a bit too old when I came here. Only the young ones get to dance there."

"So how do you get around?"

"Oh, well, it's easy to manage some green clothes. No one recognizes us in green. Except for our clients, of course. But they have their own skin to save, from their wives and families, you know."

Psyche seemed like she was enjoying the conversation now, but Henry was never a good talker. He saw too much and soaked in too much.

"Anything else?" Psyche caught him looking at her.

"Umm ... I ... can I hold your hands?"

"Here."

She stretched them out, her palms facing down. Four stones shone from four rings on her fingers. A violet stone on her right hand and yellow, black and blue on her left. He covered her hands with his own.

* * *

An orbital was formed around his weekly whereabouts. The six lesser days he labored to converge toward his Friday evenings. From daybreak he toiled to get the money needed to buy her gifts and pay her fee. Every Thursday evening, he walked from store to store in search of presents that he would feel least uncomfortable taking to the House.

Even after all this, not every week could he see her. He came to know that she did not work every Friday, but he did not inquire her of her schedule, nor did he ask the middle-aged woman, who, it turned out, was known as Artemis and ran the business in the House. He did not ask, because he wanted to miss her. It kept him occupied. He wanted to see her, and when he could not, his craving remained.

That worked well to save him from the pain of losing Echo.

On the other hand, by adhering to his own schedule, he made sure that Psyche was available for him when she was there. He savored the warmth of that certainty. Over time, Henry developed a hunch: he could tell whether she was in or not. On arriving at the House, he would look at the perennially open front door, the candles dozing off in the evening air, and could tell right away if Psyche was not in. He would go inside regardless. The long hours of his walk in the market-place weighed too much on the presents he brought, and he had to unburden himself.

After some time, he could sense her absence in the House even before reaching the Neighborhood. Eventually his sense of her presence grew so acute that the moment his consciousness revived from his whirlpool sleep, and even before he opened his eyes, he could tell whether he was going to see her that day or not. But that would not change his routine. He would clean up his clothes and wash. A good amount of time would be spent on reflecting on whether the present he had bought the night before was worth keeping, and not returning, and then coming to the realization that it would not make any difference. There was no perfect gift.

It was easy when she was there. His rites were laid out. He would walk straight into the bedroom, with the whitewashed walls and the chandelier hanging from the ceiling, and feel depressed to see his unworthy gift framed in the hazy enclosure of the frayed mirror-edges right across the door. He did not take them for Psyche. There was nothing to present to her. He could not have redeemed himself with any gift that he could afford. He took them for the House, for the warmth it provided him.

The House gradually filled up with odd little gifts. The old stooping mirror on the front room's wall was replaced by a round one. It stood straighter, but four little wedges of previously unexposed violet paint stuck out from behind. A small, stocky brass vase took the place of the larger glass one that by now had been broken. But this matter was settled after three attempts on his part. The first replacement vase had looked small in the store, but in the House, it turned out to be even larger than the previous glass one. On his next visit, he brought a sturdy vase with a top that split and flowed down on all sides like a lily. Psyche laughed and said it reminded her of a stocky client whose glistening, balding head was surrounded by combed-down gray hair that hung like peels. So, Henry tried a third one that evoked no great emotion and quietly assumed a permanent place on the uncomely table, its two predecessors disappeared elsewhere.

He brought new shades for the light fixtures, a wooden wind chime for the front door, ceramic tumblers, brass goblets, porcelain ashtrays, ivory soap-cases, and all sorts of other trinkets. While nothing he bought was meant to be personal, this assortment of things gradually filled up the nooks and crannies and slowly changed the ambiance of the House. That in turn changed the character of the women. They started to share a part of their attention to all those presents that they previously offered only among themselves. They fought over where to put the trinkets and what to replace them with. They fought over their ownership of them, and in turn became more and more attached to themselves and, in turn, to the House, and thus started to change the way they dressed. Their sinister outfits were traded for warm, pleasant ones. Visitors increased in number, and the women spent more of their time inside than outside, more profitably than playfully.

But even with the growing business, Psyche managed to keep Henry's slot intact, even though it had to be shortened from half an hour to twenty minutes. Then to fifteen, ten.

One Friday, as Henry left the House, Artemis called him back and asked for a favor.

They were running out of liquor, she said, and with business heating up, she didn't have time to purchase more from their usual vendor. There were a handful of stores nearby. But Artemis had always bought from a place that was a few villages away. They gave them a good price and their liquors were superior. At least that was what her late mistress had told her. Artemis had never tried any other store. She asked Henry if he could bring her a couple of casks before they ran out.

Henry took the money and set off right away to the domestic distillery. By the time he arrived, however, the owner had gone to bed. Henry woke him up and asked him to take two casks out from the cellar. He hung them from the ends of a thick, flat bamboo stick that the owner lent him, and placing the stick across his shoulders, walked back to the House. When he reached the House, it was close to dawn, and even though the front door was open, there was no sign of movement. Henry set the casks down in the front and guarded them.

When Artemis woke him, the sun was glaring high in the sky. She seemed surprised to find him there.

"What are you doing here?" she said. "And what is this? You didn't fetch the whiskey overnight, did you?"

Henry stood, rubbing his eyes. The sun gave him a headache.

"But you needed them this morning, didn't you?" he said.

"I was running low, but didn't mean to make you go that late. Besides, I was going to ask someone to go with you. You brought both of them by yourself?"

"It's okay, he said." The headache was killing him. Besides, his body was sore. "I guess I'll go home now."

"You really didn't have to do that."

"Yes, I did." Henry smiled over his shoulder as he walked away.

* * *

From then on, Artemis frequently showed up with chores for Henry.

On one of these days, he found Artemis standing at the door, apparently waiting for him. She asked him to help her with something urgent: the wooden legs of a bed were crumbling. Termites had eaten into the frame, and long, thin gaps now appeared along its frame. Artemis assured him that it was not going to take much time and that Psyche would be waiting for him to finish. But he ended up spending the whole evening fixing it. By the time he was done, Psyche had left the House.

This occurred more frequently. Every Friday, he worked on something or other at the behest of Artemis and returned home around midnight. Artemis started gathering chores for the whole week: repairing a shoe, sewing up a bed sheet, picking up groceries, oiling the door hinges, and all other small things that emerge from the cracks and fissures of a household. Henry hardly knew anymore whether Psyche was there. Gradually he lost his hunch, and the whole time he worked, he kept his mind busy wondering if she was there or not. Once in a while he would catch glimpses of her, entering her room with some client or leading them out. His time slot was given to others, but he kept finishing his chores in the hope of a more fortuitous week.

Soon it became apparent that this was not going to happen. He started to go to the House earlier each week, but Artemis would be ready with more work and errands. One week he went there on Thursday in the hope that he would be able to finish all the chores before his allotted time. He worked all day, then waited for the last customer to leave late the next morning, and slept on the doorstep. He slept with the sun scorching his body all morning. He woke up around noon and set out finishing the rest of his chores. When his time came, he had barely finished, but Psyche was not there that day. The list of his chores lengthened as other nearby houses on the street started calling for his help.

Then a time came when Henry lost his memory of everything but working all seven days without a break, except for a few hours in the morning under the sun, sometimes under rain.

He dragged through the long nights of winter and long days of summer through demented cycles that got caught up in the comfort of their own repetitiousness.

Until one morning, that is, when he caught sight of a man. Psyche led him into her room, almost stepping over Henry's body. He woke up as if from a long sleep and sat there for the rest of the morning as though attempting to come to terms with his awakening. He left the House at the strike of noon and returned to his own shack.

Sitting on his bed, which creaked and crackled under the feeble weight of his emaciated body, he felt as if he'd just returned from a long trip and, with his return, the gap that separated his two lives had been bridged. It felt like his living here had been a continuous affair. The memory of his stay at the House swiftly fled toward the far horizon of his memory. Only once in a while would an image, or sound, or smell, or a laughter, or sometimes a frayed piece of an event float up. Their remoteness impelled him to laugh about them and saved him from delving into the details of their context.

As days went by, the wretched state of the shack made itself conspicuous and in encroached into his delirium. It saturated his mind and overflowed into his body; his limbs stiffened, his senses gave way, and he shook himself and looked around. The furniture in his room, and even the walls, had slowly acquired a sinister look from their long unattended pose. Henry spent a few days cleaning his little shack, going through things that had long been useless. He spent another few days resting and convalescing from the scars and bruises and fatigue inflicted from the frantic labor in the House.

It was winter, but he had a handsome pile of firewood, made up of discarded furniture. When the whole pile was used up, he still felt languid and did not want to fetch more. Instead, he slipped under a blanket and tried to stay warm by thinking about why he had left the House.

Psyche had always been with other men. That was what she did. Even the miserable few minutes allotted for him had also been filled up by other visitors. It was probably the person that visited her that morning that struck him back to his senses.

It was Narcissus. He had seen Narcissus a long time ago, but there was no way he wouldn't have recognized him. But that could not have bothered him. Narcissus's lechery was known to all. A rumor had it that he kept count of the new girls brought into the Neighborhood, and took care to visit them before they were too wasted. If true, he must have already been with Psyche. Probably a long time ago. And numerous times too.

Maybe the fact that Narcissus was there with Psyche meant he had been unfaithful to Echo. Even though no one, including Echo herself, would have expected that Narcissus would stop seeing other women after he got married, for Henry, it pained him to know Echo was suffering.

Or perhaps, even if Henry knew all the time that Narcissus would not allow Echo the respect she deserved as a wife, Henry realized that day that maybe Narcissus was really not keen on preventing Echo from taking lovers. Did that realization give way to Henry's irredeemable sense of loss? But that could not be why he came back home. He had done nothing about it after coming back. All he did was fix his miserable room and then let his wretched body recuperate.

Maybe it was just a coincidence that it was the same morning he saw Narcissus with Psyche that the futility of his stay occurred to him.

Maybe that was the reason he came back. But he could not erase from his mind another thought. Did Echo still remember the piece of cloth she had torn off her body to nurse his broken finger? Henry looks at the scar. The thick crooked line around the finger and the crown on the top forms a ring. A matrimonial ring that two of them made together—a covenant that he was destined to carry on his mortal body, but Echo had no less part in it formation.

Henry slept on that thought for seven nights. On the eighth day, he walked to the lagoon where he had stood beside Echo on the night of the Green Festival. He stood for a long time with his eyes closed. Waves ran across his feet and came back with the ebb, gnawing into the sand beneath his heels. His standing body felt as if it were being swiftly dragged backward. The wind changed direction and raised eddies of confusion in the air. He felt like flying in the sky with warm clouds passing below him, caressing his feet. The sound of the sea slowly ceased being a roar, and the morning sun sent ripples down his skin.

When he opened his eyes to the scream of a few seagulls, the re-flection of the waves glared at him and attempted to blind his eyes. Henry walked into the water and then lunged forward. All the noises drowned. From the lagoon, he drifted toward the sea. And his mind drifted toward a memory that couldn't have formed from something that happened in his life. It couldn't have been a memory of a dream, either. But it was real, maybe from a different life—from a different story, rather—that didn't offer a promising fate for Henry. A memory of Henry going to the Castle in search of something that could be the memory of Echo—the daughter of a priest. And in his absurd pursuit for that memory, he had metamorphosed into a tree. A peach tree.

VII

THE MEMORY OF A PEACH TREE

When Henry reached the Castle, the night was settling toward the quietude of midnight. The nearest inn was far behind, and he was very tired. Henry did not want to go too far from the Castle. He stood in front of the large wooden gate overlooking the tall towers and the dreary gray walls against the backdrop of the gray sky. The outer wall stretched from the gate in both directions. He searched for a hint of light in the long rows of windows in the building.

A hush of cold wind blew ahead of his sight and put off any candle that could have been lit on any of the window ledges of the large edifice. If there was a smell of burnt wick, the length of night did not carry it over to him. Henry stood, waiting for the candle to be relit, and wondered how this building always sat on the fringe of the city, raising on its cold floors the soft steps of Echo's feet, its stone walls shuddering by the touch of her fingers and its large hollows warmed by the fragrance of her breath. And only now he found himself here, after such a terribly long time.

Nothing flickered for a while, and he started walking around the castle, keeping close to the outer wall. It was a long and painful under-taking, as the stone fence was intermittently strewn with thorny bushes and sturdy shrubs. Henry did not care. He brushed along the wall as if touching a part of Echo. He wanted to touch the whole of it. But when he reached the other end, he spotted a small crevice in the wall, jagged and covered in thick moss, hidden behind a large bush. It could not be seen from outside. In the dark, Henry traced the wall, brushing his body against it, sustaining cuts and bruises. Through the crevice came a feeble sliver of moonlight, spread across the ground. That light came as a portend that he was destined to see her and therefore this opening was offered to him. The premonition was so real that he felt dizzy. He had become used to the idea that he had lost Echo forever, but this real-ization was too much for his body to bear. He became short of breath as his knees shook and his wearied, cold-beaten body gave way. He knelt, and his head was brought to the level where the crack widened.

From this position, he could see through the wall and to the other side. There was nothing much: some more bushes, and, through a fortu-itous opening in that bush, a part of the gray castle building came into sight. In that small section of the wall, a light flickered on a window. Henry pressed his face toward the wider opening at the bottom. The room with the candle was on the second floor of the main building, which stood behind a row of one-storied apartments. The apartments extended on both sides and prevented access to the main building. For a moment, Henry thought he saw something moving near the window. But it was too far away. He touched the ragged crack with his hand; the thick moss felt soft. Stringy roots crept from one side of the wall to the other. He moved his hand further upward and hit something that moved. A buzzing noise came from the other side, and something stung sharply on his finger. Before he could take his hand out, dozens of bees flew in through the opening, stinging his arms and face.

Henry waited for the pain that studded his senses to subdue before he tried to measure the width of the opening. It felt just wide enough to poke his head through. But it turned out to be narrower than it looked. He bent his head toward his chest and pushed all the way to his jawline to push his head through, but not without scraping off the soft cushion of moss. He gave another hard shove, inflicting deep scratches on his jaw, but managed to push the whole of his head to the other side. From there, he could move no further. His shoulders got in the way. After several attempts to squeeze his body through, he thought of pulling his head out and look for other ways to go to the other side of the wall. But the crack was narrower toward the other side, and the edge there was sharp and pointy. So, even though he could push his head through, when trying to get back, it stuck around his chin and the base of his skull. He tried to maneuver his head, but nothing worked. Henry then placed his head in the way that he thought would offer the least resistance to the wall and gave a hard pull. All he could manage was to dislocate his jaw and get a few more gashes below his chin and on the back of his head. He was stuck.

Day broke. Birds chirped. Inside the portal, his head was safe from their droppings, but the rest of his body was not. He now saw that the hole turned out to be a pathway leading inside the castle compound for an assortment of commuters. Little frogs hopped over his body. Centipedes crept over his face. Snakes slipped through the small openings around his neck. One of them slithered between his legs, and one poked at his neck with its snout. Henry yielded and maneuvered his head to allow it to slip by. It stopped for a moment to give him a forked lick, as if in a gesture of gratitude, and, spreading the chill of its breath in the small space of the hole, left him there.

Henry's wounds began to fester. His sight blurred and his pains blunted. He no longer felt hunger, and his senses spiraled downward until he ceased to know what was real and what was not.

One morning, the sound of young female voices wove a web around his senses, trapped in the thicket of dementia, and pulled them into the glade of stark consciousness. The sun stood further north above the castle. There was no daze in his waking up; the sharp edges of his consciousness were unmistakable where the sound of the chattering girls landed. Smell of earth, moist from the morning dew, mingled with the pungent sap oozing from the injured branch of a nearby bush. A pair of squirrels turned toward him in unison, alerted by the snap of his waking up. Henry did not feel hungry. His wounds did not hurt anymore. He did not feel like moving.

He tried to focus on the approaching voices, but their words were too jumpy, as if hopping on their toes on the rocks over a dancing brook of laughter. They ran into each other, bumped, played and halted for no reason, and again bubbled up in fits of the vernal garrulity of their begetters. But from the unreasonableness of their youthful chattering sprang forth a melliferous melody that steeped into his head, ringing like a stream of cool water. Henry became slightly dizzy in an almost somnolent pleasure, but he did not want to fall asleep. He wanted to call for help, to let them know he was trapped. But in his daze he did not know whether any words emerged from his throat.

Maybe he did not use the right words. Maybe he did not even try to get the words right. Or even if he tried, maybe, in his stupor, he waited too long before attempting to enunciate them, so long that he forgot the words by then. So, it did not come out right. Or did the words come out from his mouth at all? The bubbly stream of the voices did not suffer the tiniest disruption. The squirrels did not jump in startlement. But the stream in his head kept flowing.

For a moment, he doubted if he really was awake. Trying to move his left hand, he did not find any sensation, but a mild scraping noise came from where he expected his hand to be. He tried to open and close his fingers. They resisted, but he could sense something moving up and down his thigh. He was awake, after all. He focused on his hand and brought it up to his throat. His Adam's apple felt large. There was something different about the opening around his neck. It was more spacious now. Henry moved his hand further up his face.

He expected resistance from the edge of the hole, but there was more room than before. He could even bring his hand through that extra clearance all the way in front of his face. It took him a few moments to realize that the thing in front of his eyes was a part of his body, and not some dried up cadaver of a strangely shaped snake. His arm was now merely a bunch of bones put together by a thin layer of skin that itself was shriveled and tinted dark green. The fingernails were long, and the earth underneath them hinted of vegetation. Patches of moss covered the back of his palm. He brought his arm back through the wall. On its way down, he touched his shoulders, now nothing but bones. He felt the deep gashes between the bones where the skin sunk inside his ribcage.

He made an effort to look around. The bushes and trees were full of new leaves. The laughter of the young females had long disappeared, and now he could see them crowding beside a pond. They were taking their clothes off in preparation for a bath. His neck became tired, and he dropped his head.

Henry realized that he had his full senses back, but something lingered. He felt no great urge to take notice of his physical state. With his physical transformation, his mind also went through a change, becoming apathetic to events around him. When the idea struck him that, with his body so emaciated, he probably could get through the hole, it did not have much effect on him. He felt around his head and realized that the head itself had not shrunken much. The skin had shriveled, but the size of his cranium felt unchanged, and he could not force it through the hole without fracturing his skull. And that was only if he had enough strength. It was difficult enough to move his hand.

But getting the rest of his body on the other side no longer seemed to be a problem. He simply had to squeeze his body by bringing his shoulders together, and he decided to do that, because that was the only option other than doing nothing. But he had lost significant strength. Besides, the little amount of energy he could manage had been barely enough to drag his body an inch or two. But he was not worried. For one, he had lost an enormous amount of weight. And his newly acquired indifference offered the gift of great patience.

He moved his arms to the other side and pushed his whole body out of the hole. The process took him a few hours and was dotted by pauses and resuscitations of his scant energy. His progress was so slow that, at one point, a squirrel placed a nut on his temple and ate. A few bits of shell rolled inside his left ear. Long before he managed to land on the other side, the laughter of the young women passed by him again, this time coming from the opposite direction, and night had fallen. He fell asleep.

When he woke, it was still dark; he did not know whether he had slept only for a few hours, or if days had passed. It did not make any difference; there was not much for him to know. He could not become weaker. It came upon him that he needed to replenish his energy.

He dispatched his left hand to fetch himself some leaves from the bush he was lying under. The leaves had sharp pointy tips, and they cut into his skin, but he did not feel pain. Not much blood was left. He shoved them in his mouth. It was not an easy affair with his jaw dislocated. He could only engage the right set of his teeth to chew on the thick, juicy leaves. The sharp tips cut into his mouth, but his bite of pain came from something else.

With the first hint of juice from the wounded leaves trickling down his tongue, his mouth reacted violently and, in its attempt to fill up his mouth with saliva, the base of his tongue was pierced by such a sharp pain that he almost passed out. When the pain subsided, the saliva drooled down the corner of his lips, and before he could reach to save the little stream of precious liquid, it reached the ground and wetted the earth.

After a few days, when he managed to stagger to his knees, he came to notice that his body had become a tree. The little bits of torn clothes left hanging on his body were tinged with dark green moss and smeared with dark brown earth. They clung to his body like peeling bark. His withered limbs hung like half-dead branches, and his hair congealed into sturdy dreadlocks like the tendrils of vines. His beard flowed onto his chest, bifurcated by his protruding Adam's apple. His genitalia, shrunken and creased, studded like the base of a broken dead branch. Even his movement did not betray his treelike visage. He moved so slowly that the squirrels stopped on him, snakes hung from his shoulders and birds perched at length on his head. When he peed, the dark yellow liquid trickled down his thighs no faster than the juice from the slit of a date tree; it barely moistened the ground beneath. His withered legs resembled the roots of a tree denuded by relentless rain.

The metamorphosis undergone during his dementia had another bearing. The lives around him had accepted him not only as a part of them, but they had also taken him up as a part of their communal life. That day, the squirrels brought fruits and nuts for him; birds perched on him and warmed him with their wings.

The next day he felt stronger, strong enough to move slowly when he wanted to lie down and sleep so that he did not break his bones. He had a long sleep that night. Long and full of dreams. On the following morning, Henry crept out of the bush into the sun. The light bit into his skin. But he liked the warmth and let his body collapse on the ground to soak in it.

There was a small, muddy pool a few steps away from the bush. It lay beside the earthen path on which the young women went to the pond. Getting to the pool and coming back from it would have taken him so long that he could not have returned to the bush by the time they were to pass it again. But still his body set off, as if with a will of its own. His arms and legs worked in sync at the behest of his arid throat. The path declined toward the pool, and he reached it much sooner than he had estimated. He dipped his face into the water, and its coolness sent his body into a whirl. His breath slowed down. But this new sensation left him gasping for air. As he moved his face from the water, his whole body convulsed, and the sudden rush of air into his lungs dizzied him.

The young bathers passed by when he was halfway back to his bush. This was on an incline, and it took much more effort from him to advance every inch of the way. But, once they had passed by him, he realized that he did not need to hide. His body had become a part of the place. A camouflage itself.

So he stopped getting back under the bush that had saved him from weather for so long and tried to make out something that had struck him just now from the voices he heard in such close proximity. There was one particular voice that he discerned clearly from the others. Her sound was not that of laughter, nor of a word, but just a sound, an interjection, and that, too, not in response to anyone else talking.

The more he thought about it, the more he felt that the sound was directed toward him, and he recognized the voice. From the backdrop of his memory, it peeked like a tiny fleck of cloud into a corner of his mind, then grew bigger and bigger until it raged like a monster that covered the sky and crashed down like a thunderstorm. When it cleared, he could no longer remember how many years had passed since he had heard this same voice on a boat, deep out at sea. His heart did not race quicker; he did not breathe faster. He simply went toward the pond. A peach tree stood between him and the pond, and he went in that direction. He had not decided what he was going to do, but he had plenty of time to think. In the meantime, under the nourishing sun, the minuscule vegetation all over his body were animated, and he relished the flow of blood through the dried-up canals deep within his body.

VIII

THE REBIRTH OF PENELOPE

Henry gazed upon the yet-unscathed surface of the vellum on the desk, until its frayed edges dissolved in the intensity of his reverie. After mentally filling it up over and over again with the memories of different shapes and colors, noises and melodies, smells and tastes, when he finally placed his quill, nothing came forth. The ink on its tip had long dried up. He dipped it in the well and brought it down again on the off-white center of the parchment. A black dot appeared beneath the tip, and before the ink soaked into the texture and spread, he dragged the quill diagonally, toward the upper right corner, and withdrew. The rest of the ink hung drying as Henry let his gaze wander, this time around the small, slanted line he had just drawn. He let images run around it until it conjured up the lower leg of a woman. He followed the image in his mind and drew the tip of a big toe from the bottom of the line. Then he took it along the arched and softly creased insole, turned around the roundness of the heel, bending slightly toward the ankle, the back skin wrinkled in tiny creases, then swerved away to form the plumpness of a calf, then forming the back of the knee.

Henry dropped the quill and took in the image as it dried, the foot stretched and only the tips of toes touching the invisible ground on the surface. He put his finger below the knee and traced the entire outline and then touched his lips with it. He dipped the quill and drew an anklet that draped idly on the arch of the foot. He then gave the leg its thigh, drew the other leg, drew the hips, belly and the belly button, breast and neck and long, flowing hair. Then he spent an inordinate amount of time on the face.

He held the picture in his hand for a long time. He wanted to call her by a name and searched for the right one. He listed all the names that came to his mind. Columns after columns, he put them down neatly, one after another. None worked. When the night was over, he had a sheaf of pages full of names, all of which had been struck off with precise lines. Some were deleted because of the way they looked on the page and some for the way they sounded when he read them aloud. Some for the images they evoked when he thought about them. Some for the way they tasted, the way they smelled, the way they smeared the parchment, the way they resembled the ones that he had already struck off.

Then he stopped thinking about a name and started writing.

"Penelope was left wasting her youth, by the goddess of her fate, in a House that was an absolute mismatch for the magnitude of her beauty. Lady Luck just had to oversee her entrance into that dreadful mansion. Thereon, little events that were central to her duty in the House entailed others in such seamless sequence that she never knew if there was elsewhere to go.

"Upon his first visit, Enrique met each of the four ladies of the House. Each of them had their own charm, yet, once he saw Penelope, there was no way he could want to see anyone else. But as was the case with him, every other visitor wanted to be with her only. Enrique was told that he would have to wait for a long time before he could see her. He was willing. He joined the long line of people that languidly slithered outside the House. He waited for a long time. A very long time. So long, that the man waiting right in front of Enrique in the line, even though his body initially displayed the briskness of an intense awaiting at the prospect of meeting Penelope, gradually grew an acute lack of interest that only time can afford to carve, and eventually fell off the line. Enrique lost count of how many more patrons fell off in front of him, in the same fashion. Enrique would, then, turn his head to see the line growing at his back until he could not see the end anymore.

"When at last his turn came, he had grown into an old man. But his aging was strangely selective. His hair had turned gray, but he had plenty of it. The thick locks shone in the delight of his reaching the end like a snow-covered proud mountain peak glittering in the midday sun. As he vocalized his contentment, his voice bore the deep timbre of a wizened man, but still carried over the mirthful resonance of youth. His eyes took in the events around him like that of a sage but radiated the yearning to devour them like those of an adolescent.

"But stranger things awaited him as he stood in front of Penelope. She looked as young as when he had seen her the very first time. If her eyes hinted of tiredness from sleeping with so many people through so many years, it only added to the mystery of their darkness. Her long, thick hair was a little ruffled, but still flowed like the sea he had wanted to plunge into for so long, now only a trifle disquieted as if by a brooding cloud. Her gait gave few hints of how tired she was. When she sat on the edge of her bed and straightened her left foot, her toes resting on the floor, to take the stocking off her leg, a straight line was created that stretched from the arch of her foot all the way to her knee. With her stocking off, her insole looked only slightly soiled from all this walking over all these years, but her heel was smooth and moist. Her calf looked so soft that he could drown in it."

Henry put his quill down and took up the parchment in his hands. He read it once. Then once again. Then again and again. He touched the parchment to his lips, his cheeks, and then smelled it. His body trembled, and the parchment shook. When the storm subdued, Henry relieved himself.

* * *

Penelope takes the other stocking off, climbs onto the bed and lies on her back. She spreads her legs apart, her arms resting on both sides of her head. Her hair spreads in a dark sunburst around the pillow. She rests for a moment, then pulls off the rest of her clothes and throws them toward the wall that features the only window in the room. Her clothes drift along, then, as if resisted by the air in the room thickened by the sheer extent of its existence, halt for a moment and, whirling around, land underneath the window. She lies on the snow-white bed sheet, her face devoid of expression, her body devoid of tension. Only her toes remain slightly curled, as though from the anticipation of an imminent pain, and her eyes seek refuge somewhere else. She looks through the ceiling, piercing through the sky, living elsewhere, in some other world, as if whatever happens to her body here in this room, in this world, need not have any bearing on her eyes.

Enrique climbs on the bed, and the softness of the down mattress ripples. Her thighs absorb that undulation and her breasts throb, but her eyes do not come back from oblivion. He sits between her legs and waits for her to look at him. He sits there for a long time, but she does not move her eyes. When Enrique senses a weariness landing upon him, he tears his own eyes from hers. He touches the inside of her thighs and advances upward. As he closes in, his body trembles. He pauses and sees that her eyes are still as distant as ever. But something in that distance enchants him, and his own eyes entangle with hers, as if through her eyes he is carried to another world. Another world that he could not reach any other way.

But the night does not wait. His knees become tired, his ankles hurt, his eyes become sleepy, and his head drops onto her stomach. There he falls asleep. He dreams that he is inside a cave. The cave is half-full of water, and he floats around and bounces against the walls. There is a small opening at one side, through which a pale, reddish light shines. Enrique floats round and round until he reaches a narrow, dark hole. When he touches that hole, it feels very cold and very hot at the same time. It burns through his head and freezes his heart. But he is certain that it is the only way out of the cave, so he bumps his head against it.

The hole does not give in at the beginning. But after he bumps into it repeatedly and for a long time, it starts to open. It softens and widens, and the hole does not look so dark anymore. A faint ray of light comes through, but it still feels very cold and very hot. But it doesn't matter anymore. The hole gobbles him up and thrusts him into a tunnel. He moves slowly. He cannot go back even if he wants to. Not that he wants to.

When he feels like he is coming to the end, Enrique wakes up. His time with Penelope is over. The sun is up, and even beneath the dark velvet curtains of Penelope's window, a sharp ray of light lies on the clothes she had tossed onto the floor. Penelope is still on her back, and Enrique is still on her stomach, but her bodyguards have stepped in to force him out of the room. They stand on each side of the bed, and one of them pulls on Enrique's hair. He jerks his head. He was drooling and had created a pool in Penelope's belly button. He wants to wipe it off. But as he advances his hand, one of the bodyguards bends over and, wrapping one of his arms under Enrique's stomach and clutching a bunch of his hair with the other, lifts him.

"Your time is up," the bodyguard says as he throws him onto the floor.

Both bodyguards leave the room.

When Enrique comes back the next day, before the sun has risen, he is pleasantly surprised to find a very short queue. Apparently, Penelope is not as young anymore and thus is not much in demand anymore— not even close. There are younger, heartier girls in the Neighborhood to whom people flock instead. Enrique recognizes most of the people who stand in front of him. They were all in the line in front of him before— the few who didn't fall off. They are the true lovers of Penelope, and this creates danger for him. Even though there are only a few dozen of them, none will let her go easily. The previous night, Enrique came up with a detailed scheme to remove the guards from his path. But now these lovers pose a greater problem. It is possible one of them could get to her and then refuse entry to anyone else. Enrique knows this because he has toyed with the same idea.

That thought breaks his heart. But he has come too far to abandon his quest. He doesn't know what else to do. So he stays put.

When the sun rises and the morning blood smeared on the House is clearly visible, the head bodyguard emerges and ushers all of them inside at once. He leads them through a long hallway studded with doors on both sides. Through each door, he discreetly lets one patron enter. Enrique wants to protest. He hasn't spent such an enormous amount of time waiting, just to be paired with any random woman. But isn't this the case for all these patrons? Why aren't they objecting? Is it because they know something that Enrique doesn't? Or is it that each of them is wondering the same thing: that no one is challenging this slander because they know something he doesn't?

Before Henry could make any sense out of it, a door opens and he enters. Penelope is lying on the bed. Who are there in the other rooms, then? Why am I the luckiest person? Or am I? These queries pass through his mind like floaters in his eyes before they blur and disappear. After all, why does it matter anymore? He has arrived. Again. For the second time.

By the time Enrique makes it to Penelope for the second time, she is back in the reality of the room. She glances at him and around the room, as if she has returned home after a long, long time. He stands in front of her.

* * *

"You are the first to come to me for a second time in all these years," She says.

Her gaze is too intense, and Enrique looks away. He does not tell her that there were dozens of men before him, all aspiring to the fate that awaited him alone.

Enrique quietly climbs on the bed and sits between her legs and lays his head on her stomach. Penelope ploughs her hand through his thick hair. Enrique, scared of the previous night's dream, fights sleep. He rubs his face on her stomach. Then he lays his ear on it. There is a voice. At first it feels like his imagination, her heartbeats, mingling with her other bodily noises, conjuring up a sound that he misconstrues as a voice. But slowly, the sound becomes more distinct. Enrique lifts his head and sees that it cannot be Penelope. Her chest moves up and down in a serene rhythm, and through the valley of her breasts he can see that her eyes are closed and lips shut. As she exhales, through that valley blows a wind that smells of years of sleeplessness.

Enrique lays his other ear on her stomach. The voice is much clearer now. The words are crisply enunciated, yet foreign, but they are so full of color and passion that each word conjures up a story, as if from the other world Penelope had been in the night before. Maybe it is a dream that she is having and it travels to Enrique, who has waited for so long to meet her, whether in this world or the other. Or any other. He focuses on those words and tries to experience the stories. They sound as if they were told by different narrators, and thus their backdrops are different. But this apparent disconnect seems to have a greater purpose, and they slowly draw him deep into her dream; gradually the words transcend mere sounds and become images, and he is able to experience them.

He floats from one story to another as if swimming across a lotus pond, leaping from one leaf to another. He cannot tell anymore whether he experiences her dream or if he has moved into his own dream. He wonders because all of a sudden, he spots the cave he dreamt of last night, except he is now outside it. It does not intimidate him anymore, and he swims toward it, but something intimidating remains—an aura of dread that does not touch him, but one he can sense. He is close enough to the mouth of the cave to spot the location of the dark hole. It is covered by water bushes, but otherwise it is unmistakable. He leaves the safety of the lotus greenery and swims toward the opening. As he grows near, the air of dread intensifies. Upon reaching it, the whole pond seems suffused with fear, and he swims to keep his head above the dense thicket of fright. He glances through the opening and learns the source of that fear. There is a woman inside. She looks familiar, even though he cannot recognize her in the feeble light, but the trepidation in her naked body is undeniable.

She swims from one opening to another just as he had done the previous night. When she comes to a stop and presses against Enrique, he recognizes her: Penelope. Her eyes, full of fear, dart around, and does not seem to notice him. She then locates the dark hole, and as she speeds toward it, she bumps her head, causing the whole cave to shake. Enrique is thrown into the water and fights to prevent herself from drowning as the cave shakes, sending wave after wave. He knows by now that the water is nothing but his dense, thick fear. Still, the tremors intensify with each push, and Enrique loses the strength to keep up. His body gives way, and he sinks.

Enrique awakens and finds that he is lying with his head on Penelope's stomach. He looks up. Penelope is still sleeping, her mouth agape and her head deeply sunken into her pillow. Enrique spots the sharp sliver of sunlight burning the heap of her clothes beneath the window. Afraid of the guards, Enrique grasps her ribcage and shakes. She opens her eyes and looks at him. She tries to sweep her sleepiness away with a smile that spreads from her mouth and eyes to all corners of her face and body. She stretches her hands toward him. Enrique latches onto them in grave concern.

"Dawn has broken," he said. "The guards will be here any second! Why did you let me sleep?"

"Don't you worry about them. I forbade them to bother us. In fact, you have earned me for a whole day."

"You forbade them?"

"Yes."

"So you're saying that you give them the directives? That you told them to throw me away last night?"

"Was that last night?" she said. "Could be, I don't remember who came when. But I remember every one of my guests. You are the one who came back again after such a long wait."

"Of course I would. Haven't I created you?"

"Why did you wait so long to come to me if you created me?"

"I don't know. Maybe I am not used to getting the things I want. Maybe my desire is so strong that it would have blown me way unless I softened it with a prolonged delay."

"So, what do you want to do with me now? You want to take me out of this hell?"

"You find this place a hell?"

"I don't know. I've been here probably too long for me to call it that."

"Because you got used to it?"

"Yes. But when one lives at a place for too long, any place can feel like that, I guess?"

"Unless, maybe, if you can somehow manage not to live in the place too much."

"What do you mean?"

"You know, your world is the world that you create."

"But this is the only place I know. I have nowhere else to go. How could I possibly do that?"

"But here's the thing: you don't always have to be physically present to really be somewhere, do you?"

"You are probably right. I hear so many stories from my visitors. Every day I have seen dozens of them, and they all came burdened with their tales. There is no exception. All the stories began with sadness, and then as they walk along their stories, they end up being joyful. Those stories are what has kept me going all these years."

"You mean, all they did was tell you stories?"

"No, not really. They shared them only by laying their heads on my stomach."

"That's all they did?"

"Yes, that's all . They put their heads on my stomach and shared their stories with me. Then when the time came, my bodyguards threw them out."

"They never got into you?"

"I can't recollect any such instance."

"What about the guards? They never wanted you?"

"I think they did. I could see it in their eyes in the way they never looked into my eyes, the way they always kept themselves at a distance, and took care not to touch me. Didn't you see? They are so strong, yet they always look so battered, so worn down. Sometimes I have seen bruises on their bodies, on their strong arms and faces. I cannot see what they hide under their uniforms. But I have seen blood dripping down their shirts. I felt bad for them. One day I called them near me. They obliged, but just stood there with their heads hanging, their hands clasped together in front. I even asked them why they never looked at me. They didn't say a thing. One of them had a wound on the back of his hand. I wanted to touch it. When I did, his whole body shuddered. I moved my hand and looked at his face. He looked away, his face contorted as if in an effort to hold back tears. I felt too bad and told them they could go their own way. But then something happened. The one I touched looked into my eyes for the first time. It was only for a moment, but his eyes were so full of passion that they got burned into my memory. I have never seen him again. And I never talked to any of them again."

"So, you are still a virgin?"

"That's the way you wanted it to be, didn't you?"

"I think I did, but I am not sure anymore."

"What do you mean?"

"I don't think I want you to be a virgin anymore."

"What do you mean? You wanted me to be with everybody who came to me?"

"I don't know. But I don't think I got it right. I can't have you. You … you cannot be gotten. See, I try to touch you but I cannot. You are too pure, too unsullied. It is all too ethereal. But I want to hold you. I want to hold you against me hard. How do I do that? It does not matter to you if I love you with all my purity, if my touch is devoid of all sin, if I call you using all the endearments of the world. It does not matter to you, because you have not seen it otherwise."

"Then don't love me. You can hurt me; you can abuse me."

"No, that won't work. You are not initiated to hurting. You don't know them. It won't matter to you."

"But then I will get used to it. You can initiate me. And then you can hurt me."

"But then it will be all the same to you always. You will get used to being hurt by me. What difference would it make when I do it later?"

"You can love me then. When I am expecting abuse from you, you can come back with the purity of your love."

"But how shall I be pure again, once I soil myself by hurting you? And it won't matter to you, anyway. You will have a picture of me in your mind, and everything I do you will interpret in that light."

"What do you want to do, then?"

"I am sorry, Penelope. I have to abandon you. I have to let you go."

"If that is what you need to do. But I will be here for you, if you want to come back to me. But you know that already."

"May I kiss you?"

"How could you do that? You have already left me. If you still kiss, that would be with someone else."

IX

THE LONG WAY TO THE
HOUSE

Henry gathered his parchments, dropped them in a leather folder, and fetched a large needle and a fish line. He sewed up the three sides of the folder, from left to right. The parchments stayed put inside, but the small gaps between the stitches puckered open like the lips of fish struggling to breathe out of water. He tightly sewed it from right to left.

Satisfied, he took it with him as he walked toward the lagoon. The wind was quiet and the water calm enough to set up a blurred reflection of the sky, where a few small pieces of white cloud dabbed against the blue, ignorant of their own whereabouts.

For a long time, he stood ankle-deep in the water. The sun warmed his skin. The wind blew his curls and made them tickle behind his ears. A seagull flew overhead in front of the sun, hiding its light for a broken moment. He held the folder out, intending to drop it, but waited so long that the wind grew restless and waves frothed on their crests. He went back home, his hands not relenting.

Henry looked around his room for a safe place to store the folder. The small table, which stood on two legs and was propped against the wall to compensate for the missing legs, had nothing on it but a layer of downy dust that stuck to the thin lamina of grease as if out of languor. But through that hazy overlay one could discern the outlines of objects that had stood there in the past, and had probably worked hard to impress Henry, but his preoccupation with things external to his residence was too strong for mere objects to overcome. The only seat in the room was an old, heavily embroidered cushion Henry had bought from a royal sellout market. Its intricate needlework of gold, burgundy, and dark emerald had lost their distinctions, an oily sheath making its colors indistinct and its texture gloomy. It sat on a stocky stone pillar he had salvaged from a decommissioned fountain in the marketplace. The pillar's spiral grooves inclined the shadows of his room toward the darkness beneath the table.

The bed was made of thin planks of wood. Henry had laid a few worn-out blankets to lend it an allusion of softness. The sheet was once white, but long ago lost any definition to become a gradient of gray that started mildly at the edge, then deepened at the center and slowly went lighter toward the other side, which was pushed against the wall. On top of that gray, its landscape was marked by stains of different sizes and colors: food, bird shit, spilt ink, dead flies, and things he had no idea about. Beneath the short-hanging bed sheet emerged the pointy tips of a pair of old boots.

A wooden coat tree with six or seven stakes guarded the door from inside. A blue jacket hung on the side away from the door, a pair of breeches below it. The stand was topped by a checkered hat. Like the bed, it had lost its color to the soft tones of the gray dust deposited there over the years. Nowhere could Henry find a place to hide his folder. He stepped outside.

The thoughts about sullying himself: those he could find no place to bury. To reach his Echo, his long-enforced chastity had led him nowhere, spawning only long-winded roads of deception, issuing pleasures only from the promise of a destination of love that had now descended on him as false and useless, a shimmering mirage on an unending stretch of hot and barren road. Henry decided to change this: to defile his chastity.

* * *

When he stood at the threshold of the front door of The House, getting his eyes accustomed to the dark interior, he heard a gasp, followed by a series of soft but eager footsteps. Henry saw Artemis rushing to him. It was warm summer morning and she was only in her skirts—barefooted and bare-chested. Her hips swung like those of a happily pudgy housewife, and her long, black skirt, which she held up in one hand, danced on both sides.

"Where have you been all this time?" she said. The shock in her eyes seemed so authentic that it felt almost sweet. Her face was not made up, and the wrinkles beside her eyes looked honest. Her morning voice sounded more mundane than ever, but the sweat beads on her bare shoulders and wetness near her armpits gave an air of sea-beach freshness. Through her lips, parted in surprise, her crooked bottom left canine looked yellowish. Her hair was not done yet; she had it bundled and tied up with a small shell clip on the top. Henry had never looked at her this closely before. When he finished summing up her body and came back to her eyes, her shock started to ease.

"You cannot just go away one day like that!" she said, letting go of her skirt and placing her hands on her waist. She now droned in a complaining tone. "You know, I had planned to extend the House in the back ... had the lumber ordered and even made the carpenter agree to give me a break on his fee, telling him we had a handyman."

Henry thought he should have felt angry for this impudence. Artemis took him for granted. But the way her blunt elbow tips bent sideways, and her un-tanned upper arm glowed in innocence, he could summon only pity.

"Why, you still could do it, couldn't you?" Henry said.

"Oh well, I have let it rot in the weather for too long, I guess," she said, dropping her shoulders.

"What weather? There hasn't been much rain lately."

"True."

She stretched her head as if to have a look at the "weather" through the door behind Henry.

"But every time I pass that stack, it upsets me," she said. "I did get a break on the lumber, from one of our clients, but he still did not give it for free, you know? And I have two new girls and I need more rooms."

"But the wood is probably just fine, right? It's just that you counted on me to do it that bothers you, I think."

"Maybe so."

Artemis seemed distracted. She looked closely into his face and frowned to shoo away the bright backdrop of the outside world. It was probably his sudden talkativeness that caught her attention. She took a couple of steps aside to get a better look at him.

"So you are back for some time?" she asked, but did not wait for his response. "I will send someone to the carpenter right away. You can start tomorrow."

There was, of course, no one else to send. It had to be him. Even if there were someone, she wouldn't trust that person with the travel allowance.

"What do you say?" she said.

Henry was bemused that she was even asking his opinion.

"Look, Artemis, I would have loved to help you. But I cannot stay that long. I have come just to see Psyche."

"What's the rush? Why don't you have one of the new girls for a longer slot. On the House. Whoever you want. You can have Psyche, too, if that's what you really want. But there is a new girl, quite a stunner."

"No, Artemis, I am good. I will just have a word with Psyche and leave."

"Okay."

Henry expected further dawdling, but instead, something was taking place in her face. Her frown transformed into a smile, and her lips joined in with a hint of coquetry. She pulled her skirt up and, stood on her toes, leaned closer to him and whispered, "Come with me. I have something to show you."

She turned around, pulling her skirt higher as if to offer space to her sudden nimbleness, and danced toward the other room.

Henry followed and tentatively asked, "Where is Psyche?"

Artemis stopped and giggled, saying, "She is not here today."

Henry knew she was lying, but wanted to play along. But more than anything, somehow, it now seemed fitting that his unbudding should be done by Artemis. He let her lead him into the room.

"Sit here. I will be right back." She raised a whirl in her skirt.

Henry sat on the bed and said, "You don't have to change."

She stopped but did not turn back as she said, "Just a quick wash. I am all sweaty."

"It's all right. I like the smell."

"Do you, now?" She turned and stood in front of him, seemingly at a loss as to what to do. In her eyes, Henry spotted a little girl struggling to figure out what offense she was being punished for. Henry playfully squinted his eyes and raised his brow. She gathered her skirt and Henry traced the silhouette of her legs and their curves. He grabbed her shoulders and pulled her to him.

* * *

As Henry walked out of the room following his initiation, Artemis followed him in a hurry and said, "Don't you want to see Psyche?"

"No, not today."

"She is not with anyone at the moment."

"Of course not. How could she be, when she is not even here?"

Henry turned around and looked fully into her eyes.

"You don't really mind my little lies, do you?" Her playfulness was overtaken by the pudginess of a busy House mistress.

"What happened to you, Henry? You've changed an awful lot!"

"You should've asked sooner."

"I guess so. But come again. I will cook for you next time."

"You cook in here?"

"At my own little place."

* * *

Henry went back to Artemis's a few months later, but this time the visit was merely a coincidence, and unavoidable. He went to the Neighborhood every week, visiting a new woman each night. He started from the first House on the street, taking the first woman he found waiting. From there, it had been a mindless traversal of almost a lunatic frenzy to connect as many dots as he could to conjure a picture too intricate for him to perceive or even to care about much.

But he kept an account of all his encounters. Every morning, back at his two-legged table, he wrote in his journal. Page after page he filled up with details that rivaled, at the same time, the diligence and the detachment of an accountant. There was hardly any time to sleep because he had to leave home shortly after his writing time for work. He worked because he had started to save money. Then there was the matter of paying for his nocturnal adventures.

He found a job in a flower shop, the smallest and dankest one, at the end of a row in the Marketplace. Henry's employer bore more than a few similarities with his store: small, crabby, and alone. Hermes was his name.

Hermes's clientele was made up of those who realized that quality flowers were out of their reach and who happened to pass the dank little store at the far end of the market, where a rotund little man tried hard to conceal his perennial grumpiness with a smile as magnanimous as his broad, shiny head. They might not have cared for his grin, but they did care for his prices.

When Henry offered himself as a helping hand, Hermes dropped his smiling charade and seemed ready to spew a flurry of profanity. He didn't make enough to make his own ends meet, he said, and paying an employee was out of the question. But Henry explained that he was willing to get paid only from any additional business he could bring, and wanted only half of the profit for each job. This offer sounded safe to Hermes, with nothing to lose.

Hermes indeed had a lot to win. Within days, Henry had reversed Hermes's fortune. Henry had a way with flowers and produced magnificent arrangements. The touch of his fingers brightened the colors of the most wilted and dullest of flowers, and each arrangement emanated a unique and captivating fragrance. Henry's prowess rapidly spread through the market, and sales catapulted.

Demand soon far outstripped the store's sales capacity. Hermes hired a few more hands, and they helped with other chores. But his bottleneck was Henry, who could conjure up only so many arrangements in the hours he worked. Hermes offered him full-time employment with pay higher than the market norm to squeeze the most out of his prodigious employee. Henry also received better offers from the competing flower shops, but he wanted none of it. He could not allow anything to gnaw into his time for the Neighborhood. In fact, he was certain that his success could not be sustained if he stopped visiting the Neighborhood. He drew inspiration for his themes from each visit, and his morning journaling foretold that day's work in the flower shop.

At any rate, the business flourished. Orders were placed for special events, and Henry's stamp of excellence was immediately apparent in this capacity, as well. These events brought big money to the business. Henry did not cash out his ever-increasing share, however, but instead arranged with the owner an agreement for safekeeping Henry's money after his daily expenses were deducted. Hermes realized that the initial profit-sharing deal with Henry had not been as good as he initially assumed. But it was too late now. All Hermes could do—not without a great amount of consternation—was watch as Henry's fortune grew. Of course, this meant equal earning on his part, too, but Hermes found it increasingly difficult to stomach the agonizing parity of riches between a mere employee and himself.

On the romantic front, Henry found it very easy to get carried away. His relative indifference to the surroundings meant he did not notice anything out of the ordinary. His newfound way of channeling his passion was no help, either, and after a few months of weaving through one house after another in the Neighborhood, spending each night with a different woman, he stepped into Artemis's house in due course. For him, it was just another connecting dot, and he failed to even recognize the House as special. Nor did he recognize Artemis when she led him into the room where he had first met Psyche a long time before.

Psyche sat on the bed in her standard pose, her stretched arms resting on her raised left knee, her right foot tucked below, and the familiar, albeit faded bruise peeping out beneath her short blouse. That pose hit something in Henry, and he was brought back as if from a months-long reverie into which his affair with flowers had induced him. He recognized Psyche, and subsequently recognized the room. And the House.

Not that Psyche recognized Henry, which was obvious from the way she let a smile play coquettishly. She jutted her midriff, stretching her belly button over the smooth expanse of her stomach, her arms squeezing in to form an ominous cleavage. More than anything else, her inadvertent flirtatiousness created a mirror for Henry, in which he could see how much he himself had changed since he last visited the House.

Part of this was physical. He had shaved his beard, his mullet was gone, and his hair was short and neatly trimmed. His body had lost its dirt-brown layer. His unruly moustache was reduced to a geometric certainty. A duality of his shirt and breeches in bright white and black had replaced the infinite possibility of his previously mud-colored shirt, which carried the stamps of his myriad adventures. Starkest of all his changes was the dullness of his eyes, which previously burned with insatiable lust.

Now, dipping into the distance in Psyche's eyes, Henry was aroused for the first time on account of her lustiness, as well as in the loss of the Psyche whom he once knew. And because of this, he decided that the desecration of his chastity was now complete.

The time had come to see Echo.

"What are you looking at?" Psyche said in an apparent attempt to break his reverie. "The night will not wait for us, you know."

"It won't matter." Henry was amused at the cruel tenor in his own voice. "You don't have even a window to see the night leaving."

He stood straight and let his eyes lustfully poke at Psyche's bodily goods with a lewdness that would rival Echo's infamous husband.

"Clever. But there is a door all the same, and it never closes," she said as she bent the toes of her left foot upward. Then, she whispered, "You think you could shut them out ... for me?"

Henry smiled coldly and worked his way through the tiny opening between the footboard and dresser. He stopped to glance at her foot to try one last time to scavenge, even if a tiny speck of, his Psyche.

No, she had not changed. Only the bruise under her blouse had paled, and there was a new scratch mark on her neck. But none of her immutability could bring the old Psyche back. Before that pain of loss could prevent him from touching her, he embraced her and unhooked her blouse from the back. All the while he kept his eyes on hers, and when a smile of appreciation rose on her lips, he planted a long smothering kiss on them, leaving Psyche wanting for air. Once Henry finished the kiss, and even before Psyche could come to terms with her breath, she was lying, her clothes strewn on the cold floor and his face buried between her breasts.

When Henry was putting his clothes on, the night might not have been over, but, in the meantime, he had done enough to push the dense thicket of her unfamiliarity for him, even if a just a little. When he took one last look at her, she recognized him at once.

"Hey! It's you!"

Henry smiled and turned .

"Wait a moment, will you?" Her voice started to break.

But Henry had already left, and there was no way he could return.

* * *

The next evening, Henry skipped Artemis's House, even though there were three other women there for Henry to visit. When he got back home, he found Psyche sitting on his bed. Henry stood at the threshold for a few moments, stunned at the difference in her appearance. Were it not for the symmetrical spots on her cheeks, he would have taken much longer to recognize her. She wore a long, dark cloak. But more than that, her face was shrouded with such dejection he wondered if it was only the previous night that he had seen her. Before she could tear through her thick screen of melancholy to speak, Henry grabbed his pajamas from the tree hanger and stepped out the back of the house and into the yard covered by trees and sprawling, untamed bushes. When he returned, Psyche was in the middle of the room, prepared to stop him from evading her once again.

"Where have you been all these days?"

"What do you mean?"

"Why did you suddenly disappear?"

"I don't know why you ask," he said.

He started toward the table, but Psyche sidestepped to block him. Henry stopped and looked into her eyes.

She waited.

"I don't know why you ask," he said again. "I never even saw you in those days I stayed at the House."

"Yes, yes. I know. But..."

"But what?"

"But I saw you! I knew you were there for me. All those days ... all my days ... they were so much more bearable for me, knowing that someone was there for me, waiting and longing for me."

"You cannot have missed me, can you? I never even touched you."

"I know, I know. Maybe that's why I missed you."

Psyche raised her hands as if to grab his shoulders, but stopped short and clasped them together in front of her stomach.

"The moment they touch me, they lose me, and at that instant I lose them, too," she said. "It's the longing that keeps them waiting for me."

"Why do you want me always waiting for you?"

"Because that's how I live. That's how I've learned to live, ever since you came."

"But I cannot live that way."

"You cannot? You cannot. But ... but I don't care, Henry."

"You don't care about me. And you expect me to care about you?"

"Yes. Because you do care for me. You care for me, anyway."

"How do you know?"

"Because, after that, you never ccme back to the House again. Everybody knows your story, Henry! The story of Mr. Henry. I knew, too. But I didn't know you were the same person. Until you showed up in my room the other night. Then you left. And did not come back again. Even though three other women were available. That is not how the story of Mr. Henry goes. Mr. Henry goes to every woman. But you didn't. Because I was there. You didn't want to come back! Why? Because something changed in you after seeing me. You didn't want to see other women with me being there. And that's because you do care for me."

"There could be other reasons."

"There could be. But there isn't. And you know that."

"So, what do you want from me?"

"Come back to my place and be there for me."

"And what do I get in return?"

"I don't know. I don't care. But at least you know that there is someone, someone who lives knowing that you are there for her. That would work for you, wouldn't it?"

"It could."

"So you are coming back to the House?"

"I'll think about it, Psyche." Henry started toward the table again.

"You will think?"

"Yes."

Psyche stepped up and grabbed his shirt.

"Henry!" she whispered. "You want me to get killed?"

"No, I don't."

Henry pulled her hand away from his shirt, but didn't let it go.

"I will see about coming to your place," he said, stifling an urge to kiss her fingers before letting them go.

Psyche stayed until Henry finished his dinner and was ready for bed. She leaned on the wall, undulating against it. Her cloak slid from her shoulders, and she curled her hands under her chin and followed Henry's every movement through the haze of her tears. The bed was narrow, and when Henry sat on the edge and looked back at her, she walked over, grabbed his shoulders and kissed him on the mouth. His cold, unrelenting apathy shocked her. Before her face shattered completely, she let him go. Her scorching steps raised angry chatters across the wooden floor, and her cloak whirled in the small enclosure of his dreary room in her tempestuous exit.

X

⚜

FINDING ECHO

At the flower store the next morning, Henry took stock of his savings from Hermes. Business was good. Despite all his visits to Neighborhood, he had accumulated a very healthy amount. Henry took a few bills to lease an expensive suit and a pair of nice shoes. He then rented a carriage and started for the Castle.

As the carriage slowed to a stop at the towering gatehouse, the pebbles that shot from the wheels carried on their squabble with the wooden spokes before settling on the gravel road. The gray edifice loomed, an impregnable, sprawling giant. The quiet was replaced with the grating of the heavy portcullis climbing up, almost as if on its own will. This surprised Henry to no end. Half of the city people would sacrifice a limb to get behind this gate. The overlord of the Castle, Narcissus, held unfathomable power and unimaginable wealth. And Narcissus was known for his relentless desire to keep them inside these walls. When the iron gate opened at Henry's mere arrival, he didn't know whether to be elated or alarmed.

No soul emerged on the other side, but from the barbican above came a voice that complemented both the rasping of the opening gate and the hospitality of the burgeoning tranquility this morning promised.

"Come in, please!"

One of the four narrow windows upstairs opened.

The metal grille did not completely disappear into the arched ceiling, and the tips of the heavy rods hung threateningly in the air, but there was enough clearance for the carriage as it creaked and squeaked through. Once inside the gatehouse, an armored sentry was visible, standing rigidly in a depression in the left wall. One of his hands hung straight, and the other held a long spear, signaling for the carriage to halt. The sound of descending footsteps came through an open door leading to a dark staircase on the right.

Ahead, a long stone pathway ran straight into the inner section of the castle. This ended at another gate, rather ornate, of wrought iron with elaborate floral patterns. Beyond the gate there was a large garden with trimmed shrubs and manicured floral beds. Fountains were interspersed with trees, their water reaching different heights and creating various patterns in the air. Henry heard the stories of the lavish and extravagant parties held in the garden and in the grand ballrooms. At this time of day, however, the din of those hedonic hours was replaced by the serene rustle of the fountains.

Henry strained to hear the sound of the water, but the impending footsteps on his right materialized into a person, whose uniform bore less severity than that of the guard's. The middle-aged man exuded a gravitas that came more from his posture than his attire.

"Welcome to the Castle!" he said, squinting slightly at the darkness inside the carriage and smiling in a way that seemed too amicable for his authoritative countenance.

"May I ask whose presence the Castle has the pleasure of, sir?"

"Henry."

It was the only moniker he had used in a long time. It hung in the air but did little to quench the flicker of inquiry in the eyes of his questioner. In that interval, the faint murmur from the downstream canals of the garden fountains wafted through the wrought iron gate and reached Henry. Henry dived, almost unwillingly, into a part of his memory that raised a cloud of dust and a smell of rust. As he faced the man, he found something inside himself as strange as a life from a time long gone.

"Apollo," he said. "Henry Apollo."

The smile on the other side of the carriage window broadened a trifle.

"The famed Henry Apollo! It is a great pleasure to have you at the Castle, sir, Mr. Apollo."

Doing what suggested a quick bow, the man produced a piece of paper from his vest pocket and glanced at it.

"I am very sorry to inform you that Mr. Narcissus is not in the Castle at the moment. He is out of town on a business trip. We expect him back in two weeks."

He bent forward, putting his right hand on the top of the carriage window, and asked. "Did Mr. Apollo have an appointment with Mr. Narcissus today?"

"No."

"Is Mr. Apollo carrying a letter from an acquaintance of Mr. Narcissus?"

"No, I have come here uninvited."

"My regrets and apologies, sir, that you have missed Mr. Narcissus. He left just yesterday."

The man straightened and clasped his hands with an air of finality, then added, "Nevertheless, Mr. Apollo is most welcome to stay at the guest house for the night."

Henry waded through the information and weighed this offer. This must have been a mere formality on the staff member's part. Besides, despite Henry's inexorable desire to see Echo, in his reckoning, gaining access to the Castle so effortlessly had seemed the most unlikely prospect. The only proper thing was a polite refusal. But that would not help his cause. Henry was not impatient, but his arrival at the decision to meet Echo bore the burden of a longing far too great. His unfaltering patience meant that the finality of his decision carried a great weight of definitude. For him it was not a matter of propriety, but of preference. If accepting the offer to stay in the Castle that Henry assumed to be a mere decorum increased his chance of encountering Echo, he did not bother with propriety.

"Pardon me, sir, if I am meddling, but do you have a business matter with Mr. Narcissus?" the staff member said, apparently mistaking Henry's deliberation as indecision.

"Yes," Henry said as he looked into the staff member's eyes and then beyond. "Yes, I do."

Henry pondered how individual lives were broken into pieces, and how each piece was compressed to fit all the bits of that life into a narrow flow that was allowable to, and by, the partakers of a conversation.

"In that case, I suspect I have something to offer," the staff member said, smiling graciously. "Mrs. Narcissus looks after business in absence of her husband."

Henry looked into the eyes of the staff member and tried to figure if he had somehow recognized Henry's real motive. But in the backdrop of amiableness, all he found was a wall. Could it really be this easy?

"It would be my pleasure to meet Mrs. Narcissus."

For all his composure, Henry could not be sure if he was able to make the word "pleasure" sound as aloof as he intended. Again, that wall of eyes stared back at him. He added, "Unless, of course, I am a bother."

"Not at all, sir," the staff member said as he looked to his right, straightened up, and waved. "Puck here will lead you to the guest house, where you can relax. I will inform Mrs. Narcissus, and hopefully we will be able to arrange a meeting for this evening."

Henry found himself in an enormous, elegantly decorated room. It required a great deal of effort to come to terms with its excesses. Standing at the threshold, as he looked from left to right, he appreciated the sheer size of the room only as a source of awe. The bed was exceedingly high and wide, the floor covered in too-soft carpet, the room too dark from the excessively thick curtains hanging from the impractically large and almost unusable windows. The chairs and the tables were overly ornate.

But as he stepped on the stool and sat on the bed, he picked up a perspective that allowed him to make an observation regarding himself: that he was even assessing the extent of luxury had its own implications. Were he to be in this same room a few months earlier, before he had renounced his chastity, he would have barely registered such profligacy. But even though the licentious nature of his own recent behavior did not have much bearing on his outlook, it did acquaint him with the habit of "excess," and he had developed the faculty to discern as such. The evidence that people spent so much time in such repetitive and inherently useless objects indicated to him a senselessness that verged on brutality.

Henry had not brought a change of clothes. As he lay down with his feet dangling over the step stool, the vaulted ceiling jumped into his vista, almost half of which was concealed by a huge chandelier that hung directly overhead. His tired body sank into the mattress, which was softer than anything he had ever touched. But his aversion to extravagance caught up with him, and besides the physical relief, a weariness landed upon him. With his body wedged in the bed's cool caress,, he closed his eyes. The crystals of the chandelier started to move and noiselessly tinkle to melt into a pale mush of smoky glass when a soft rap at the door brought him back to his senses. He waited for a second rap to make sure the first was not a part of an impending dream. It never arrived. His sense of time was blurred by the haze of his swing between sleep and wakefulness before the crystals stopped moving and the chandelier was reinstated with its original demeanor.

They just want to announce the time of the meeting, Henry thought. Or postpone it. Or cancel. Only if the rap on the door was real. When he finally disentangled himself from his repose and opened the door, he found a lady holding a tray. She was dressed as if she were going to a ball, and her face was bright with a smile he could not decipher.

"If you feel like indulging yourself, sir," she said as she lifted the tray a little. Four white china bowls, serving vittles, on four corners, were centered by a scarlet, oval plate arranged with freshly cut fruits of an assortment of hues.

"Thank you, but I'm not hungry."

"Then I can leave it here, if you wish."

She stepped forward, and her right foot, strapped in a high heel, peeped from under her long, flared skirt.

"Just in case you change your mind, Mr. Apollo."

Henry found it interesting the way she addressed him as Mr. Apollo. He darted outside of himself to see how "Mr. Apollo" would react, expecting a response idiosyncratic to the gentlemen he had seen with women in such settings. Nothing followed, and the lady raised her brows in tension as her right hip clearly strained from her forward step. Her knee quivered, and the frill of her skirt, draping from the knee, waved in the air.

"I don't change my mind frequently," he said.

Her forward knee now straightened, and her foot was taken back to meet the other. A thin cloud of pain formed in her eyes while the rest of her face sustained that meaningless smile.

"I will gladly take it back," she said, changing her posture. "Please ring the bell if you need anything."

Henry did not remember seeing a bell. He could find that later, of course, but meanwhile, the lady had not moved. Is she waiting for permission?

"I did not mean to be rude," Henry said.

"You were not, sir."

She attempted to brighten her face as if Henry's notion was absurd. But she seemed to realize the truth in it and ended up smudging her smile with the frail cloud in her eyes that rushed across her face.

Henry could not understand why she had to deny his rudeness, but he was not wont to argue. He took her distressed canvas of a face into his heart to stir himself; he had been numb from all the extravagance in the castle for far too long.

The lady lingered for a few moments before turning around. She stepped down the stair gingerly, her skirt swaying with each step and its hem stroking her ankles. She looked so pitiful in her slow gait that Henry wanted to step down and kiss her nape. But something kept him tethered in the room, almost as if in a spell. When she disappeared, he closed the door and lay down on the bed, staring at the ceiling again. He savored his sadness for her and let the spasm in his throat grow a cushy lump.

* * *

When the coupe horse carriage trotted down the stone pathway and entered through the wrought iron gate, the restless water sprays that formed the fountain tips were wiping the last traces of crimson from the western sky. The carriage stopped in front of a large entrance to the main building. Henry was led through long, shadowy hallways with rows of closed doors on both sides, ending up in a sitting room.

The room was cavernous, but after just a few steps, Henry realized that all the space and decoration in the room, all the paintings on the walls, the sculptures of differing sizes and media mounted on various stands around the space, the rugs and the chandeliers and potted plants—all of this was meant to accommodate a rendezvous of just two people. All the flamboyant redundancies fashioned a round opening, centered near the corner opposite to the door he entered through. Two elaborately ornate armchairs were placed on one side of that negative orb, facing each other and separated by a low and heavy table. The longer sides of the table bulged slightly, its lacquered top glistening in checkered tone of gold and mahogany. On some of the squares stood single ivory figurines. Together they suggested a sense of careful dis-organization. But Henry discerned a queen, a knight and a bishop in the taller ones. The smaller statuettes were easily recognizable as pawns, encircling the genteel.

His escort offered him the chair that had its back toward the open space. When he sat, he found himself in the locus of the cold, blank eyes of all the chess pieces. The daunting energy they directed at him was unmistakable. It was not in him to discern a battleground. Henry never picked a fight, never appreciated hostile elements of any sort, in any way. But when one can be fearless, or rather indifferent, in a battle-ground, it does not prevent one from getting hurt. But this did not matter to him. He looked at the walls, which were dappled with lights from the chandeliers.

A soft wind blew from the entrance and crept past him, over his head toward the other side of the room, raising tinkles from the crystals of the chandeliers. They glistened, and the rugs came to life as the dapples danced over them and across the walls. With the wind wafted the fragrance from the flowers on an exotic plant across him. It was unlike anything that he ever smelled, but it brought myriad scents that he had known well on the long journey of his love life.

When Echo stepped into the room, dazzling in a peacock-blue dress, Henry stood. He was disarmed.

XI

❦

HESTIA INTERVENES

Her pale skin looked soft but it had lost the intensity the lagoon sun had imbued in it. Her lips looked thinner, as if from the weight of years of silence. Her hands embodied the work of a sculptor, perfected to the last crease on her knuckles. Her fingers posed the moves of a ballerina, each arrested in the same stupor that soaked the whole Castle to its last hallway, halted only by the glitter and weight of her jeweled rings. When she asked Henry to sit, her lips smiled, but her eyes retained their distant apathy. She sat upright, then slanted a little toward her right, touching the armrest with her right elbow, to look fully at Henry.

Henry was disarmed. As Echo looked at him, the smile from her lips abated, and her eyes took on a tinge of apprehension.

"I welcome you to the Castle, Mr. Apollo."

Henry sat motionless, his eyes acting as the window between an unstirred exterior and an interior that raged in a gale of emotion at finally seeing her after so many excruciating years of longing.

"What brings you here?" Echo asked.

Henry could not begin to answer—not without setting off the avalanche that had grown into a monstrosity over the long, unbearable winters of his pining. Still, even the quietest of seas had ripples, even if the minutest ones. Despite the glaring blindness on the faces of the chess pieces, the fragrance that preceded Echo into this room now surmounted the miniature ranks, and flanked his defense. More than anything else, the scent reminded him of the Castle itself, which assisted him snatching himself from the edge of the abyss.

"I came to discuss business with Mr. Narcissus."

Did the sound of his voice accentuate the apprehension in her face? Did her brows knit a little? Did her eyes wade back through her memory for an instant?

"You can feel free to talk to me," she said, regaining her composure. "My husband and I have no secrets. But only if that is not a problem for you, of course."

Henry smiled at this assault on his emotive bastion. She asked him to feel free. To talk to her. What else could he have come for? But the time was not ripe. Not yet. Besides, her words were imbued in the same darkness he had walked through just a moment earlier: the long cold hallways, as if the Castle's musty air devoured its inhabitants and gnawed at the depths of their souls. No less Echo. Henry held to that thought to safeguard his stronghold.

"It's not a problem, but this matter I should only discuss with Mr. Narcissus."

"Then I am afraid you will have to wait until next week."

She straightened, clasped her hands on her lap, and said, "We expect him to return by then."

"I can come back."

"Do you live in town?"

"Yes."

"Then it is at your discretion. But you are welcome to stay at the Castle in the meantime. Of course, I don't presume to interfere with any other businesses you may have."

"Nothing to interfere with. But I prefer to leave tonight."

"As you wish. Anything else I can do for you?"

"Yes, if you don't mind sitting for another few moments."

To Henry's proposition, the trepidation in her eyes attempted a return, but all that could form on her face was a misty puzzlement. Her brows slightly rearranged, eyes donning a tinge of unmindfulness.

Henry sat back and looked at her hands, then traced upward. The translucence of her organza sleeves meddled with his memory, but the opacity of the thick draping on her skirt indulged him in reliving the splendor of her legs from the night they she had swum by his side during The Green Festival. Her pale chest sported a locket with a too-familiar coat of arms. When his gaze returned to her face, her lips were parted a little, her breathing deeper, and her eyes melted.

As if on cue, she rose and said, "If you change your mind, or if things change favorably, you may talk to me about your business."

"Thanks for staying ... for me."

"My pleasure." The puzzlement left her eyes.

"We will see you at dinner, then," she said before turning and walking away

* * *

Back in his room, Henry sensed a burgeoning emptiness in his heart. As if something he cherished for a long, long time stood to lose its worth. Something that accrued value primarily in proportion to its unattainability. Her voluntary invitation to dinner daubed a mundane brush across something very precious.

Henry thought about the woman from the afternoon and entered a pleasant longing for her. He wanted to fill his emptiness with that yearning. When the time came to attend the dinner, Henry was happy when the woman failed to appear. The fullness of his void was un-interrupted.

* * *

If the sitting room table was fashioned in an arrangement of ag-gression, the dining room was a rampart of epicurean visuals. The only other chair that flanked the massive, round table was shielded from him by an array of dishes; none matched the other, either in color or form. Nevertheless, they conjured up a wonderful gastronomical composition against the backdrop of the heavy mahogany. The butler stood a few polite steps away, facing Henry, with a hint of a bow that insinuated readiness to serve at command.

"This," Echo said from her seat. "I have prepared myself."

A small china dish steamed with what looked like meat with thick pieces of onion.

"Goat liver. A little experiment."

"Kindly tell me when it is enough, sir," the butler said as he picked up a silver spoon from the outer part of the table.

The blunt tinkle of the silverware against the china perturbed the repose of the comestible and stirred up a voluptuous aroma of sautéed cumin and ginger. Henry allowed himself a generous helping and, impaling a forkful, placed it in his mouth. He chewed and moved it around, his tongue pressing it against the roof of his mouth to feel the touch of her hand that was infused in the thick gravy.

As he swallowed, he found her gazing at him, her hands petrified on either side of her plate. Her eyes were so bare that Henry could see the deepest of her interior, where jade caterpillars crept through the greenest of grasses beside creeks that were dark and mellow, their water raising dulcet murmurs around stones covered with colorful frogs. Soft branches swayed in the cool breeze and stooped over the creek, almost touching the water, only to retreat back up against the sky that dripped intense blue around milky clouds.

"What else would you like, Mr. Apollo?" The butler took a step forward. "These sardines, fresh from the lagoon, braised with dill and lemon—"

Henry acted with such a force to tear himself from his reverie that the butler halted. Then the butler smiled, his eyes twinkling, and Henry made his way deep into those eyes, moved around, looked back at himself from their depths, and at Echo, from a different frame, in different light. When he returned back to himself, he himself could not help but smile.

* * *

Back in his room, Henry took the leather folder from his inside coat pocket and ran his fingers across the sutures. He looked around for something sharp, to tear through the reinforcements he had inflicted upon it. He noticed a golden rope hanging from beside the bed that went over a pulley wheel and out of the room through a small hole in the back wall. Henry recognized it to be the bell pull. The two bookshelves on each side of the bed was full with neatly arranged books with spines printed in golden watermarks. Nothing else. The room offered too many hideouts, too many nooks and crannies, and his urge to ransack the room for a knife swiftly receded. He brought the folder closer to further inspect the stitches and found that they had coalesced with the hide. The smell of leather repulsed him, but then he lifted the folder to his mouth and let his canine teeth dip into the taut line.

Henry disinterred his story. The story that he had woven in order to find a path to reach Echo seemed to start losing its pertinence. But the persona he had started to create in Penelope to proxy Echo in his lovelorn mind—at this moment, at least—struck him as an act of infidelity on his part. He felt a great urge to remove any evidence of that betrayal. The story he had buried had to be exhumed now, so that Penelope could be effaced.

The silver quill and inkwell on the writing desk did not remain mere embellishments any longer.

* * *

Penelope needs to get down from the bed to prepare for the next client. The rain has let up after pelting the garden beyond her window all day, but the sky still wears a thick, gray cap just over the horizon. The sun has crept down into that thin opening under the cloud to brighten the world before dipping headlong into night. The trees are still sodden, glistening against the backdrop of the sunset.

He wouldn't be in for a little while. Penelope plays a ruse with herself. Hasn't yet knocked on the door, anyway. She gets down from the bed. The cold marble sends a shiver through her feet. She crosses her arms over her bare torso and walks to the window, pressing her bosom against the cool glass panes. Her nipples stiffen, and she feels a blunt pain. She props her breasts with her hands to relieve the pain. The sun has now turned crimson, dissolving swiftly against the horizon, the trees dripping blood. Penelope lifts a white shawl from the armchair beside the bed. Wrapping it around her nakedness, she opens a window, and climbing through it leaves the room.

Her feet land on the wet, muddy ground with a squelching sound. The shawl gets splattered with small, dark blobs. Her feet are cold, but the sun's last rays spread a sugary warmth across her body. She strolls through the trees like a needle weaving aimlessly through a crocheted doily in an effort to flee from her semi-nudity. As the sun sets and everything around her un-dabs from the wet reds and oranges, the sky slowly uncaps itself, and the trees loom darker and taller. A gust of wind howls through the forest and shakes droplets of water from the leaves and branches, saturating her flimsy cover.

Her body shivers. She wants to head back. Her client must be in by now. He can wait, but she needs to go back. It's getting cold. But she has lost her way. It's been a while since she last came out here. There is no milestone to guide her way back. The trees appear identical in the dark, the sky spotlessly blank. The wind is deflected by the trees, blowing from every direction, swaying branches to create diabolical silhouettes against the pitch-black sky. Penelope runs, splattering mud all around. The end of her shawl flies behind her. A large, dead tree looms before her, its stiff, naked branches protruding ominously. She moves her head sideways to save her throat from being impaled by a branch, but it sticks to her shawl and tears it away. She loses her balance and crashes.

As she finds herself lying on her back, large drops of rain pepper her breasts and face. She crawls to an open space that appears to be the far perimeter of the garden. The ground slopes toward low-lying farmland with a little, wooden hut at its base. Penelope cannot remember the hut. But she scrambles closer to it, and losing her balance again, rolls down the decline. She lands at the door of the tiny room. The door is open and it is dark inside. She crawls inside and pushes the door shut against the wind, which is now a full-fledged thunderstorm. The hut is empty, and its wooden walls are dotted with holes. Water trickles down the walls, creating a puddle on the earthen floor where she has seated herself, embracing her legs, but this is better than the pelting ice-cold water outside. She puts her face between her knees. Her client must be waiting in her room. He can wait there for her. He will wait for her.

* * *

After he returned the carriage and walked home through the burgeoning buzz of the night, Henry sat on his bed, still in his boots and breeches. The tenacity of the nocturnal languor surrounding his room outlived his reminiscing and he remembered the previous evening again and again until he could no longer distinguish between what he remembered and what he borrowed from the recollections of previous nights. He brought out the newly scribed parchments from his folder. The moment he looked at those words, he knew that they, too, were destined for the same anachronistic ordeal that his memory had started to suffer. Memories were so conniving, even when in black and white. Instead of writing, Henry left for a walk.

The lagoon offered him the shelter he sought, with its detachment. The sky hovered indolent with a few scattered patches of listless clouds, the sand impassive, and the water bumping languidly on the shore with dull waves. He walked along the beach as the moon slid surreptitiously to the other side. He hadn't yet been able to remove Penelope from his story. But he had taken her very close. She could wait in that bare, lonely hut for some time. Because, for all the hospitality and warmth Echo had offered him, none of those had brought her even an inch closer to him. Echo's gesture possibly was a scripted formality availed to any guest of the Castle. Henry felt the need for something more from her, to win a borough or two from the expanse of her mind, in order to give his unwarranted guilt at least minuscule of substance. As he walked toward the impending dawn, Henry scoured his thoughts for an idea.

The darkness in the eastern sky faded, and with the stars decimated, Henry's legs gave way. He sat on the sand and waited until the lagoon water passed through all the matinal colors before the sun peeked over the simmering horizon. An idea descended on him. He walked to the marketplace, the sun clambering up his back.

When he reached the flower store where he worked, Hermes rushed to him, barely noticing Henry's disheveled clothes and hair and the drying wrinkles of sleepless eyes.

"Thank goodness you're back!" Hermes raised his hands and shook them. "It's been a riot! I turned away two weddings and one spring fair job yesterday. How could you do this to me? Don't you relax yet; we got two big orders before Sunday. Not a single moment to waste."

"I want to buy the store," Henry said dryly.

"What store? You want your own shop? Let's talk about that later, shall we? We got work to do here. And I mean work! The wedding is tomorrow night. I ordered the flowers yesterday. Thanks to my good judgment, they are already here." He lifted his chubby arm toward an indistinct location inside the dark interior of his shop. "And would you believe?" he said. "Those slackers haven't shown up yet! They are driving me crazy, you know. Thank goodness you are here."

"Hermes, I want to buy this store."

"What? You want to buy what?"

Henry blinked hard, hoping to moisten his unslept eyes.

"This shop! Are you crazy?"

"Look, I need to make a good amount of money in a short time. You know how poorly you pay. How much do you want for the store?"

"Hold on! Hold on! Have you lost your head? Why do you think I want to sell?"

"If you get its worth in cash, why not?"

"I don't even know how much to value it at. Never thought of selling. And. .. and I don't want to sell, anyway. What would I do if I didn't have it?"

"You could go on vacation. You've been working for too long. You deserve a nice getaway. Or if you want, you can work for me."

"Stop right there! Why am I even talking about it? Tell me this, where have you been? Where did you get this crazy idea from?"

Henry could not tell if the little man paused because he really wanted an answer or he just ran out of words.

"And, you know what? Even if I do sell this store, I would never sell it to you. And even if I had to, I will not work under you. Never!"

"You don't have to work. But if you change your mind, you are always welcome to work in my store."

"Your store! This is NOT your store. And it never will be!"

"See, I have saved a big portion of money you paid me. I will give you the whole of it. It's more than four thousand."

"What, are you crazy? I won't sell it even for ten thousand—if someone were to offer that much, that is."

"Ten thousand?" Henry ran his hand through his hair. "Would you sell it for twenty?"

"Twenty thousand! W-what if I did? You don't have that much money. No point talking about it."

"All right, twenty thousand then. I will be back in two days."

Henry turned and began walking away.

"Wait! Where do you think you're going? Get your twenty thousand when you can, but first we got to finish these orders."

"Never mind those orders," Henry said as he stopped and looked over his shoulder. "You don't have to worry about any orders, for that matter. Just plan your vacation. And if you do want to work for me, I am giving you seven days leave now. Paid."

Henry continued on his way.

"Stop this now, will you? This is my business, and it will remain so. You don't want to work, you can quit—after delivering these orders, that is. But stop ordering me around in MY store."

* * *

Henry paid heavy fines for returning the clothes dirty and crumpled, rented a change of new clothes and went home to wash. He then rented another carriage and ordered the driver to take him to the Castle. Then, he opened his folder and withdrew the quill to write shakily on the parchment.

* * *

Penelope wakes up by the knock on her door. Not from a sleep. She wakes up into a time that keeps resetting for her. She looks out the window—the garden is twilight red. The knock on the door repeats. Penelope abandons her comfort of impropriety and receives her client at the door. It isn't the convention to receive clients at the door. In fact, she doesn't remember when she last did so. It is a rare exemption for the patron, and it retains its worth not from the magnitude of occasionality, but rather, to the contrary. This is one vernacular custom that gathers its weight from the sheer extent of its existence. That somehow everyone, including Penelope, knows without being told that breaking the impropriety of receiving the guest half-lying on the bed with a postural disdain carries some weight. Tonight's guest heralds a special occasion. Penelope does not know the nature of the occasion, but her ignorance does not spare her from standing up to it.

As she opens the door, her guest stands there and looks inside the room with palpable apprehension. Penelope doesn't cajole him to enter, nor does she step aside. There is something weirdly familiar about him. The way he gets lost in bouts of distraction after each of his attempts to act attentive, the way he just stands there and offers no inkling of intention to step inside. Those eyes, and that apprehension in his eyes, are born out of prescience of something. An unmistakable foreknowledge of something sinister that lies in the not-too-distant future.

The evening has already been tumultuous. The sky drenched Penelope's garden with a blunt, gray downpour all day, and though it has now let up to finally allow the sun to play its scarlet farewell solo, the wind picked up again as the night encroached from the eastern sky. Now the wind is already howling around her room, and has been joined by incessant thunder.

His eyes do not flinch at the lightning. When finally his gaze arrives at, and rests on, her eyes, though fleetingly, she bends forward and, holding his large bony hands in hers, pulls him inside. She leads him to her bed and has him sit. At that moment, a glaring lightning floods her room, and deafening thunder follows. Penelope is so shaken that her knees give way. Before she collapses on the floor, her guest grabs her at her waist and pulls her up so she can lay her down on the bed. Her face is pallid and her lips, dry. She opens her eyes and looks at him with a lifetime of tiredness. He pulls the bed sheet over her.

"I will find some help," he says as he tries to get up.

Penelope snags his hand.

"Don't leave me. I will be fine."

She struggles to take a deep breath and says, "Just get me some water." She points to a jar and tumbler near the door.

Penelope struggles onto her elbow and takes a few sips. A drop of water slides down from the corner of her ashen lips.

"That was so close, that lightning," she says, pulling the sheet to her chin. "It cannot be too far beyond the garden."

"Something has burnt," he says as he turns his face to the window as if to confirm the source of the smell.

"There is a hut at the south end of the garden. Do you think the hut took the hit?"

"Or it could be any of those dead trees."

His urgency to negate her guess leads her to suspect he might know something. But she is too tired to protest.

"Yeah, it could be." She lies down again. "Do I know you, Mr.—"

"Henrique."

"Henrique! Even your name sounds familiar. Have you been here before, Mr. Henrique?"

"Penelope, you are not feeling well." Henrique looks away and says, "I can come another day."

"Another day! Yes, that is it." Her eyes suddenly become sharp, her voice belligerent. "You can always come another day. You so like to come another day. Why don't you stay here tonight for a change?"

"You are too weak, Penelope."

Penelope smiles wryly. The expression fails to exude strength.

She says, "I can send someone to see what happened to the hut."

"It's okay. I can go there for you and see."

"Of course you would do that. For me? I don't know. You won't listen to me, even if I ask you not to go. Because you want to do it for me. You want to do everything for someone else. It is your little trick to live unobliged. If you don't want to stay with me, you can go. You can go; you are free, but you won't. Because you want to do it for me, to go check the hut for me. Here, take this shawl with you. It is cold outside. But wait, what if there is no hut? What if I am just making it up? Who cares what happens to a miserable little shack? But it doesn't matter. You will go. You have already left. Just watch out for those cold, cruel, naked branches on the trees."

"I will, Penelope."

"Of course you will. You will carry out all my requests. You can make one feel so obliged."

Henrique drapes the white shawl over his shoulders and prepares to step to the hallway.

"Stop!" Penelope shrieks. "I don't want them to see you going to the garden. Just open the window."

Henrique steps out of the window. Penelope sees him outlined in lightning three more times before he disappears beyond the swaying trees.

* * *

On his return to the Castle, Henry was given the same guestroom. Or that's what he thought. From the great chandelier on the ceiling to the immovable curtains on the wall to the quill and inkwell on the desk, everything looked the same. Except for the linens on the bed and the table. He could not tell whether the upholsteries of the sofas and chairs were the same or not. The intricacy of their needlework and the multiplicity of their hues bought them a peculiar generality he was not sure the designer had aimed for. Henry, however, did not mind this slight relief of uncertainty.

He sat on a couch to savor the anticipatory shivers running down his body. A soft, almost unnoticeable, tingle danced on the heights of his fingertips and the plains of his palms. It hinted at his body coming to terms with the fact that the enormous distance it maintained from another body, of a very special person, was receding. It churned a weariness in him: the thought of landing on a new odyssey into the unfamiliar landscape of the mind of Echo, his love. But his lack of excitement was followed by fear—fear of losing something that he had come to appraise as most valuable. As if to parry the fear away from him, Henry looked toward the door and brought himself to long for that door to open and to see another face–a face that had worn a meaningless smile for him. The door did not budge, but the heavy curtains on the opposite window slowly swayed, and a thin opening between the curtains let a slice of afternoon sunlight sneak through. It danced lazily on the wall in the shape of an urn, and he thought about how the lady had stepped down his stairs the other day.

As the nugget of sunlight crept up the wall, unrest arose in him. Henry got up and savored its warmth, grateful to the lady, wanting the moment to linger. Just as his legs ached and then became numb, a rap came from his door. The sound did not herald the familiarity he waited for.

Henry opened the door to find a man holding a tray.

"Do you know the lady who came the other day?"

"Sir, I am afraid I don't know."

"Never mind." Henry stretched his hands to the tray.

"I can take it inside for you, sir."

"It's okay."

"And were you talking about the lady who served you the day before yesterday?"

"It's all right. Don't worry about it," Henry said with a smile. "Thank you."

"My pleasure, sir."

Henry put the tray on the table. He examined the colorful items in each of the five dishes. Five silver spoons, glittering, beside them. But the china bowls were too immaculately clean, and the food was served too neatly. He could not bring himself to disturb their quietude or upset the balance of their composition. But their aroma flanked around his defense.

Henry had not eaten all day, and he longed to have the first meal with Echo. Another soft rap, this time familiar, sounded on the door.

Henry closed his eyes and searched for a fragrance that might have wafted alongside the sound of the knock. But the flamboyant mélange of the alimental aromas from his table was too strong to be drowned out.

He resigned himself and reached for the door. It was indeed her, his lady with the meaningless smile.

She looked different today. She did not carry anything, and her hands were gathered on her stomach, giving her a dignified look. Maybe she just felt dignified and important; she was asked for, after all. Or asked about. She smiled still, but the effect was ambiguous. Behind the smile that attempted to light up Henry's room, there was another part, lurking in the crevices of her pretty features, sparkling in gleams of triumph and vanity.

She had painted her face, piled her hair on top of her head, and put on a dress that Henry would not have expected of a servant. She was a different person. Henry missed the sadness in her posture. She was gorgeous, but Henry now found her less attractive.

Is it her loss of melancholy? Or was I prepared for a grander, more beautiful picture of hers? One that my longing extrapolated over the intense expanse of my visit in the Castle?

The lady could not have been aware of her own depreciation. She stood with her head held high, her vain smile now more of a dim smirk. Her ignorance roiled up a pity in him, enough to make up for the beautiful sadness she wore, two days ago. Henry could finally return her smile.

"You asked for me, sir?" The proud gleam in her eyes made them look so pretty it cloaked their conceit.

"Do you mind coming inside, Ms.—?" Henry said as he stepped aside.

"Hestia. It's an honor, sir."

Hestia walked on her heels with surprising quietude.

Henry thought it appropriate to offer her a seat. But he couldn't. Maybe he felt it was fitting for her to sit on the table, propped on one of her onyx black heels, her other shoe dangling beneath her cream chiffon.

"You are searching for someone, aren't you, Mr. Apollo?" Her eyes sparkled, now more authoritative than vain. She stood against the table and crossed her ankles.

"Why do you say that?" Henry tore his gaze from her shoes.

"Someone you have been searching for a long, long time?"

Henry's smile barely penetrated his tired face. He sat on the bed.

"No," he said. "Not really. Not anymore, anyway. But why do you ask?"

"Your face is such a giveaway, Mr. Apollo. Your weariness outruns your age by eons. You haven't found her yet, have you?"

"It doesn't matter if I find her."

Henry was glad that he did not need to keep up with her gaiety. His eyes crept down to the large ruby that glistened on a locket, settled snugly in her valley. He did not try to look up before he said, "I never really lost her."

"Because you never really had her?"

She shimmied, seeking more comfortable support against the table. The ruby bobbed merrily between the soft orbs before settling. Putting her hands on the table, she pushed herself to sit on its edge, propping up her foot.

"You don't always need to lose someone to find her, do you?" she said.

Her pause let a smidgen of thoughtfulness mingle in her voice when she said, "Why were you looking for me?"

"I simply asked about you," Henry said, fighting the distraction the alluring angle of her legs created at her loin. "Didn't mean to bother you."

"Bother?" She smiled, but it was more mischievous than redeeming. She lifted her right leg on the table, sidewise, dangling her shoe from under the cream chiffon. "So, you are not happy that I came?"

"I am happy, all right. One might not want to see someone, yet still be happy to see them."

"But you wanted to see me anyway."

"I can ask about someone, can't I? Without really wanting to see them?"

"No, you can't. You may not give in to your urges, but that doesn't render your urges false, does it?"

"Why have you come? I didn't ask you to."

"Because I like you."

She shrugged and gathered her hands near her lap as the tip of her dangling shoe bobbed up and down.

"Even though you knew I was searching for someone? Someone else?"

"Yes, but I knew you wanted to see me, too," Hestia said with a giggle.

The sliver of sunlight that had breached the curtain disappeared. Darkness grew thicker, but Henry did not want to turn on the lights. Hestia's silhouette blended into the light backdrop of the wall, the frill of her skirt swaying in the wind, and the twinkle in her eyes and the ruby swinging along with it. As the brooding darkness smudged the whole of her body against the wind of the room, Henry knew he wanted to talk to that disappearing persona.

So, where does that put me?

What?

That I have been searching for my love all my life and still want to see someone else?

I don't know. But why the need to define it? Why the need for a name for it?

To understand my act. To understand how I behave.

How does naming explain an act?

I don't know. But don't we try to classify our behaviors, anyway? We give names. Names that tell us how we perceive our acts. Then we rank our acts to fit those names.

It makes things easier.

It is, then, not a matter of judgment. If the idea is to understand acts, the names can have some value so long it serves that purpose. If, or when, it doesn't, there is no need for it.

Maybe a better question would be, "Why did I act the way I did?" But that cannot replace my original question. It's too direct, too one-dimensional.

Merely looking for a reason, instead of trying to understand the phenomenon and the need for the question itself.

Maybe we really don't want to understand our actions. We just want to put everything in its place. To have a picture of juxtaposed images of our actions. After all, naming is not such an effective way to explain our deeds.

Or is it the other way around? We try to explain so that we can know how to classify. So that we have the picture sorted out for us. When that classification becomes insufficient, we break it. We come up with new names.

But we are not always comfortable with new names. Not until we become familiar with them. We don't go about naming whatever strange deeds we encounter. That would be anarchy.

Then, there is when a name is accepted. This mere recognition offers behavior a certain extent of acceptance. Just for having a name.

Maybe it's not the name, rather the familiarity that gives it the level of acceptance it gets.

It seems, then, the way we talk shapes our norms.

Not every behavior, with a name attached to it, earns approval at the same level. But each takes a certain leap, however minuscule, in their acceptance with the recognition of their name.

As the impending night led the room through the first stroke of darkness and then toward the bleary light that, given enough time, even the darkest of nights can offer, Hestia stopped swinging her leg for a moment, then resumed, putting her hand on the table to lean back and bobbing her hair around her shoulders.

Henry tried to remember if her lips had glistened when she had walked in. He wanted to think they did, and he wanted to plant a kiss on them. But the languor from his rambling was too much for him to overcome.

"Is this why you wanted to see me?" Her words wafted from where he assumed her glistening lips might have been. He could smell the gloss and see the way the gloss twinkled.

"I think I'm trying to offer acceptability to my behavior by going on and on about it."." Henry could not be sure if he said the words aloud,

There could be other ways to do that. *To earn acceptability for that behavior.*

Such as, asking why it has to be questionable.

Because we have accepted it is not right to act in that way?

No. "Right," "wrong"—they sound too overbearing.

Because this is not such a normal behavior?

Suppose it is not. But, what is wrong with not being normal? If it is not harmful?

Maybe we think it is harmful.

Harmful? For whom?

For this matter, maybe for none.

That brings it down to this. My act harms no one. But it could, if I were married. Married to the one for whom I search. That could disquiet the matrimony. To save that nuptial bliss, we condemn certain acts as unexpected, or even unnatural. That attempt, by virtue of having some homogeneity, carries over to my bearing. Though there is nothing harmful in this instance, no conjugal life to be disrupted, no marriage to be disquieted. This for the sake of an idea we call marriage. What is the other side of the story? What if one were to say, since this behavior, this act of mine, is natural, since it happens, and since it is, by nature, counterintuitive to marriage, why can't marriage be seen as unnatural?

People shouldn't get married, then?

It's not a question of ought. If I marginalize a behavior for its harms, it can work the other way around, too. Marriage being unconducive to this behavior, one might also argue against marriage.

But marriage is too important, not to mention too complicated, to look at it from the level of such a small issue, isn't it?

Then, it is not about being natural, or normal. It is not about benevolence; it is about what we deem important.

Did Hestia laugh? Henry couldn't be sure if it was her giggle that broke into his trance or the jangling smell of the gloss over her lips; his auditory and olfactory senses crossed over for a moment.

"What does it matter whether I approve of your act or not?"

"Because I feel comfortable."

There is more, then. My need for comfort begs for acceptance.

"What do you want to do with me now?" Hestia asked.

"I don't know. I wanted to see you but decided against it. So, I have no plan. I am happy that you are here, but I have nothing to offer."

"You can kiss my nape if you want." She bobbed her head and her hair swung to the front.

Henry got up and stood in front of her. Hestia looked into his eyes, a thin mist hovering on them. Her brows raised; her lips parted. The enormous ruby heaved up and down in its cozy fold under the swirl of her intense breathing. Henry held her neck in his hands and closed his eyes. The sweet smell from her lips intensified. He pressed her head on his throat. The shadows turned dark red and gleamed like the huge ruby on her chest. The air got denser until he could not breathe anymore. After he let her go, he lit the candles on the table.

"You wanted to see my nape?"

Henry blew out the matchstick and smiled at the white after-smoke that added pungency to the air in the room.

"Then why didn't you?"

"The picture in my mind—from the other day—I wanted to go close to that moment." He turned to face her and said, "That I did. Thank you for coming."

She stood and said, "You didn't ask me to come. You could have done with a little more gallantry."

"That's the best I could do. I could have affected dignity, but it couldn't have been better. Because for that I had to affect my own dignity. You see, I cannot give more than what I can. You understand, don't you?"

"I think I do. You won't forget me, will you?"

"I might have," Henry moved as if to escort her toward the door, "If I tried to offer more than I have."

XII

ECHO AND PENELOPE – A TUSSLE OF STORIES

A shadow emerges from the garden and forms the shape of Henrique. He trudges toward her room and stops outside the window. Penelope cannot remember how long it has been since he left. The recurrent initialization of time adds to her woes. Henrique, pale like the belly of a fish, looks at the windowsill as if it were a mountain.

Penelope gets down from the bed and reaches out to him.

Henrique's eyes, restless and pensive, avoid meeting hers.

"What happened?" she asks.

The weariness in his gaze gleams of pain. Henrique labors to say, "Nothing." His voice trembles, and a tremor spreads through his body.

"Nothing? You are shaking like a leaf," Penelope says as she touches his shoulders through the open window.

"It's nothing."

"You've been to the shack!"

His eyes flutter around hers for a moment.

"What did you see?"

"I—I cannot tell."

"It was struck by lightning, wasn't it?"

Henrique casts a blank look.

"Was someone in there?" Penelope asks, concern infusing her tone, but then confusion comes over her and she cannot be worried anymore; an unmindfulness lingers, as if from her attempt to understand the reason for her concern.

It is cold. Penelope now senses Henrique's hair under her hands.

He presses his lips to muffle the clatter of his teeth, but his mouth curves at the corners and quiver.

"I am cold," he manages to sputter.

Penelope brings her hands down to his elbows and helps his staggering legs over the windowsill into the room and leads him to her bed. His body is spattered with mud, his clothes torn and frayed.

She calls for warm water, and sponges his body. The shawl she lent him is soiled, an ominous tear down the middle. She tosses it beside the door. Penelope pats him dry with a fresh towel and slips him under the blanket. A cold draft has entered the room, and she gets up to shut the window. She takes a few steps and forgets what she had in mind and instead goes to brew some tea.

As he sips the tea, she sits by him and combs her hand through his hair. Color returns to his face slowly, his body calmed and relaxed. His eyes are closed. Just when his breath finds a rhythm and depth, hinting of an impending sleep, he opens his eyes and takes her in fully, as if he has forgotten what was bothering him from the garden.

Penelope smiles.

"You are beautiful," he says.

"Sure, I am."

Her response hangs between affirmation and introspection.

Her uncertainty lets him relax a little and he says with a smile, "But where is your modesty?"

Her face brightens, and then, hiding a mischievous smile, she purses her lips and narrows her eyes.

"You tell me. You should know better. Where is my modesty?"

"You figured me out again."

"Yeah." She swings her leg like a gladdened youth.

"You could've taken another name," she says. "Henrique is too close. But your smile is hard to miss. You almost never smile."

"You make me smile."

"Such a pitiful creature you are." Her grin is not unabashed.

"And how does it feel to be created by a pitiful creature?"

"Pitiful, I guess?" Penelope stoops over him, looks into his eyes and whispers, "But it doesn't feel that way."

"No, it doesn't." Henrique sounds unmindful, as if from the strain to look at her large eyes, hovering so unrelentingly close.

He gives up focusing and gazes past her. Then, as if to make good for his distraction, brings his right hand out from the blanket and reaches to the locks hanging loose over her ear and twines them about his fingers.

"Then again, how much can we know about someone just from what we see?" he says. "There can be in me, somewhere, in some locked-out corner, something that might not loom as pitiful, that basks in some inextricable glory, and that could spawn something so sprightly, like you. You never know. When you look at me, all you see is what I have left out for you to see."

"What have you *chosen* to leave out you mean?" she asks.

"Maybe. But it's not as easy to choose as one wishes, is it?"

"Or, it is not easy to shape one's own will."

"That, too."

Henrique ponders the idea for a moment and says, "Or maybe just that. I wonder how much of a reflection of my creator I am."

"Your creator? You have one of your own?"

"Mustn't I?"

"So you do. That is so hopeless! So despairingly repetitious. And why must we be doomed to know of this endless chain of our creators?"

"Why would you want to know?"

"Because you brought it up? Because it came up?"

"Because you wanted to know, or I needed to bring it up. The way we are. The way they fancied us to be. Their way for us to want that way."

"Why are they the way they are?"

"Because their creators are like that, I guess. Their creators like them to be that way, because they wish to live through them. They try to make good for what they miss out."

"They must be very lonely and wretched," Penelope said. "Are you lonely?"

Henrique smiles.

"You don't like to say."

"I could answer, but that would leave out a lot. You tell much less by saying anything at all. I only possess the loneliness that I was given. But that may not be all about loneliness. Then, who is to say that I might have had more than my fair share of loneliness? After all, who is to set rules for our creators to be fair? They don't have to be fair."

"Do you think they may try to avenge themselves if we talk ill of them? Would you be angry?"

"The creators themselves are the ones doing this. So there is no reason for them to avenge themselves."

"And free will?"

"It'll hurt them more."

"We need not care about theirs. We have to think about ourselves."

"But we are closed by our creator's will. There is nothing we can do that is not in their hands. We do what they make us do. Your fear is their doing too. But take comfort in this if you want–they act so because they are themselves afraid."

"Are you afraid?"

Henrique does not seem to listen to her anymore. Or see her, or feel her hair entangled with his fingers. It grows dark.

"If there is nothing for us to do, it is because we are bound to their destiny," he says. "We are them. Our pain is their pain. The only way to transcend this pain is to sympathize with their pain. But that is possible only through their own empathy."

The darkness seeps inside the room, and the walls blend with the window. The room has become a shapeless void. Only the cold draft remains, in which Henrique's meaningless words float.

* * *

Henry met Echo in the same sitting room as before. The ivory pieces on the chessboard table were rearranged, but stood with the same keenness, flanking his chair with the same geometric intensity.

"You have changed your mind, I assume," Echo said from the same sedentary height befitting her propriety.

"About what?"

"Talking business. With me."

"Oh, yes. That. This matter has taken an abrupt turn."

"They always do."

"You would know." Henry paused to weigh the remoteness he sensed in her retort. "I had wished to request from Mr. Narcissus a partnership in this flower business that I am trying to procure. It calls for a larger amount of money than I had previously envisaged. I wonder if Mr. Narcissus would be willing to lend me the amount."

"What amount do you have in mind?"

"Sixteen thousand."

Echo waited a moment before moving her eyes from Henry, as if weighing Henry's proposal. As she stood and approached the chessboard table, Henry's memories of Echo on the day of the Green Festival rushed back. Her present unhurried and dignified gait contrasted with her previous youthful nimbleness, the protective dullness in her facial expression belied the younger face that always bustled with passion and alacrity.

Echo picked up a white knight and put it on a square two and half steps behind.

"Mr. Apollo, your reputation has long been known in the Castle." she said, killing the small smile that formed, and looking directly into Henry's eyes. "And beyond. Yet we don't have any information of you having run any enterprise before. I would like to ask you what led you to this decision to own your own shop? We must find out before we put so much stake into it."

"We?"

"Pardon?"

"I," Henry paused not to ponder what to say, but how to arrange the words. "I would answer any question you may have for me. But only from you."

Echo's eyes formed a small squint. But she erased that promptly, and went back to her seat. She then smiled and said, "But the money belongs to the Castle. And to Mr. Narcissus."

"Mrs. Narcissus, I said I would answer any question that you may have for me. Goodness knows how much is longing to spring forth from my heart at the behest of a single question from you." When Henry paused to breathe, the silence in the room congealed, heavy and dark. "As for the business, I offer nothing except for the deal. You are at complete liberty to refuse."

A great deal of time passed, and Echo opened her mouth she spoke in an almost inaudible whisper: "I will have the money ready for you tonight."

Louder, she added, "May I invite you for dinner?"

***

Penelope lifts her mouth from a kiss, retreats toward the wall and says, "I don't like this life."

Henrique rubs the side of her neck and nibbles around her ear before asking, "What do you mean?"

"Do you call this a life? There is no respect, no freedom. And ..." Her search for words almost feels like a necessary allusion. "And no love."

Henrique raises his face to scrutinize her.

Penelope relishes the warmth of his stare for a moment and then says, "What?"

"That was so trite!" Henrique chuckles.

"Don't you laugh at me!" She tries to hide her embarrassment with a frown.

"Where do you get these ideas from?" He kisses her brows and levels the tiny, pretentious wrinkles with his lips.

"I don't know. But why can't one want to change?"

"Well, people always have wanted to change … into things."

"Yeah, they always did. That's what I am saying."

"Like birds, and other things. What's up with these unreasonable desires?"

"I'm not being unreasonable, am I?" Penelope senses the sarcasm but cannot bring herself to care. "I don't want to be a bird; I just want to get out of the House."

"You cannot help it. You are bound by your creator."

"But my creator is not bound."

"How do you know?"

"I don't. But maybe he can think about it?"

"We will see to that. What kind of life do you want?"

"I don't know. Maybe a writer's life?"

"A writer?"

"Yeah, like you. How can I think of anything else?"

"Like me."

* * *

At the dinner table, Henry searched Echo's eyes for the lush meadow, the fluttering leaves on the swaying branches, and the rocks washed by the creek water. But Echo shut herself out today. On the other hand, she was so vivacious that Henry feared he had been too eager to get into those eyes and had slipped. He made a second attempt to plunge into her through her eyes, but her joviality had rendered her impregnable. He then looked at her from the outside. Her face glowed with sparkling bits of smiles dancing around her eyes, the corner of her lips, the eddies of her frown, and the ripples on her cheeks.

Her slender fingers danced as she introduced the dishes she had prepared: fattened duck liver, fish eggs, exotic mushrooms and warm loaves of bread that she made with rare grains she ground herself. She showed him some blisters on her palm as proof. Henry wanted to kiss her reddish tender skin, but too many hurdles stood between them.

After this introduction, Echo excused herself from eating and with a move of her eyes signaled him to start. Henry had to refamiliarize himself with the faces on the numerous platters. Echo rooted her elbows on the table, her forearms straight and her fingers loosely clasped in front of her face. She tilted her head as if to see around her hands, her smile donning a tense eagerness.

There were enough distractions to keep Henry engaged, but she settled down, and he attempted another foray into her eyes, evading the defense of her hands. There still hung a curtain that fluttered with each of her smiles, shivers of her fingers, jingles from her earrings, rustles from her satin. When the curtain moved, he tried to catch hold of the world behind it. It was not all that sunny, with a glade pockmarked with fleeting flutters of lights and shadows from a tree's rustling branches. Once he thought he could hear the emerald stream breaking onto the gray stones. Yet again, the moan of wind wove through a maze of cold dunes.

Henry finally finished his odyssey, sailing from one platter to another, and put his napkin on his plate and sat up straight, which created a stillness at the other side of the table. Echo's fingers stopped fidgeting, her face apparently waiting for a kind word on her culinary exploits.

"May I ... inspect your blister?"

The suddenness of the question let her relax.

"You practice medicine, too?"

"I wish."

"I would rather you consider yourself a physician." It sounded more like a request than a proposition.

"Physician it is, then!"

"I will meet you in the lobby."

* * *

Penelope waits on her bed, pressing a quilt to her bosom. She stopped seeing anyone else. She doesn't know when he will show up again.

It could be months.

It could be years.

Or it could be now.

She ponders. Was it a mistake to ask him about her life? Imprudent to have a hunger to be a writer? Did she hurt his ego? His writer's ego? How? He is nothing but an imagination, a shadow of a higher contemplation. How could his ego feel pain?

Scorn comes over her, and she feels even colder. The window is open, and through it comes a cold, dark wind that flutters her quilt. She presses her face into her palms and sobs. She waits. He could be here in a few days, or months, or years.

Or now.

* * *

"What are you working on?" Echo asked Henry.

Henry wiped his quill and gathered the pages, put them neatly inside the leather folder, and bound it with a lace.

"My musings."

He placed it in his coat's inside pocket and rose from the chair. He had been making use of his early arrival while waiting for Echo.

"So, you are a writer, too!"

Henry smiled and said, "I hope it wasn't too much trouble."

"What?"

"Wanting to see you."

"Don't worry about it. I have other business matters to take care of tonight, though. I'm afraid I have to leave soon."

"It's not all tranquil for the mistress of the Castle, I see."

"Not at all. But I am wont to bring troubles upon myself. Makes it more bearable I guess. It can be quite dreary out here."

"Dreary!" Henry pounced on the word. "That's the very word that came to my mind when I first stepped inside the Castle."

Echo didn't blink.

"So you wanted to have a look at evidence to the contrary?" she said.

"Evidence?"

"Yes, painful evidence of something not as characteristic of the dreary life in the Castle."

"Your hand?"

"Yes, you wanted to have a look."

"Inspect!"

"Inspect."

Echo sat on one side of the small, round table and signaled Henry to do the same. She straightened her back, placed her right hand on the table, her palm turned upward, and pushed it toward the center.

Henry held her fingers and over him came tumbling a rock that had gained mass over years of his waiting and yearning. He trembled, shuddered, and his chest, for a moment, filled with a deafening beat that submerged all other sounds. The moisture that screened his eyes precipitated to his bottom lashes and, after the sound of his heartbeat mellowed enough to let the small things in the ambient peek their heads, he waited for his eyelashes to lose their salty viscosity.

* * *

Back in his room from the most momentous rendezvous of his life, Henry had a dream. He was lying on Penelope's spotless white bed. Beside the window stood a dark wooden desk that glowed in the morning light. Penelope sat at the desk with a quill in her hand, scribbling on a piece of paper. In his dream she was clothed, and as beautiful as ever. Her hair flowed over her shoulders and down her back, covering her face from the side, but Henry could still see her profile. Her cheeks looked somber and her deep eyes thoughtful, the long lashes looming like a dark awning. She had put on a white blouse that was cropped, but modest. It gave her a childish air of innocence, as if disowning the obscenity of her abundant sensual beauty. But at the same time, the curves of her bosom and her shoulder that were conspicuous through the ubiquitous transparency of dream aroused in him a desire to hold her in a long embrace. But she looked too engrossed, and her detachment formed an insurmountable barrier around her.

Soon, Henry found himself looking at Penelope through the window, from the garden. She stopped writing and poked her lips with the tip of the quill. Her lips brought forth such an enormous expanse of sweetness that if he were to kiss them, he would have to crawl around to gather all the softness from them. As if just to further aggravate his travails, she smiled. It was a drawn-out affair. The wonderful fissures and crevices her face formed were too beautiful and too much to fill up with the nectar of her smile, like a net of rivers and tributaries in a rising flood. When the expanse finally became saturated, Henry could drown in it and sip in long, peaceful draughts.

Penelope stood up to stretch her arms, against the colorless ceiling. Colorless, not dark. Henry had never thought of the ceiling of Penelope's room, and now the absence of that memory offered him a backdrop that gave her a strangeness. Her hips loomed voluptuous on her long legs, and she looked distant, her thoughtful face wading through the thick torpor of loneliness at the height of her beauty. Henry gazed at her from behind as she walked toward the door. But, as it often happens in dreams, he could also see her front. The door then turned into a window and she walked through it. The light behind her blurred her clothes and, against that light, Henry saw that she was no longer clothed, and he felt the chill she must have felt in the cool wind of the garden. He waited for her to come back and look down over him so her warm breath would blow away his chill.

But the dream ended. Henry woke up and, when he realized that he was in the lavish room of the Castle, the memory of his dream became muddled, and he could not be sure whether he had dreamed of Echo, Hestia, or even Penelope. When his confusion brewed so far that he no longer cared, he got up and went to the window to push the curtain open. Outside, opposite his room, a short building stretched from far left to far right. Beyond that was another building that was just as wide, but taller. A light was visible only in one window on the third floor of the taller building. Someone was seated on the window ledge, or at least it seems that way to Henry. The sky was dark, yet he found nothing in that darkness that could lull him back to sleep. His ecstasy from the last rendezvous with Echo filled up that darkness with a so much bliss that Henry finally decided to redeem the guilt for his authorly betrayal with Echo. He took out his folder and parchments, and the quill.

* * *

Penelope gets up from her bed and walks to her hamper. She pulls all the clothes out, trying to remember which one is her favorite—her most favorite, as of now, anyway. After going through all the colors and hues, she finds a long, crimson, satin dress with golden straps, and puts it on. Its flared bottom rises a little to expose her calves. From under her bed, she takes out a pair of golden shoes with golden laces that wind around her ankles and all the way up to her calves. She tilts her head from side to side and fluffs up her hair. She goes to the mirror and gathers her hair and holds it at the back of her head, then on top of her head, a bit on the right side, and then decides to leave it alone. From her jewelry box, she takes out a pair of long, gold earrings. They jingle and twinkle as she puts them on.

Standing in front of the full mirror, the bright sun that comes through the window glitters on her dress, and her hair glows. She smiles, turns to view her profile, and then steps out of the room. The long hallway is bright with the sunlight from the rooms on both sides. Penelope ignores the chatter coming from the rooms as she walks down the narrow hallway, all the way to the other end, where a single door opens to a sudden drop. She puts her hands on the threshold and bends outside. In front of her lie rows of mountains that meet a foamy sea at the far left. She looks down, but cannot see the bottom. A warm gust of wind comes from above and disarrays her hair. She closes her eyes and lets the wind touch her face. When the wind quietens, she stands straight, holds her skirt in place, smiles, takes one step beyond the threshold and lets her body drop.

XIII

A FLIGHT TO THE
CHILDHOOD

The Castle's high walls held the morning light at bay for a trifle longer. The wake of dawn is preceded by the golden hue trickling down the gray buildings. As Henry waited for his carriage, the Castle's harsh features mellowed in the moist air. He wanted to see Echo against this backdrop of that melting color.

Henry had declined Echo's invitation to breakfast, and the tortuous way of Castle protocol offered him no option to see her before leaving. As his horse approached on the stone pathway, Henry breathed eagerly to get all the color in the wet air.

"Is Mrs. Narcissus up and ready for the day?" he asked Puck, the footboy.

"I'm afraid Mrs. Narcissus left before sunrise, for the town, sir," Puck said as he lifted Henry's hamper. "Does Mr. Apollo have a message to leave?"

"No." Henry's happy run suffered a trifle hit. What could be this sudden, and undeniably urgent, plan Echo had come up with? Something was off. Terribly off.

Henry said, "There is nothing."

Puck placed the hamper on the back of the carriage.

Henry reached the marketplace at noon and found two ladders perched in front of the flower store, two men standing atop them, taking down the store sign. Glancing inside, Henry found unfamiliar people moving things around. Hermes stood by the entrance, dressed in an old livery, demonstrating a curious air of subservience, his hands folded in front of him. He made a face at Henry that resembled a smile.

"Welcome to Narcissus Flowers," Hermes blurted out.

"Narcissus Flowers?"

"May I help you, sir?" Hermes said, clearly avoiding eye contact with Henry.

"What's happened, Hermes? And stop acting so strange."

"Mr. Narcissus has bought the business," Hermes said under his breath.

"What! What do you mean he bought the business? He is not even in town!"

"He is not. But his lovely wife oversaw the transaction on his behalf. A magnificent young lady she is! A treat to ..."

"His wife?"

"Yes."

"But you agreed to sell to me for twenty thousand."

"I never said I would!" Hermes lurched forward on his toes. "Besides, thirty-five is better than twenty, wouldn't you agree?"

"Thirty-five thousand? She paid thirty-five thousand for it?"

"In cash. Why would I lie? I can show you the receipt if you want. Come to my house later in the evening. I am throwing a party!"

"That won't be necessary. But what are you doing here?"

"I work for Mr. Narcissus. The charming little lady offered me quite a good pay. She is one lovely—"

"Did she now?"

"Indeed."

Hermes took a quick step toward Henry and lowered his voice and said, "She asked when she could see you."

"What did you say?"

"I said she should come back today."

"Today? When ... never mind."

"You are not leaving, are you?" Hermes asked. "She hinted at a big raise for you."

Henry looked at him and scurried toward the door.

Hermes followed at a brisk pace to keep up and said, "See, I don't care if you work here or not, but she wanted to pay you really well. Will you listen to me now?"

Once outside, Hermes resume his place by the door and grumbled at one of the old employees, "There he goes. And he was part of the deal! Oh well, I can't force him to stay if he doesn't want to, now can I?"

* * *

Henrique trudges through the open door, spreading the musty smell of despair throughout the room. His hair is in dreadlocks. Beneath his unkempt beard, the hollows of his cheekbones shed dark shadows, and his worn-out clothes expose his emaciated torso.

"What's happened to you?" Penelope asks.

"Nothing." he says, his attempt at a smile drowning in the labyrinth of his beard. "What are you up to?"

"What is there for me to be up to? I waited for you for so long."

"But you have your clients."

"I don't take anyone. Not anymore."

"You shouldn't have done that."

"You would say that. I should've known. I know you hated me for wanting to change my life."

"It's not that. It's been such a long while. I don't even remember all those talks."

"Yeah, it's been quite a while. So what reminded you of me?"

"You tell me."

Penelope takes a long breath and looks at what she is wearing. Upon Henrique's face descends a weariness in surmise of repetition of a dreadful narration.

"This poor little thing jumped over the end door." Penelope starts. "They say she looked like an angel flying down the mountain. Her golden hair fluttered in the wind, her red dress glowed in the sun and flapped like the wings of a seraph. And she looked happy, they said, before she disappeared beneath the rocks."

Penelope catches Henrique staring at her, his eyes burning.

"What?" she says. "What happened? Who was that girl? Won't you tell me?"

Henrique lowers his eyes and says, "Do you really want to know?"

"No." Penelope looks away. "No, I don't want to know. Don't tell me. Just come to me. Come here."

Penelope holds his hand and leads him to the window. She lets him sit on the sill. Calling for some warm water, she digs into her hamper. From the heap that does not contain a crimson gown with golden laces, she pulls out dresses of all colors and hues. She puts on a plain white dress with long, wide sleeves and fetches a bucket of water that was left inside her door.

She pulls at his clothes and they tear off, unearthing a soiled and emaciated body with thick, dried scars near his cheeks and collarbone. His dreadlocks are entangled with his beard, which covers a good part of his chest. His hands have long nails, tinged in green.

"But that was not why you came back," she says. "Not because of the death of that girl."

Penelope dips a towel in the bucket and dabs at his dirty shoulder as she says, "I don't know why you keep it from me. But I am getting some ideas. You know what? I have decided to write. I will write. I will write my stories. I don't know much about my stories. But you keep coming back to me, carrying all these new stories on you. New stories of me. New but same. Same but different. Like new moons, those cease to be every lunar month. But their periodic deaths are all so unique. I will write about my deaths. Would you get upset? I don't care. Why should I care? What is the worst you can inflict upon me? Another death? That you will do anyway, won't you? I don't care anymore."

Penelope presses the cold, wet towel to his stomach.

Henrique shudders from a coldness that came not from the water, but from a different world.

* * *

Penelope sits at the dark wooden desk near the window and picks up her quill.

""Am I getting the idea that the chronicles of my life keep changing and recapitulating in cycles because of an endless divorce between the idea of my existence and the backdrop that spawns that idea?" she asks.

"The divorce is rather between the state of mind and the idea it engenders," she replies. "But that is a mere rewording of what you said. What you call 'a backdrop' of the idea, is the state of mind. It breeds a notion, an inchoate mass of feelings, that throws its arms to catch hold of something, anything, that offers it a terra firma. Perchance, a band of dissociated words comes to help, and it holds on to them to shape into something that is not as flimsy as its existence by itself. While that formation goes on, the state of mind transforms, and then, to the dismay of the rescue words, that formless notion can no longer find those words or the construct those words construct relevant anymore, and the cloud of their divorce looms inevitable. The prime mover for the construct is then something else, something so painfully complete in their dissociation with the state of mind, something that is born merely from the urge of those words to succeed in their construction, their own solidification."

"So am I the states of that mind, or those formless notions, or the constructs of the words?"

"It's not about you. It's about his struggle."

"But I am his struggle, ain't I? What is his struggle?"

"Struggle for the state of his mind, maybe. But really for those murky notions that spawn spontaneously from the state of his mind. And his words would not leave them in peace."

"Why bother with his words, then?"

"Because his mind won't just go by, his forgetful mind. It wants to register. All of it. To keep records, so that it can maintain the conviction that it was true in chronicling his states of mind."

"His nostalgia?"

"One could call it so."

"It's all about truthfulness, then."

"Sadly, yes."

"What is sad about it?"

"It is sad because honesty need not have any bearing on the state of mind."

"Maybe it is just intrinsic to the state of mind, or the essence of the feeling that it generates, that it demands a truthful reproduction."

"Preference, rather? It prefers the truth."

"But it cannot care for exactness."

"No, it can't. After all, the future of memory is so utterly hopeless. It transforms relentlessly, perpetually morphing into its own new reality. It doesn't know how to go back and rectify. Only a dull sense of dissatisfaction remains, that it might have transmuted."

"But that dissatisfaction has its state, too. It itself can change. And even the memory of that dissatisfaction may blur."

"It does, and that is why it strives to bring on the vise grip of the feeble words into action. And his struggle is against that."

"But it's a losing battle. He cannot go anywhere with this fight of his. He is doomed to play catch-up with his notions," she says.

"Yes, and that is why you never grow, you never go anywhere, you die at will, and yet you can never die," she says."

* * *

Henry pulled his boots from under the bed, where they had lurked in the darkness for years, unused, covered in a thick veneer of grimy dust. The left shoe felt heavy and wobbly. Something peeked through a hole near the big toe. Henry shoved his hand inside, and something ropey and squishy resisted. A thin snake squeezed and slithered through the hole. It scurried over the floor and out the door. The sharp pain that had bitten Henry's heart over and over again since Echo's inadvertent act of betrayal—Henry yearned to find such a hole, a doorway, a portal to abate that pain.

Henry made sure there was nothing else living inside his boots. He cleaned them to their approximate color and tried them on. They fit all right, except that the arch of the left one felt a little tight. He took the shoe off and felt inside with his hand. Something hard and smooth stuck to the vamp. He pried it with his nails and yanked it out. It was a green clamshell he thought he had lost a long time ago. He tried to remember when he had put it there for safekeeping, but nothing came to him.

He ran his finger over the tiny engravings: "Henrique" and "Penelope" bridged by a scribbling that he never could decode. It was Penelope who had had the engraved shell, a trinket from a shell store. That was a long time ago, in his childhood village. She called him Henrique. Henry did not like the name, but she would not care. Penelope was not her real name either, and she, too, did not like that.

Henry brought the shell to his ear, as if to hear the sound of ocean. It sounded nothing like the sea. Not even like a lagoon. Penelope promised he would hear the sound of the sea if he held it close to his ear. Henry protested that it would not work with a clam shell. It had to be a conch shell. Penelope challenged him and demanded that he put it to his ear. Henry refused. He put on a show of pestering her, but, in truth merely did not want to prove her wrong.

Later, Penelope would crouch behind him in an attempt to place the shell close to his ear. But all her efforts were futile. Henry could tell her smell from far away. He always knew when she was around and caught her right at the last moment. She would get mad and grab his mullet to shake him back and forth. Henry let her do that a few times, then, holding her hands, he would pull his head forward to let her crash against him.

As the years wore on, like the garments and pranks and blues of their childhood, they grew apart. Long before he left the village, she quietly slipped into the role of a mere acquaintance to make room for her new friends, festivals, and a string of more flamboyant courters.

But when, bereft of his parents, Henry was leaving, she came to see him off with the current suitor under her wings. She palmed off the green shell into his hand and whispered her wish for him to keep it safe for her. Henry had not seen her since.

The shell was the only thing in his room not smothered by the dust of remembrance. He pressed it close to his ear again and thought he heard an ocean sound, but it did not offer him any inkling of the meaning of the cipher inscribed on it. For all these years, Henry didn't want to know what it said. Maybe he hadn't been adequately curious. Maybe he thought he had time to ponder it later. But today, indifference caused by the passing of time suddenly turned into a piercingly acute eagerness to know. There was only one way to find out. He dug out the only decent set of clothes he possessed and headed for the lagoon.

The sun was past its prime, and it was five hours' walk from his home, but his mind was made up, so he let himself soak in the lagoon, washed his clothes, and spread them on the white sand to dry.

* * *

By the time Henry reached his childhood village, the sun barely hung on, its white glare mellowed to a tint of dim yellow. At Penelope's home, he met her father, who didn't recognize Henry, but told him that she was not living there anymore. He instructed Henry on the way to reach her new home. Henry knew her parents' house by heart, and he barely registered the changes in the path his long absence allowed to creep in. Now that he followed a route made of fresh words, with the sounds of new places and persons, and delivered by a voice that was changed not only by age, but also by estrangement with Henry, the same neighborhood suddenly loomed foreign. But Henry took it in with the serenity of a river inevitably reaching its mouth.

By the time he neared his destination, the small veranda in the front was flooded with the orange of the day's last rays. A small, round table stood on one side with two chairs behind it. A potted plant hung from the ceiling at each corner, small leafy twigs dangling and swaying in the breeze. A bassinet sat on the table and a woman sat on a chair, her black hair flowing past her shoulders and blending with her black blouse. Her long, black skirt was neatly draped over her sandaled feet. Her shoes were black too, with silver accents to match her polished toenails.

She was pretty, but her face and posture emanated an unsettling unawareness of that prettiness. Her face was also flooded in orange and glowed with youthfulness, but her eyes were calm—too calm and too serene to let even a glint of passion dwell in them. Her body was artfully devoid of sensuality by an all-engrossing contentment that was so intense that it was almost dark. Her hands, with which she slowly rocked the bassinet, were artistically slender, but not without the roughs of maturity. They were no longer pink and plump, like they had been decades ago, nor did they sport dirt under the nails. They were beautiful, but her silver nails were dull. She looked content.

The day's warmth receded, and Henry sped up to catch her in the last bit of the evening orange.

It took Penelope a long moment to realize that Henry introduced himself not as a stranger, but as an old acquaintance. And when she did realize that, she barely shook the expression of meeting a stranger from her face. Or she could not, or she did not think of doing so, or it just did not occur to her. But she got up from the chair with a contented slowness and allowed a smile to spread across her face at a leisurely pace.

"Henry? Are you really? How have you changed!"

"Penelope, do you remember the shell you gave me?"

"Penelope? What is that? Wow! Penelope! I forgot that name. Nobody ever called me by that name after you. I had a name for you too, right? What was it? Rick?"

"Henrique."

"Right! Henrique!"

"Do you remember the green shell you gave me?"

"What shell? Wait, don't start with the old times already. We can talk about those later. Come inside. You look awful. Come! You need a wash. I will heat up some water for you." Penelope carried the bassinet inside the house, put it near the bed and left the room for the courtyard through the inside door.

From there she yelled, "What brings you here? Business?"

Henry followed her voice to the threshold and said, "No, I have come here to see you."

Penelope was pouring water in a pot from a pitcher.

"You haven't!" she said with a chuckle as she carried the pot to the low stove under a shed, arranged with firewood. She wiped her hands on her hip. "You look tired. Why don't you have dinner with us?"

Squatting in front of the stove, Penelope tried to start the fire. Her stomach sagged a little and padded up between her breasts and her thighs. The lower side of her cheeks had started to fill, and the lines beside her eyes lingered even when she was not smiling. But when the fire caught and the light danced on her face, she was brought back to the life of their shared childhood. It staged the theatricals and mischief that was a fixture on her face. But her hair did not fling around and nestle in front of her eyes like it always did. She tucked away a few innocent strands behind her ear, anyway. The red stone on her ring glinted like a drop of blood.

Pleased with the fire, Penelope stood and said, "What? Will you have dinner with us? Or have you committed elsewhere?"

"No. I will, if I have to wait for that before you talk."

"What are you talking about? I am talking to you."

A soft cry came from inside the house.

"She's up again! Could you please rock her a little for me?"

Henry went inside to place the basket near the door. The baby stopped crying while airborne but whimpered once on the ground. Henry rocked the basket with the alacrity of those unaccustomed to tending a baby. Soon, all there was to be heard was the crackling of firewood.

"She is four months," Penelope whispered. "She takes after her father."

"Who is her father?"

"You don't know him. They moved to the village long after you left."

She stoked the fire with an air of uncertainty and said, "When did you leave again? After the plague, no?"

"It's going to be difficult talking to you."

"What do you mean?"

Henry waited, frightfully aware of how dangerously her all-consuming contentment appeased her conflicts.

"So, you were here during the pestilence?" she said.

"You don't remember when I left?"

"Oh, it's been a while. So many things happened after that." She bent her back as if to stretch, but it could have been an attempt to shrug.

"You've lived at the same place for too long, Penelope. Your memory could never get hold of any context. All your pasts are jumbled like a mushy porridge."

"Henry, you talk the same way you did before!" Penelope said as she stoked the fire again, though the flame was just fine.

"You haven't changed, have you? Hey, didn't you like the porridge my mum made!"

"You remember that much, then."

"What do you mean? I remember a lot."

"Do you remember what you wrote on the green clam shell?"

"What is this shell you are talking about?" She dipped her fingertips into water and said, "Your water's ready."

She carried the pot near the well and poured its steaming contents into a pail.

"Come here and wash yourself. I will take the baby inside; it's getting cold."

Henry let sink in him the quietude of the brooding night creeping out of the well, from the dark crannies of the house, the shrubs at the back of the yard and the trees beyond. The wet stone floor around the well shimmered in the terminal vestiges of the day's light. The buzz of the day melted into the vapor swirling over the bucket, and when it became too mellow to bear, a cricket from a nearby bush worked up its courting carol.

Henry splashed water on his face. The liquid warmth reminded him of the seashore of his childhood. They used to meet on the beach on summer afternoons. In spite of the scorching sand, they would take their shoes off and run along the shores, chasing each other. Her breathless laughter would mingle with the stupor of the afternoon heat. When they stopped, she would sit, propping herself on her hands behind, her hair spread all over her face.

Another cricket joined in, shortly followed by a third. Henry looked in the direction where Penelope's singsong voice wafted through the courting cacophony. She became so calm, Henry thought. Calm and beautiful, yes, but less pretty. Her beauty morphed, becoming intensely minimalistic and so full of grace that it hinged on a grotesque dullness. Only the way she spoke bore any childhood flamboyance.

Henry stood up in the darkness. The well floor had completely deserted the pale blue of the sky, and he let the cold breeze wipe away the warm wetness from his face and his arms. His tired lungs filled with a freshness he did not know what to do with.

Penelope approached him with a towel. Henry waited for her to close in. When she offered him the towel, Henry clutched her hands over the towel and looked into her eyes. "Do you really not remember?"

"Remember what?"

"The shell."

"Help me remember!" Penelope said as she released her hands from his. "I'm sure I will."

Henry dropped the towel and retrieved the shell from his pocket.

Penelope took it.

"Ooh! You still got this piece of junk?"

"What do you mean, junk?"

Penelope looked at it with a distant curiosity and said, "We were so childish, weren't we?"

"We were children."

She picked up the towel from the ground and looked up at Henry without trying to hide a smile. "And, after swimming, you preferred not to dry yourself even back then."

Her motherly cleavage tilted under the dark eclipse of her neckline.

"So, what did you write on it?"

"I don't really remember. Let me see." She stood up, squinted at the small inscription, and muttered, "Something ... in code."

"Yeah."

"Oh, right!" she exclaimed. Narrowing her eyes, she said, "You're not playing with me, are you?"

"Playing what?"

"You really didn't get it?"

"No, I didn't."

"Then, you don't want to know." She folded the towel and proceeded toward the closet.

"But I do."

"No, it's silly."

"What's wrong with you, Penelope?"

"What?"

"Why are you trying to forget everything?"

"Trying to forget? I am not trying to do anything." She turned back and looked fully at Henry. "There is nothing to forget, because there is nothing to remember."

"Then why aren't you telling me?"

"Because it is silly."

Henry waited.

"It is very easy. I just wrote it upside down, and left to right."

"That's it?"

"Yes, and you couldn't figure that!"

Henry took the shell and said, "But that reads, 'Henrique is silly; he is crazy for Penelope.'"

"That's right."

"I've tried to read it so many ways ... never saw it."

"That's funny."

"I think I just didn't expect it."

"Guess so." She puckered her lips and raised her brow. "Tell me about yourself. What do you do? You got married?"

"Penelope, I need to go."

"What do you mean?"

"I must go. I am done here."

Henry stepped on to the veranda, walked down the steps, and disappeared into the black night.

XIV

❧

THE LOSS OF PSYCHE

To return from his childhood village, Henry had to plod through a stretch of forest, two villages, and wade across three shallow tributaries. He could not tell if any of the channels was the primary stream, because each one was unique. They varied in width, warmth, and color. They also tasted different when he quenched his thirst from them. The forests gave him relief from the beating sun, but had their own perils. They teemed with snakes, coyotes and venomous spiders. When passing by one village, his body longed for a cold wash, warm meal, and the comfort of a bed, yet when he walked through the other, he wanted only to pass through it as quickly as he could.

The route had not changed since he ran away from the plague that shrouded his childhood village and took his parents' lives. Trudging through the same course after a life of many lives, Henry realized that he had always yearned to go back to the village. But now, after finally returning and then leaving it behind, something had transformed that desire. As if a tether had been unbounded. Prior to this journey, this desire to go back had pulled him so tirelessly, so incessantly to this place that he had become forgetful of its presence. Only now did that tug cease to exist, and its absence dazzled him with the pain of its loss.

He suffered the emptiness like a strip of woods freshly cleared, naked and exposed under an unrelentingly clear and daunting sky. A void that he could only think to fill up with more emptiness.

Henry pondered whether to return the green piece of cloth to Echo. He could pay her one last visit and tell of his long odyssey that was on account of her. He didn't want to vindicate himself, nor did he want pity. He only wanted to relive all the sufferings he cherished and all the memories he suffered that had been burgeoning in his life, that had suddenly become burdensome.

But instead of making plans to see Echo on the rest of the path back home, he recounted to himself all that happened to him since the Green Festival. It was no easy undertaking. The time was long, and all his memories, as if each had a life of its own, jostled and shoved each other to stand in the midst of his anachronistic recollection. A particular piece of memory added to his woes, a rather vague sense of a memory, like a washed-out image, impinged on the frayed periphery of his mind, breaking down his attempts to organize all this. Much as he tried to push that distraction aside, it came back with ever-greater force. By the time he reached home, the young sun creeping behind his back, Henry realized it was a futile battle. He stopped at his door and yielded.

This was a fitting place to allow that image of that memory to descend upon him: the face of Psyche in tears, whose beauty was the comfort it offered Henry. After Psyche left his place, her existence barely disquieted Henry's life. Because she had offered him something too generous: a gift that was free, like all the great presents of life, like the warmth of the blue water of his lagoon. The magnitude of that generosity he could appreciate only now, when he decided to let go of all the offerings he had accepted. He wanted to see Psyche, and that urge loomed more pressing than anything else.

* * *

By the time Henry reached the House, the sun had reached its height. The flimsy candle shades on the front façade perched with indolence after a mirthful night, their colors dulled under the scowl of the glaring sun. Through the front door that never closed came the sound of a late-morning commotion. Henry heard the busy steps of soft feet, raising the discordant jangling of silver anklets. A shrill voice confirmed the owner of those footsteps as Artemis. Henry stopped at the threshold to let his shadow beyond the doorstep usher in his arrival.

"Is that you, Henry?"

Henry listened to how her voice suddenly mellowed through the thinning darkness inside. "Come on in, darling!"

Henry stepped inside. Artemis stood in the middle of the front room in a long skirt. She had grown older, her body sporting the interim grace that reigns for a short while before giving in to age. Her breasts had lost a mote of their voluptuousness, but this broadened the grace of her valley. A motherly indifference crept into her eyes and gave her face a defenseless attraction, but the brooding hollows on her cheeks offered a youthful insolence. Her lips were fuller and the only colored part of her body, a burning crimson that spread flame up his loins.

Artemis turned to give some directives to her charges inside, and her large silver earrings jangled. She then stepped forward to hold Henry by the hand and pulled him inside.

"You forgot us completely, didn't you?" she said, her voice carrying a tinge of motherly affection, but before that maternal tone could throw water on his flame, Henry pulled her to him.

"Take me," he whispered.

"What? Now? I ... I haven't washed yet."

She gathered her hair on top of her head. Her nape glistened with the dews of labor. "Lots more to do, too."

Henry looked on, his breath starting to steer her reluctance into confusion.

"Okay." She let her hair drop. "Since you never ask. Get to that room. "

"Just come with me," he said. He grabbed her wrist and led her to the nearest empty room.

"Your hand is burning! Are you well, Henry?"

"That's not how you keep your clients interested, is it?"

"This is so unlike you," she said as she closed the door behind her. "There, I've done it again!"

The golden rectangle of the cloudless day near the front door threshold slowly rolled itself up. The dust in the air floated in and out of the sun. Artemis came out of the room alone and went on preparing the House for another evening. No one disturbed Henry's postcoital nap until the shadow of the house draped the tree trunks across the road. Henry woke and sat on the bed for a while. He stepped out of the room. Artemis was dressed up, her face painted in heavy, almost sinister make-up that reminded him of the first day he had seen her, standing in front of the House. He remembered why he had come.

"Are you expecting Psyche today?" he asked.

Artemis turned toward him, and her face softened. She reached out to Henry and picked up his hands.

"So, you haven't heard," she whispered.

The pressure on his hand told Henry the news would be ominous. He looked for confirmation in Artemis's eyes, and it was indisputably there.

"When did it happen? Wait, don't tell me." Henry could see his own journey of progressive realization of the news through the gradual transformation in her face.

"I am sorry, Henry. I didn't know she meant so much to you."

"Neither did I."

He jerked his hands out of hers and trudged toward the door as he repeated, "Neither did I."

* * *

Henrique yanks his foot from his last step in the backyard muck and reaches the window. His struggle with the boggy yard has worn him out. Panting deeply and trembling from the cold wetness, he is relieved to find the window open. But then he realizes it is not open, just that the window has no sash at all. There is no sign of any sash ever being there, in fact. It is just an open window frame with only a translucent screen hanging from inside. He clambers through that open window and ignores the mess his muddy feet create on the sill and the floor, and tries to chase away the last flimsy obstacle, the gossamer screen. But as he flips through the folds with quivering fingers, he cannot find the end to it. He tries on the other side, with no better luck. In his restlessness, Henrique tries to grab the frail-looking textile to pull it down, but it slips from his fingers. He throws his hands in rage to push the screen away. It does not resist. Nor does it yield. He loses his balance and plunges into its endless length. His pushing and shoving only soils the wall of confusion he finds himself inside.

When he gives up and breaks down into a sob, Penelope is heard: "Is that you, Henrique?"

Darkness in the shape of a familiar silhouette approaches from where the voice came, and when it congeals enough for him to smell the fragrance from the body, Henrique stretches his hands. This time his fingertips find resistance. He grabs the cloth hard and rips it apart. In a rage, he keeps tearing the screen into shreds. When his fingers drain the last mote of energy from his wearied body, he stops and finds Penelope kneeling in front of him. She looks confused, as if she has forgotten why she is here. She stands up unmindfully and walks toward her bed. Henrique sits in the middle of the textile massacre and looks around. In the slowly adjusting light, he finds the room full of people. So many, in fact, that he cannot see the walls. By the time Penelope reaches her bed, he finds the bed full of people, too. As she jostles into the crowd to make room for herself, she gets infused with others, and Henrique cannot find her anymore.

Someone else approaches him from the left side of the room. She wears a beautiful green dress that smells of the lagoon water, but as she comes closer, Henrique notices her diamond necklace and rings. As soon as she starts to look familiar, she walks past. As he labors his tired head in the direction she went, she is nowhere to be seen. With that, the smell of the sea fades away, replaced with a medley of other aromas.

Then yet someone else comes. She walks in no particular direction, walking only because she wants to walk, or not even that. She does not know whether she wants to or not; she just finds herself walking. So she walks, raising moist thuds from her heels stabbing the soft earth of the crowded room. Her skirt sways like the screen Henrique tore into pieces. Her hair is mounted on top of her head, her nape emanating a sad fragrance of sandalwood. As a matter of course, she blends into some other nook of the bustling room.

Henrique moves around to get away from the bleary humdrum on the side of the room he is facing and looks about the window, where, out in the bright green garden that is no longer a quaggy deathbed, he finds her standing in the midst of the trees.

She appears pensive in her small, red blouse. As she walks, the scars beneath her ribs look like henna, depicting colorful stories of other lives. As she strolls among the trees, they sprout flowers, and their brilliance wipes away the gloom in her face. When her smile outshines that of the brilliant sun above, she walks close to Henrique and stands in front of him, her hands gathered on her belly, her translucent veil stoking her golden earrings and her long, red and gold skirt glinting in the mild breeze.

She does not look at him, but her smile acknowledges his presence, here or elsewhere. Henrique wants to reach her, but extending his hands ushers in huge clouds that cover the last speck of blue in the sky. A wind arises around her, and large drops of rain splash onto the earth. She stands there, her hands unclasped, her smile untouched and her body un-drenched. Soon, waves rush through the window and wash away the bleary picture that has conjured up the walls of the room that did not have any walls a moment ago.

* * *

Henry wanted to wipe off the tears that had splashed onto the parchment, but they were soaked up before he could reach them. The wet greyness on the page spread at a violent pace.

* * *

Henry closed his eyes against the cool evening breeze from the lagoon. The pain in his heart started to congeal. The evaporation of tears around his eyes felt soothing, and that repose made him weary. He waded down the water and lay on his back. On the quiet surface of the lagoon, his body bobbed between the warm water and the cool air. He drifted along for a long time.

Coming back ashore, the truth of what Psyche had said last time they met descended upon him. His need was for her to need his presence. That was all he ever had, and that was all he could ever have. Possibly that was all anyone could ever have. He had it. And he lost it with Psyche's death.

The comfort that his pain churned up from his melancholy dwindled. He became restless and did not know what he wanted to do. He could attempt to get back what he had lost. For now, he wanted out.

He took out the green piece of cloth from his pocket and pressed it in his hand. It did not spawn anything, like it had always done before. He touched it against his chest and eyes and lips. It did not provide any warmth, other than what it borrowed from his own body. Maybe that was what it had always done, returning the fervor that he himself lent it. It offered him no smell other than what it had from his own sweat.

He could send the piece of cloth back to Echo. Or he could do nothing with it. It did not matter. He hurled the parchments into the evening offshore wind and watched them spread in the air and float toward the sea. The last page landed on the water too far away for him to know if it really touched down. It did not matter. He left them to soak in the clear and transparent water, no less saline than his own tears.

* * *

Henry left his shack and walked toward the other end of the village. He was leaving for a long time and did not expect to find his abode undamaged, unharmed, and above all unacquired on his return. A long walk loomed ahead, the baggage of his memories weighing heavily on him, so much so that he could have laid them around and walked, waded or swam through them for another lifetime.

From the thick of those reminiscences one piece of memory stood out. He couldn't decide if it was from the life that he has been living, or from elsewhere, a distant recollection of deserting his life for a voyage—a journey in quest of a father that was not as burdened with memory as was the case this time.

It trod a treacherous path, scheming up a labyrinth of routes that met itself endless times with different faces, and conjured a loop that brought him back to the very place he wanted to flee from. There was no running away from one's life. It only added to the woe that life already was.

This time, Henry's story plotted the other way around for him. He intended to come into the folds of life, to grow something from inside of it. But he pursued it too hard, and when the futility of his effort rebounded, it struck him with the same force. Now that he was on the path again, the same sun beat on him harder, the dust that the day let settle upon him was drier, the sweat that caked the dust on his skin felt thicker, and the haze of the rumination that he waded through felt more onerous. When he had no more sap, he stopped.

He passed the weekly marketplace, the carnival grounds, some farm-land, the school, a few neighborhoods in between, to the end of the village. A gaping stretch of swampy land flanked the village. Henry had his last meal a long while earlier.

He came across a small diner on the fringe of the neighborhood marketplace. It was part of a domicile and was run by its residents. The kitchen was apparently inside the house. Outside, in a large, covered space that was an extension of the main building, seating for the diners was provided. The space was open on three sides, and some dark and crooked wooden pillars stuck out from the elevated plinth to hold up the roof.

Henry wanted to avoid getting caught in the web of daily livelihood. The open dining place did not betray him regarding that. He dropped his sack on a low bench and stepped outside in search of the water tank. He found it on the right side of the house.

With a mugful of water, he squatted beside the tank. He washed his hands and splashed water on his face. The coldness made him gasp. To intensify that choking sensation, he splashed a few times more. When the screen of water thinned its haze on his eyes and his dizziness from gulping for air had worn out, a pair of feet in sandals appeared beside the tank. They looked clean, even though the dust of the dry day had left a thin layer on them. The pink tinge on the toenails suggested a hint of health. The ankles and the plump cuffs emanated a glow of beauty of pubescence. He looked up to find the owner of the legs, and a shock almost tipped him over on his back.

It was a young girl not quite in her teens. She maintained a distance in a polite effort to give him his space. But she looked at him, her curiosity barely concealed in her large eyes. Her dark, shoulder-length hair flanked her deep-colored, round face and gathered beside her soft little mouth. Her nose exuded the freshness of the beauty that comes from finally coming of age from the prepubescent stubbiness, and her neat eyebrows bent upward in an expression of innocuous curiosity. The ruffles on the chest of her floral frock obscured the maturity of her bosom. She held with both her hands a brass pitcher, swaying in front of her.

She carried an uncanny resemblance to Psyche; had he not broken his own delirium with the cold splashes, he might have taken the girl to be Psyche herself in her childhood. His shock must have shown even with the muddy water camouflaging his face, which had been rumpled by the long walk. A smile formed on her face, but it froze for a moment before being replaced by a curious apprehension. He staggered onto his feet as a gesture to let her get the water. But even more, he did it to escape from her. A violent attraction roiled up, and if he weren't able to stifle it soon, he could foresee some cruel consequences. The girl, on the other hand, resumed her smile and took a step forward.

"Take your time, sir."

Henry discerned an underlying authority in an otherwise hospitable tone.

"I'm done."

"But you're really not."

He looked down at his hands, which were dripping murky water from the fingertips.

"I guess I'm not," he said, lending a force to his face that, at other times, would have translated into a smile.

"Okay then, take your time. I'm not in a hurry."

She dangled the pitcher from her right hand, shifting her weight on her right foot, and placed her left hand on her waist. The frilled hem of her frock swayed around her knees.

Henry took his time. More than he needed, as if to honor the girl's request. But that also meant that his struggle to keep his eyes off her would be longer too. When he decided he was done, he stood up with an exaggerated effort and turned away, attempting to avoid eye contact. He caught a glimpse of her face anyway, and by the time he turned the corner, Henry registered that she had offered a goodbye smile. It was too late to turn back and return it, and only then it descended upon Henry that she was just a child.

When he came back to his seat in the diner, he barely noticed the lady of the house walking up to him.

"Welcome to our village, sir," she started. "Today we have a special—"

"Just bring me something, please," he said, managing to drag out a smile with the effort he took to look at her.

"Okay, good sir! You want some of our special tea afterward?"

He nodded.

Food was served and, as Henry used the distraction to gather his thoughts, he felt something happening around him—something familiar, to which his senses reacted agreeably and unfavorably at the same time. He tried to focus on the fish on his plate. He forked open the flakes of soft, white flesh to unveil the translucent bones underneath. But the steaming smell of fish was soon overwhelmed by another smell that was part of the thing that had been prying his senses. That other fragrance intensified until it shaped into a person, who placed a glass of water in front of him. Henry looked up to find the girl from the water tank turning away, her face bearing the confusion of whether to smile or not.

Thereafter, Henry could barely concentrate on his food. The girl evidently worked there. Now that he thought about it, she was probably the daughter of the proprietress. As she moved from table to table, picking up empty dishes, asking the customers about their needs, Henry found it impossible to keep his eyes off her—her smile glowing in innocence and spawning perfect dimples, which were so much like Psyche's.

The girl glanced at Henry with the frequency found in childlike curiosity. When she once got caught in his fretful eyes, her smile smudged into confusion again. Henry ended his meal before he was done, and walked up to the lady to pay. She said some kind words that Henry did not have the presence of mind to grasp. As she extended her hand with the change, he turned his head to look for the girl. She stood beside an empty bench, resting her elbow on it, a duster in her other hand. She evidently had waited there for him to look at her. As their eyes connected, she smiled, and his heart started rushing. He wanted to return the courtesy, but it proved too difficult. He swiftly turned around and stepped out of the place, ignoring the woman's outstretched hand with the change.

XV

AN ODYSSEY OF SUFFERING

Before plunging into the thick of the swampy land, Henry stood at the edge of the village for a moment. A strange quietude ensued, as if embodying the inarticulable confusion of this farewell. As he stepped into the marshland netted with veins of narrow pathways, a thick blanket of mugginess replaced the dusty, dry air. Breaths were no longer abrasive, but they became more laborious.

The incidental walkways among the shapeless pools conjured a maze. Some long, circuitous way would lead to a dead end, overlooking a long stretch of water. Some places, the water wouldn't be as deep, or the stretches as long, and Henry would wade or swim through. Other times, he turned back to return to the last intersection to pick an alternative path. Swimming was not an agreeable undertaking. The lack of a change of clothes meant he had to let them dry on his body in the sweltering sun, inflicting rashes and itches on his skin. Despite that, if, at times, he avoided swimming, it was not because of the inconvenience.

The fatigue of his strained muscles, the pain of his bruised feet, the stink from his sweat-soaked clothes offered a respite of distraction from his sufferings. He did not want to let himself be troubled with the words that formed at the backwoods of his mind, words spawned by memories of Psyche, and danced in the reverie of their misery. Only when the regularity of his routes formed patterns in his mind as if to liberate it from its pain would those words seep out. Henry would opt for a harsher route. A swim through a long stretch of muddy water, a haul through an unkind incline, or a dash through the resistance of bushes wielding sharp-edged leaves.

He never relented, not even when it was dark, unless his body gave way and dropped unconscious. His sleep was his unyielding enemy that crouched around him without reprieve before lunging and rolling him over to enwrap him in a cruel embrace. It was then when his most dreaded tribulation commenced: he reeled into his dreams.

After days' effort to disengage his mind from his sufferings, his dreams would undo the hard work with the cruelest apathy. Only when the morning came, cracking into the keep of his nightmares, sun perching on his cheeks and arms, or a beaver or a fox checking him out, would Henry wake up to his horror, his memories disinterred for him to pick up where he had left off before his surrender to sleep. His self-flagellation would resume.

Not before numerous cycles of such regression did he realize how clueless he was of his whereabouts in the swamp. The intersections repeated themselves, water bodies came in shapes and sizes that he thought he had seen before. The foxes, lizards or snakes he encountered looked the same. The only thing that changed was the air, which became increasingly thick, the sun glowering with ever-mounting heat.

The repetitions were not futile after all, even if their only point was to manifest their existence. Henry had no other way to recognize the futility of his exploits but from their repetitiveness. The dialogue that he had been pushing to the back of his mind remained no louder than a remote whisper which could be the murmur from a distant ravine, the rustling of leaves in a tranquil breeze, or the buzzing of bees ruffled up from their nocturnal doze.

Henry decided to force his way out of the marshland. He followed the sun and reached the other side of the swamp. Standing in front of an empty road, Henry realized that in his effort to fight his dreams, or in spite of it, his dreams had increasingly featured the girl from the diner, and less the subject of his suffering, Psyche.

XVI

THE CAMARADERIE OF
ZEUS

As his sunburn cooled and the blisters and wounds recovered, Henry looked back at his long arduous travel through the swamp rather as a long break, both in distance and time. By the time he convalesced, his wounds were concealed under the indifference of scars, and he had broken up the daunting dialogue around memories of Psyche into parts, each sent to faraway lands. The blanks that the absence of those bumbling words left conjured for him a clear picture of what he wanted to find: a relationship that he lost with the death of Psyche. Despite the clarity of his objective, he was not sure of the means. He did not know where to search. All he could do was look. He hit the road.

Henry frequented the local markets and the fairs and festivals. Marketplaces were too vigilant against people who approached women uninvited, particularly those who bore the signs of stranger in the land. Festivals were too few and far between to match his urgency.

When he stepped into a barber shop, it was more to gather information than to have a good trim. All but one of the five chairs stared at their empty images in the long-frayed mirror. The lonely soul that occupied the one chair jumped up to receive Henry, and introduced himself as Oss.

Draping Henry with the barber's cape, Oss placed his hands on his head to measure the impending work, and rested his eyes on the face of his customer to weigh its foreignness.

"How do you go about meeting people in this city?" Henry asked.

So, he was a foreigner, after all. Satisfied with his judgment about the stranger, the barber merrily started his work. His smile could reflect his rapport with his equipment, which he took out to arrange on the counter. But it could as well be to cover up his preparation in answering Henry's query. He picked up a sturdy-looking brush and tried to force it through Henry's long-unattended hair.

"You haven't been to the Saturday market, I assume. A marvelous place to start. Joyful tables are as numerous in the tea stalls as the gloomy ones. It won't hurt to hit on some gay table and offer a round of tea. The sad companies can turn out equally profitable, if not more, at times. That, of course, is contingent on my friend's preference, and bearing. And, may I add, current state of mind."

It turned out that the brush was of no use for Henry's hair. Oss gave up the idea to disentangle it. He brought out a heavy pair of scissors and started cutting the dreadlocks.

"Temples are a good place to meet people. Inns are, too. Then there are festivals. But we are done with festivals for a few months," Oss said as he rested his brush on Henry's head for a moment. "Unless you are not averse to traveling a little. The Green Festival starts in a month or so, in a western village not terribly far from here."

"Anything else in this city?"

"Private parties, of course. Since you are a stranger, you better acquaint yourself with the elites of the town."

Oss took off Henry's cape and gave it a neat shake like a masterly matador before putting it back on Henry

"The mayor is a chief candidate; party is what he is elected by and elected for. Then there is this widow, Selene by name, who inherited a handsome fortune from her husband. Each party she throws stokes the rumor about the way her old husband died." Oss said, then paused.

Henry waited for the barber's theatrics to suffer their demise. Oss patiently finished working on the right side of Henry's head before violating the air of discomfort that brooded from the absence of Henry's follow-up.

"It hadn't been a week before the widow invited half the city to a party, apparently in gratitude for the condolences she received from all the invitees due to the husband's passing. As per the invitation notes, anyway."

He snipped a few more locks and then said, "Sure enough, the gala had no semblance of mourning in its proceeding."

Oss spared no details as he went on chronicling the "proceedings." When done, he tugged on the knot of Henry's cape in order to undo it, but stopped short and mentioned as if just as an afterthought, "Oh, and there is, of course, Milkman Zeus."

"Milkman?"

The hazy image of Oss on the old mirror smiled. A mildly triumphant one. He could impress his strange customer, at last.

"Yes, Milkman Zeus. That's what they call him, even though he is the richest trader in the city."

Oss let go of the cape and inspected his work.

"I think we need to work a little behind your right ear," he said as he picked up his scissors and resumed. "He was a Milkman. He dragged his rickety cart full of dimpled milk cans in front of my store. That's all he did. Selling and delivering milk to stores. Until one fine morning, he caught a glimpse of the lady: our widow. She was a dazzler, all right. Her beauty was so intense that she made everything around her look beautiful. Zeus fell madly in love with Selene. Despite his lowly social status, he tried his luck and asked for her hand. Goes without saying that it wasn't successful in any sense of the word success. But he was not a person to give up so easily.

"He opened his own store, made cheese and other dairy products. Then he started a farm. A dairy farm. In a few short years, all the milk

business in the city was his. It did not stop there; he started export-
ing his products to other cities. In a few more years he made enough
money to buy half of the girls in the city. He started building a house
that would have been the largest, most expensive in the city. Talk was
that he was planning to request the widow's hand after the house was
built. But just a month before that, Selene got married to the old bag
of bones, who had one foot in the grave."

It turned out there were many spots on Henry's head that Oss
had missed.

"It was devastating for Zeus. He left the house unfinished and retired
from the business. But that was only for a while. Something happened,
and he was back. He found a very pretty girl and married her. The wedding party was too elaborate, and the way he invited guests was his way
to take his revenge against his flame. The old bag of bones was invited,
but him alone, no mention of his wife. By that time, Zeus expanded his
grip not only over the trader's realm in the city, he also had acquired a
clutch on the local politics. He played his strings in a way that Selene's
husband could barely afford to refuse his invitation. This was a very
expensive way to show disrespect, but Zeus could afford it. At the
least. But there is no telling how expensive it is. He has been throwing
bi-weekly parties ever since."

Finally Oss was done with all of Henry's head. Henry stood up, and
without looking into the glass to see his new coiffure, he said to the
proprietor, "I am sorry I cannot pay you now. I will be back soon and
pay the full due."

Oss weighed the proposal for a moment, then smiled graciously. All
the chattering he was allowed in that wee hour of the day, might have
been commensurate with the charge for his labor. He said, "That should
be fine, sir. Welcome to the village."

Henry got the whereabouts of Zeus the Milkman and went to see
him at his house. He was denied both a visit and information as to
whether Zeus was at home or not. Henry went to his workplace and
waited in front of his office early in the morning. Zeus never showed.
Henry waited until late in the night when all the activities of the

marketplace had died down, and he had just decided to give up for the day when a carriage came rattling from a stable somewhere behind the buildings, and came to stop in front of the office. A minute later, Zeus stepped out of the office, hurrying toward the carriage. Henry calculated the point where he was to meet him and started toward that point. On closing up, Henry proposed, "Sir, I offer you my help with your parties. I am a master flower decorator."

Zeus did not stop or look at him, but his steps slowed.

"What the hell is this?" he said.

"I don't ask for any payment. I will do it for free. I just ask for access to your party."

"Get rid of this vagrant," Zeus directed his assistant.

"Does the name Henry Apollo ring any bells?"

Zeus stopped and looked up at Henry for the first time. Even though Henry just had a haircut, looking at his rundown clothes, a suspicion brooded in Zeus's eyes. But on reaching his face and then focusing on his eyes, the mist of suspicion cleared.

"So, you are the famous flower designer?"

"I wasn't aware of the extent of my fame. That was just a random attempt."

"So, you are saying you'll do it for free?" A new suspicion crept into his voice.

"No. Not free. I want access to your parties in return."

"So you are asking for an invitation?"

"Whatever way it works."

"All right. See me next Monday at my office." He poked into his chest pocket to produce a piece of paper. "Give this to the doorman."

* * *

Even though it turned out that Zeus did not throw parties as frequently as Oss the barber had claimed, he was not too far either. There will be some occasion or other at least every other month. The otherwise languid townspeople had nothing to complain about that. When devoid of matters to collectively ponder on other than the uneventful local weather, they had the flowery stories of Zeus's banquets and flamboyant soirees to prattle on. The tales of Zeus's heartbreak and curious ways of his revenge were legends that lent a faint sense of refinement, a backdrop against which the dull colors of their lives borrowed some freshness.

In any case, Henry got to work without delay. For each special event, Henry used different themes. The themes came to him in an order that bore no connection with how and what Zeus himself planned. Nonetheless, there was an order, which followed the way Henry had sent out the severed and portioned ruminations of his stories, his dialogs on Psyche's memories, to faraway lands.

For the purpose of the themes of his floral responsibility, Henry allowed those dialogs to make their way back to his mind one at a time, to grow, bud, sprout, branch, leaf and flower.

He kept himself busy for days and nights at the venue, working meticulously at details, often tearing a completed part down with fierce indifference to his own creations, redoing the undone work with increasing intensity, the deadline shoring up fast. His last moments' rushes would mean a brooding sense of incompleteness, and his charges would brace themselves for the brunt of their chief for their part in a looming disaster.

Those fears were always put to rest, as a calm demeanor always ensued with the commencement of the night's program. When all was done, the guests' amazement was so enormous that no one would have comprehended Henry's frustration, unless they were to experience his frantic spells of tearing down and rebuilding his floral creations themselves.

If anyone had any insight into Henry's restlessness and how everything he did followed what transpired in his mind, the dialogs that he had with himself, it was Zeus. Because, with the hiatuses between

Zeus's disappearances and reappearances, it was those introspections that kept him going, too. Zeus and Henry were partners in crime when it came to love.

If Zeus allowed Henry to hover at the gate of his parties, anonymously, even in an attire that would fail the dress code he himself enforced, it was only because he found an avatar in Henry, a delegate for himself who was free to act in ways Zeus's standing in society wouldn't allow.

On Henry's part, at each of the parties, hiding behind the primly clothed ushers, an unkempt and uncouth Henry searched the crowd for a woman whose face and bearing could have caught up with his state of mind, which was built around that night's party theme that he had worked on for weeks.

Henry's indomitable thirst for a face meant he never took too long to find one who fit the bill. Once spotted, he followed the chosen woman from a distance that at the same time preserved his anonymity and allowed him to cherish her every move, to descend into every detail of her smiles, gestures and speech, and relishing every bit, until he was completely consumed by the intensity of that passionate perusal. At that moment, he would introduce himself. Despite the blinding passion that led him through those cycles of monstrously arranged meetings, he would accost the women in an utterly dispassionate manner, so that the sheer weight of his passion would not wedge and nestle between the two of them.

He didn't have any problem if his lady of interest was engaged or married. The only thing that deterred him was the false smile they wore when talking with him. Not that Henry registered that falsity in its face. For him, that deceit manifested as a phenomenon of something missing in their smile that was the very thing his whole pursuit centered on. Something that was not only unique to Psyche, but also what defined Psyche.

As luck would have it, that pretentiousness was ubiquitous in all the ladies Henry zeroed in on at each of those parties. And every time, that realization descended upon him like a physical blow, so much that he had to parry it off with a wave of his hand, his face contorted in pain. With not much as an adieu to the lady of his interest, Henry would retire and leave for home. He would allow to descend upon himself the weariness from his vigorous work over the previous weeks.

But those breaks were only to replenish his ardor and to prepare for the next venture, at the next of Zeus's parties, which was never too much of a wait.

This cycle went on for months. Then for years. Until one day, when Zeus called Henry to his office. For everything he did for Zeus, Henry had never had to meet his employer before. He ordered flowers and other materials as needed, without having to know how they were paid for. They were always paid for. The assistants he needed were always at his disposal. So, when he was finally summoned for a one-on-one meeting, Henry didn't know what to expect.

When Henry knocked on the heavy wooden door of Zeus's office—a dark, large stone building at a quieter corner of the marketplace—it was opened and held by a doorman in uniform. Another attendant led him into what looked like a foyer and asked him to wait. It was spacious, and decorated with such extravagant arrangements of furniture, statues, and leafy and flowering plants of such flamboyant colors that, sitting on one side of an enormous couch made of dark mahogany and teal velvet, he expected Zeus to appear any moment. He even readjusted his position so as to face him comfortably around the huge colorful urn set on the center table between him and the single seated sofa on the other side of the room that exuded the confidence required to seat a magnanimous host.

Instead, after a few minutes of waiting, Henry was led by several other attendants through several other rooms, each larger and darker in their ambience than the previous. The final room was so dark that, between the two persons engaged in an anxious chat, standing on the opposite sides of a huge wooden table, their hands planted on the dark varnished surface, Henry couldn't tell which one was Zeus. They stopped talking as soon as Henry entered. Henry waited for his eyes to get acquainted with the darkness. Either the time passed too lazily, or there was nothing to get acquainted with, as he didn't see anything more clearly even after a lengthy, awkward silence. After blinking at both figures beside the humongous table, Henry focused on the dark surface and appreciated the shiny lacquer's perfection. The reflection of the wall behind it was so immaculate on its surface that it could just as well have been a pool of water, still in the windless room. Henry even started to see, by all means mere figments of his imagination, fish swimming beneath the surface, so discreetly that no disturbance was invoked at the surface of that body of water.

Before Henry's distraction could solidify into a conviction, someone said something—a sound, a noise, a directive—and one of the two persons walked out through a door on the right side of the room. The remaining person walked toward Henry, made another noise and turned toward the left side of the room, where Henry could vaguely see a seating arrangement for several people.

After taking a seat, the person finally talked in the voice that Henry recognized as Zeus.

"It doesn't get brighter," Zeus said.

Henry tried to look where Zeus's eyes were supposed to be, but couldn't be sure that Zeus could see his confusion.

"Nothing," Zeus answered, nevertheless. "Nothing gets brighter. Not the things you try to fix. Things that you try to build. Nor this room. This is how it is here. When you came through all those rooms, your eyes adjusted to the layered darkness. It won't get any brighter. If you saw your pupils, you would see that they are as big as those of cats."

Henry blinked once more, anyway, before asking, "You want me to cut the costs?"

"You don't understand, do you?" Zeus said. "What are you doing, Henry? What exactly are you doing?"

"I don't believe that you don't understand what I do. And why."

"No. But I think I can ask you this, because I am a bit ahead of you. Even if only by a single step."

"We don't even tread the same path."

"I knew you would say that."

The words floated on something that Henry would have thought was a smirk.

Zeus leaned back and took a breath, then said, "That gentleman that just left? The last of my creditors. The last deal that I signed with. For the last job you will do for me. Yeah, the last one. Why on credit, you will ask? Last one? There were more? How many of these parties were on credit? You ask questions. Or maybe you don't. You don't care. So long as you have your stories to settle. Your stories. You haven't run out of them yet, have you? I don't really care. But what I do care about is what you have been trying to get. Do you really think perfection is separated from your reality? Do you really think you will find what you are looking for? You say you don't care if there are no more parties. Well, you do care. This is how you are set up now. This is the only way you get what you look for. This is how you have set yourself up. All I wanted to suggest to you is ..."

Zeus let out a rugged sigh and said, "Okay, I will get there a little later."

The words stopped coming from the direction of Zeus. Henry didn't know whether to wait or ask the questions that had replaced his original queries for Zeus. The room hosted no motion. Nothing stirred that Henry could hold to materialize his thoughts into words.

"You know why he agreed on one last credit extension?" Zeus resumed. "Even after knowing that it won't get paid back? Yes, my foray from opulence to destitution has been my own doing. Yes, he won't get back anything, but he gets to meet and make advances to plenty of customers he doesn't get to meet otherwise. You see, these parties have been the harvesting field for a tremendous number of opportunists.

They all have reaped a great deal from them. What did I get? Nothing. In fact, I lost quite a bit. I lost all my money, right? But that's the least of it. I lost my love. Not the person, that little miserable bag of gluttony. Not that person, but my love. My love for her. It perished. No hatred for her, either. Nothing. I did hate her at one point. That was just another side of my love. But all that is gone now. Nothing is left for her. Selene. I get nothing from all these extravaganzas. Not that I expected anything. But I got nothing, anyway. Until now. Yes, until now. You ask what that is. Or maybe you don't. But I will tell you. I will tell you, anyway. Before I do, though, don't you want to know why I am trying so hard to throw this party that may have no meaning for me?"

Zeus paused in a way that Henry inevitably saw coming.

Henry could make out Zeus standing and spreading his arms to indicate the room.

"All this will be gone in a few weeks. They will liquidate everything. All this and everything else that I have. Zeus will no longer be entitled to something that he didn't have any business having to begin with. Yes, you said we don't tread the same path. That's not true. Because it doesn't matter what path it is, for us they are just that, the paths. We are willing to tread a tremendously long length of it to get to where we want to go. And none of us know where we want to get to. Nor do we care. But this realization offered me the sight of the biggest reward. See, I don't have anything to gain. It was never meant to be. But you do. So stop beating around the bush. Open your eyes. It's about time, anyway. I have seen the path that you have been carving out with your themes. It's about time. Go for it. Get it for me. I know you will. That's the reward I see at the end of all this. And that's why I have put every last bit on it."

Zeus sat back down. Henry stood up and, as he started toward the door, unattended, the last words floated from Zeus: "Maybe it can, after all, get brighter."

* * *

When Henry spotted a lady in a graceful, pearl-white gown, he pondered why he had never seen her before. Maybe because he never waited long enough before settling with someone to stalk. Because he feared, if he really set his mind to it, he might as well have found someone—a suitable substitute for Psyche. Even if that were the sole reason he hooked up with Zeus, he wasn't really ready for that; he couldn't really bring himself to do that. And it was for the same reason he never waited too long and allowed himself to settle for the first face that attracted him. Now that he knew this to be his last chance, he offered himself time. He had a chance to weigh how his heart responded to each of the faces that attended these parties.

There was another thing. Henry couldn't help being amazed at how Zeus saw through his dialogs, his stories. He realized only after this brief encounter with Zeus that his need for the conversations had come to an end. That night, Henry found himself waiting for the right person to arrive. He knew it was an open-ended undertaking; there was no keeping track, no going back to select someone he rejected on the first pass. Either he would find her, or he wouldn't.

So, when he smiled to see the lady in the pearl-white gown, he did so because he felt as if he had been swimming in the lagoon on the Green Festival, out of breath, out of energy, counting the strokes before his body gave in and drowned, coming forth to a monitor boat that came from out of nowhere right before fate stepped in. After that smile spread an ecstatic warmth all over his body, he looked intently at her face. It bore such humility that it contrasted violently with her unprecedented beauty. Henry did not bother to follow her. He walked up and stood in front of her.

"This is Henry Apollo," he said to introduce himself.

"The famous Henry Apollo!" She let go a smile that was tinged with pain, but that brightened up the world around her. That smile removed any doubt Henry might have had.

"I have been trying to find—this—for a long time. But now I have found it."

He paused, not to add to the drama or to pay dues to the weight of his avowal, but to collect himself from the waves of euphoria her beauty sent to his way.

"I am severely in love with you," he said. "I don't want anything from you. I just need to know if I can be the one, who, you would always be certain, would be the one waiting for you when you need him. Even if you never have a need."

Henry felt utterly drained upon finishing his words as he instantaneously knew how meaningless they sounded. There was no way to elaborate on them or explicate them. It wouldn't work that way. It had to happen, and happen by itself. There was nothing he could do about it, no matter how badly he wanted to. It had nothing to do with how she smiled. His legs felt heavy, and his eyes became dazed. But while he wanted to recuse himself, the lady was still smiling and shining with that same beautiful melancholy. Her eyes rested transparent, where he could effortlessly enter, bathe in the cold creek streaming down somewhere within, and let go of his weariness.

She knew what he meant and that way she was a friend, but there was nothing she could do, she said with a smile.

Henry felt a hand on his shoulder. It was Zeus, who smiled, and whose smile was merely a reflection of the lady's.

"Henry, I see you've met Selene!" Zeus said before taking the lady's hand and kissing it.

Henry realized why he had never seen her before. When Selene turned her smile toward Zeus, Henry finally understood Zeus's stories. He nodded unmindfully and left the party. He left the city that night.

XVII

⟨≈⟩

PSYCHE REINCARNATED

There was something in the wind blowing inland from the lagoon. With relentless resolve, it changed the landscape of the terrain. Or of the mind. If it were both, Henry couldn't have told. His feet ached not from the long trudge back through the vicious swampland, but from the chagrin of not being able to mark the house he looked for—the small diner in the village adjacent to the swamp.

After encircling the small neighborhood several times, he noticed the gradual increase in curiosity in the looks of the kids playing in the area and in the growing suspicion of the housewives lurking outside. An urge to look behind, which started as a faint graze in the back of his mind, grew into an irritation that made him pause torturing his battered feet. With that, stopped a faint but unmistakable band of noises behind him.

He turned back. There stood an arrested cavalcade of children at a distance required to maintain an anonymity in the backdrop of its collective curiosity. They had been silent, except for their ambulatory shuffles and brushes that they couldn't drown out. Now that they were discovered, their stealth was dispensable. Their whispers, which he had mistaken as a conversation seeping out from the window of the passing houses, their suppressed laughter, which he had mistaken as a figment of his fatigued imagination, the grazes of their huddling limbs, which he had taken for the noise of his own languid shuffling, at once revealed their real faces.

He resumed his walk. So did the procession behind him, now louder and merrier than before. Henry weighed the situation. Night was closing in, and he wanted to retire for the day. He stopped again and looked around. Only then did he recognize the old water tank, which he must have passed by a number of times already.

Henry approached the tank and brushed his fingers against its wet wall and wiped his face with the wet hand. He pushed the cover to open a dark crescent. The tank was filled up to its neck. The water was so clean and calm that the stars reflected on its surface. He shivered in the anticipation of the touch of the cool water on his body. He raised his hands to dip into it and his dirty, bruised hand came into his view. He stood, undecided of defiling the pristine water.

* * *

"Gaia is all grown up now. Why, she is almost seventeen, and what a beautiful lady she has become!"

The pride in the speaker's voice was laced with a sorrow that she herself did not want to recognize.

"My sister took Gaia under her wing," she continued. "She is studying art—has already made a name as an artist—my little Gaia."

She wiped her eyes with her palm, then brightened up with a smile and said, "She's always been a little artist. Those paintings on the wall? She painted them all!"

Her thick and coarsened finger pointed and shivered, and her stout elbow moved uncertainly in the air. Her breath became heavy, and she sat down on a bench.

"Last autumn I caught this bug, a vile one passing through the village, when twenty-seven died in this neighborhood alone. I was lucky enough to survive. But the pain and suffering! Couldn't eat, couldn't sleep, couldn't get on my feet. And my head felt like something was eating from inside."

She paused, as if trying to recollect memories that she still didn't quite believe were hers.

"I thought I was dying. My sister came over from the town. I saw Athena after a long time. She wanted to take me to the city hospital. When she found out that Gaia did all those paintings, he wanted to get Gaia into the art academy. Her husband knows a few people, you know. Athena caught a big fish, unlike us. I am stuck here three times a day serving food to all these vagabonds, while she is having tea with royalty. I know I couldn't afford the school expenses. At least I was sending something for her boarding. It's not much, I know. Not for my sister, no. She got herself a big fish, and now she treats her own sister like a poor relative from country."

She forcefully wiped off the frown, conjured a smile, and said, "But I should not complain. She takes good care of Gaia. My little Gaia."

She started to choke up again. "Only if my buttercup remembered me once in a while—and visited. But I know it's all my sister's doing. She won't allow it, oh, no."

* * *

Under the spell of twilight, what was an attachment to nostalgia became an obsession, before the dying light of the day dwindled perceptibly. In Gaia's face, if Henry now found any resemblance with Psyche, it was only because he labored hard to do so.

But now, in front of him, stood a devastating beauty. They stood on the top of the tall building of the academy for arts, near the parapet. Her long, lush hair flew in the cool air from the lagoon, her body glowing in the setting sun that smiled red and orange on the graceful landscape of her face. The unmistakable dimple was the only indicator of what his voyage out of the town for the last several years was about Henry didn't know what to do after he found whom he was looking for. Or whether there was anything to do at all. But, on setting his eyes on

Gaia's face, all his undertakings in his recent life lost significance. And he failed to glean any significance of what was surrounding Gaia.

That wasn't completely true, though. There was the melting sun. Gaia appeared inseparable from the sun. The smile on her face, orange and gradually turning crimson, was as if made of the very sunlight. The sun was setting quickly and, he apprehended, would leave him with nothing of her. He couldn't settle on whether he should savor this flitting eternity and let it get lost into the despair of inevitability, or renounce this glory and seize and scrape whatever he could of that eternity. His uncertainty was short-lived though, because to wait was to default into inaction.

So, he waited, painful though that was, and when the sun's theatrics were over, the wait became excruciating. He moderated the dispute between his virtue of patience and its travesty, while the water of the lagoon shone brilliantly on her face and, with the help of the breeze, her tendrils caressed her smile, which spread over her face with such intensity that it shrouded everything else. If Henry plunged into a world that was only for him to dive into and then leap out and squirm through its waves, there was still the other world, which managed not to be perturbed and to carry on at its own pace.

* * *

It was a daily ritual for many of the art students to watch the sunset from the roof. They came in flocks and settled into groups. Gaia was there with a friend. A friend whom she had decided to tie the knots with, a graduate from the year before. But their union was not incidental. Gaia's aunt had her hand in everything that transpired in Gaia's world. Gaia's fiancé belonged to a family whom her aunt was intent on getting closer to.

Gaia stood there with her hand in his. The sun, the lagoon and the breeze became a formality, as even her touch in his hand had lost intensity, if there ever was any. But they passed their lives together like those innumerably repetitious waves in the lagoon, one pushing to the next one, that to its next, and so on, until it disappeared in the textureless vastness of the water. The collective life could smooth the creases and crimples in its bosom so that it did not occur to one very often to ask oneself why one needed to still hold someone's hand and still stand on the roof of a building that bore nothing more than an affectation, in front of a sun that had been made commonplace by uncountable pairs of eyes for innumerable years and a sea that was as vacuously excitable as the earth and time itself.

Gaia unclasped her hand from her friend's, which was damp with the sweat of dutifulness and too overly official to bear any warmth. The uneasiness that she knew she caused by detaching her hand reflected on her face, and she glanced to her right. There stood a person whom she did not recognize, but his look had something very unsettling about it. She smiled nervously at him and realized he was focused, with his entire self, on something in her general direction. She didn't think it was her. She might even have been in the way of his subject of attention. She swayed her body, as if to the tune of the music that the lagoon's breeze raised, and discovered that the sight of the stranger followed her movement like a bee hovering on a flower swaying in a breeze. Her smile died, but she attempted at something that came out as a nervous chuckle. She looked forward and crept her hand back into her friend's, as if there was more to life than signifying and justifying the sequences of events.

* * *

Henry left Gaia in front of the drowning sun because he wanted to soften his own fall from that height of joy from finally finding her. The next day, he went back to the Arts Building. His single-minded drive made it inevitable that he would find her. But those encounters did not last long enough to adapt themselves and make those meetings favorable for him to make useful or even harmless moves. In one such instance, he spotted her in a class, painting a nude male whose sole function seemed to be staring at Gaia. For her part, Gaia never let the bliss of receiving the constant flattery of that stare leave her face.

Another day, he recognized her voice coming from a teacher's room.

Through the slightly parted door of the middle-aged male teacher, Henry heard them discussing something that couldn't be related to the class. Inveigled by a stinging envy, he peeped through the narrow opening. The way the teacher touched Gaia and the way she reciprocated, Henry became more concerned about Gaia's fiancé than anything else. Yet another day, he found her watching a play in the front row of the theater flanked by whom he recognized as her aunt and aunt's husband and her fiancé.

Days passed. It was not always another person that Henry would find engaging with. Some days she would be in the library reading books, the themes of which would keep Henry at bay. Sometimes he would find her walking down the street bearing a demeanor he didn't feel conducive to accosting her.

Other times, he would find her sitting alone in a park, in different moods on different days: melancholic, joyful, thoughtful or excitable. But never once would he find her in a mood that was approachable for him—not that he knew what that would be, an approachable mood—until one day, when things transpired a little differently. Different in the way Gaia herself carried her own bearing. She didn't look to be quite her usual self—almost as if a part of her mind oversaw, alert and circumspect, how she herself acted.

Among all the paths he trod in the arts building and around stalking Gaia, one path featured every day: a colonnade joining the main arts building to the library. Every few pillars of that covered pathway featured a small sitting area on both sides. Gaia met her friends at one of them every afternoon. As part of his stalking routine, Henry would walk the arcade from the arts building to the library and then back to the arts building. He would wait inside the main door of the library in the foyer for a few minutes before starting back—long enough to make the interval between his coming and going look unsuspecting. While in the arcade, he made sure not to look at Gaia, or her friends. His gaze would scale the stone pathway, focusing to catch words from her voice, something he could sift out even from a sizable throng.

One day during his afternoon drill, when he just entered the library to wait for his customary few minutes before starting to walk back, he sensed things transpiring a little differently. His premonition made him sweat. As his foreboding sensation peaked, as if on a cue, Gaia walked through the door, with an affected expression of looking for someone or something. She halted for a moment as it was evident that the only other person in the foyer was Henry. But she gathered herself and let her eyes wander, seemingly making up in her mind something to do to justify her presence there. She took a few steps forward and stopped right by Henry, in front of a stand that had a few books on display. She distractedly picked up a book and flipped through the pages, but there was no doubt in Henry's mind that that page-flipping was just a pretext to linger there to let Henry approach her.

All this time she has noticed me following her, and now she is here to let me talk to her. I need to talk to her. But I don't know what to say. I even don't know whether I want to talk to her. I don't know what I want from her. Do I want her? I don't know, I don't care. She is here, standing in front of me, expecting me to talk to her. But I don't know what to do.

She put the book back on the stand and turned toward Henry and shooting what felt to Henry a piercing glance for an excruciating moment, she dispersed her focus from him. Henry still stood petrified. Gaia pursed her lips, took a deep breath and, throwing an uncertain glance back at the books on the stand, sighed with a condoling smile, and let her shoulders droop. That picture of her, Henry thought, perfectly described his tribulation.

Then, suddenly excited, she turned around and returned to her friends in the nook where she had left them earlier.

Henry was mortified. He wanted to tell her something. He had to tell her something, and he did not know what. There was nothing to tell her. He never told anybody anything. After spending that whole night awake, he assumed he never had anyone because he never talked to anybody. The real talk. Because everybody needed him to talk to them. And it seemed fair to him. Talking was not something he could have justified in order to get someone. But something had to be done to reach someone, now that he thought about it. There was nothing else, it seemed. Nothing other than talking.

So, Henry's agenda remained the same, except that he started looking for a chance to talk. To Gaia. He spent days thinking about what to tell her. From all his efforts to glean words that would make sense to present her, the only thing he could think of was, "How have you been, Gaia?"

How have you been ... How have you been ... Henry pronounced this in his mind innumerable times. Why he could pack so much fervor into those four words he couldn't explain to himself. Might it be that, boring through his infatuation for her beauty and her resemblance with someone whose enormous loss he would never recover from, and his intense desire for her presence and her touch, Henry had reached a place where all his love could care for was Gaia's well-being. Each time he uttered those words—How have you been—his consciousness jangled in his want for her well-being.

He settled on that: How have you been, Gaia? That's what he would utter. What would happen after that—Henry didn't think through. He resumed his afternoon walk through the arcade to the library and back to the arts building, hoping she would give him another chance. Just one more chance.

But it wasn't to be. It took three more torturous weeks before it descended on Henry that Gaia had set up a chance for him to accost her, and he had failed to grab it. So, it was now his turn to do the same: to set up a rendezvous.

He resumed the trip to the arts building roof during the sunset on the Wednesdays when he knew Gaia would go, too. Her fiancé did not accompany her most of the time anymore. She just stood there in the evening breeze for a few minutes and then stepped down the stairs and walked back home. There was a landing mid-way up the staircase, where he realized he could scheme a solitary encounter with her, even though only for a few seconds. Gaia left the roof right after the sun set. Henry calculated the time for her to reach the staircase, and he positioned himself at the bottom of the staircase at the right time. When he heard her footsteps, which he recognized with his whole heart, he started climbing up, synchronizing a rendezvous at that landing, where the encounter always appeared sudden. There was not much free space to fret either. It was shadowy, and there was minimal traffic at that moment.

"Gaia!"

His prolonged silence had taken a toll on his voice, and were it not for the tiny enclosure of the staircase landing, his groaning mumble might have got lost in the air. But Gaia halted and looked at his face.

Her smile told him that she knew Henry had set up this encounter, but it also told him that she did not depreciate it because of that fact.

"Gaia, you recognize me, don't you?"

"No." Her response was too quick to be fervent, but too blunt to be pretentious.

"You remember me from your mom's diner, don't you? Six years ago?"

"Six years! That's a long time. Why should I remember you from that long ago?"

"At your mom's diner."

"Wait. My mom has no diner. She never had one."

"In the village."

"Village? She never lived in a village. Well, she might have, but not since I remember. She has always been here in the city."

"Isn't that your aunt?"

"Who is my aunt? Okay, you are talking about my aunt. Yes, she lives in the village and owns a diner. And speaking of which, I think I did visit her a few years ago. Only for a month or so."

"Gaia—you are Gaia, right?"

"Yes, that's what I am called."

"I don't understand this."

"See, I need to leave now. My mom will be worried."

She sidestepped Henry to cross him, brushing against his body on the way, but stopped a few steps down. Turning back, she said, "And you don't understand quite a few things."

She smiled again and left.

Henry stood there for a moment as a bitterness seeped into him from that meaningless and worthless bit of conversation. She was not, or at least she claimed not to be, the person he thought she was. *But what was that about me not understanding a few things?*

Henry thought about starting it all from the beginning—to meet her at a place that gave more space to think and talk than the shady landing of a steep staircase in late afternoon, and tell her what he wanted to tell her, and let not the confusion of her identity distract him from his plan. He had no doubt about who she was. For one, she never denied that she was not Gaia. Then, she did stay over there in the village. But he did not care about that anymore. He never did, but when he met her, that confusion had disturbed his bearing.

XVIII

THE DESECRATION OF
GAIA

As Henry started to chalk up another plan to meet Gaia, he received a letter that was signed by Echo Narcissus, and addressed to no one. The envelope had H. Apollo inscribed on it.

"Have you ever suffered the dilemma that arises when passion dictates your moral orientation on how you conduct with people? One's world often does not accommodate sufficient choices as to let you overlap among them and still allow you to maintain your moral integrity. I was banished from the Castle—accused of adultery. This was merely a scheme, and the allegation was wrong in its literal meaning. But I could not bring myself to deny it in front of the courtiers. Because I have had, in a sense, committed an infidelity of much graver import. I don't rue the consequence either. Because it allowed me to introspect more freely and understand a few things of highest significance.

"After you left the Castle, and I purchased the flower store from Hermes, a thought bothered me to no end. My action threw me into an unbearable dilemma. I had grown a strange affinity to you that, for me, had bordered on adultery. Not in its usual sense. But the feeling I grew for you infringed upon something that kept me alive for the last two decades. I need to talk about the genesis of that.

"It happened on the night of the Green Festival twenty years ago. I had decided to join the competition not because I loved Narcissus or wanted to get married to him. I wanted to be near Narcissus, so that I could kill him. He had stolen the life of my closest friend at the Festival the year before. A few months after my best friend's murder, my mother took me to an official for a favor—an unlawful increase in the allowance she received as the widow of a deceased priest.

"I stood there on this beautiful rug, looking at its exquisite patterns as my back dripped a cold sweat of fear and indignation as I was fully aware of the reason why I accompanied my mother. I remember that moment vividly because a pair of admiring eyes offered me a warm relief—someone who stood on the other side of the room, whose eyes burnt with a passion that won't be matched in decades to come. My tender youth, my mother used as bait for that official. My mother's plan succeeded, but for the crooked official it was more lucrative to lead me to Narcissus. He gets paid in both ways—in kind and in cash. He poisoned my mother to force me into participating in the swimming context. What she did not know I was more excited to join the contest than I was scared, as I already knew the fate of my friend the year before. I was prepared to defend myself from his hitmen and then avenge her death by killing Narcissus. But I had underestimated the danger. Were it not for a fellow contestant, that night I would have had the same fate as my friend.

"That fellow competitor saved my life, and in the process, broke one of his fingers. It had been a long swim and he was worn out after the fight. At that point, I couldn't trust anyone. I thought he also had some purpose of his own for saving me. But before he passed out on the boat from the trauma, he smiled at me. There was something in that smile that changed something. That smile—of that of a soul utterly and completely hopelessly love-stricken—got burnt into my memory. And those eyes. It was the same pair of eyes that bore the burning love in that official's house.

"When he lay there unconscious, I nursed his broken finger. I left him in the boat to himself, and swam back to shore, because I still wanted to kill Narcissus. But that night, when they started the preparation for the wedding ceremony, the love-stricken face of my savior came back. I had been delirious on the boat. But that night, the whole night, I had time to ruminate, and by the time dawn broke, I had a different reason for living: I was in love. And this saved the life of a person whom I hated all my life—Narcissus, my newly wed husband. Because there was no way for me to kill Narcissus without getting caught and executed, something I couldn't allow to happen anymore. Though I never found a trace of that man again, I never lost hope to see him one day.

"For the first few years, I didn't know what to do with my life in the Castle, which was essentially a prison and whose overlord was a paranoid psychopath. I was the first and only person who got to know his cruel game and then successfully arrived back at the shore. I had thought the first thing he would do after the ceremonies were over was to have me murdered. I had to win that contest to come out alive. But when I decided to live on, my sole task was to save myself from his people. But he didn't look that intent on killing me yet. At first I didn't know why. Over time, I realized he wanted to exploit the situation in his favor. He didn't stop his womanizing ways, but used me as a trophy wife, as a presentable consort whom he would take to business meetings and dinners and galas. I played my part very well, over time buying his trust so much that he asked me to be his representative with his guests when he was abroad.

"But that wasn't getting me anywhere. So, I decided to get out of the Castle. To build my own funds. When I showed interest in business, Narcissus found it helpful and let it be. I grabbed all the business opportunities that came my way.

"Then you came along with your proposal to buy that flower store. The first night at dinner with you, I looked into your eyes and knew that you came from a different world. A world that I myself belonged to too. And then something about you... something unexplainable struck a violent blow on me. An emotional turbulence that impinged upon my love for my savior on the boat. Then there was that day when you wanted to inspect my blistered palm. I noticed a scar on your ring finger in the shape of a wedding ring. That spawned a memory that was so old that I could not put a finger on its source. At least not at that time.

"I felt something was different about you. Something very strange about you that wouldn't let me put a finger on, nor would it let me feel at ease. After closing that deal with Hermes, the whole thing started to drive me mad. The struggle among my lifelong faithfulness to my love, my unconscionable passion for you and the confusion about your identity. I was not in a sane state of mind, and Narcissus used this to his advantage and accused me of adultery. He set me up, which I could have easily refuted. But it wasn't about the truth. It had never been. At the Castle, it was all about power, and by then I myself had a few strings in my own hand, not to mention a few powerful connections that could match Narcissus. But I did not care anymore.

"I agreed to be sent off with a settlement to live in the village— essentially a self-imposed punishment. Then one day it descended upon me: The man in the boat was you. And so was the man at that official's house. And the wedding ring-shaped scar on your finger was the one that *I* had nursed, with a piece of cloth that I had tore from *my* green chiton in the Festival. It turned out that it is for *you* that I had deceived you, albeit I had been looking for you for the last twenty years, in which I never lost hope of finding you. But when reality descended upon me, it accompanied an inextricable mixture of feelings, and memories of feelings, and feelings of memories that wouldn't let me rest for days on end. When that storm wound down, I found in myself a different person, whom I don't recognize. She has nothing to do with the memory of twenty years ago.

"Last week I came to know that you are back in the city after a long trip.

"I have nothing to long for anymore. It's just that, today, looking back at my life, I only see a monstrous void. And even if that is behind me now, an unredeemable sadness lingers. Coming to recognize your identity, I thought you deserved to hear this out—no less than I deserved to let this out. So here. That is the long and short of my life."

Henry sat with the letter in his hand and could only look at it as a story that belonged to someone else. Never before did he hear a word from Echo that was meant for him. Now that these words finally arrived him, they changed everything so completely that they sounded foreign to him. Those words unearthed the pain and sadness, even if of such unfathomable magnitude, they belonged to such a mundane life, it attempted to breach the ethereal and heavenly portrait he had maintained of Echo in his own mind. The apparently indifferent and sententious face that he had witnessed of Echo at the Castle—now he found them more agreeable. It did not put any dent on her beauty, nor on her personality; it hid, and at the same time protected, the image of her that Henry had created in his mind.

This letter attempted to breach that image. He wanted an excuse to defend it. He pushed the advent of this reality, this long long overdue advent of the reality, away. Echo herself had offered him that weapon: her moral dilemma.

What would have happened if the man in the boat were someone other than him? She would still have deceived him, this Henry, with the flower store. If she couldn't love the other man, then she couldn't love him. It therefore followed that she couldn't love anyone. It didn't matter how long she waited for him; it could've been for anyone. It didn't matter. It took him some time to let the thoughts sink in. Once they sank he felt good. Or so he thought.

He resumed his pursuit of Gaia as normal business order, as if nothing happened, merely a new coat of paint had been added to his life. Only, at daytime, when he stalked Gaia through the maze of the arts building and library, he would frequently find himself lost, even though he knew the place like his own palm. At night, laying on his back and fixating his eyes on a particular dot on the ceiling, his thoughts would turn his mind over.

He assured himself that Gaia was his life. But when he extended his hand to touch that life, his fingers reached a lacquered screen and their tips burnt with longing to feel the texture—smooth and rough, downy and bristly—and the temperature—the burning heat and freezing cold. When occasionally he breached the distance from Gaia that he customarily maintained, and wanted to let himself soak in the aura of her beauty and her smell, he couldn't help but feel an acute dullness.

Days passed, and Echo's revelation quietly relegated all the elements that gave his present life a face. When he became aware of a hovering mist of insanity around him, he had to calm himself by a draught of that very insanity, and he chalked up a plan. He schemed with such composure that he thought he had finally coped with his troubles. He felt no need to revise the plan before its execution.

Nonetheless, the dullness persisted, which actually helped him run his plan. Henry's difficulty in approaching Gaia had been partly due to the fact he didn't know what to talk to her about. Now that he had set himself a completely different goal, it suddenly became much easier to walk up to her. And talk.

He had a proper wash, a haircut, a shave, a clean and freshly ironed set of clothes and waited in front of her classroom. When the hour struck, the bell startled Henry. Students started walking out of the class, and mistook Henry for a visiting professor or something to that effect, pausing to offer him respectful gestures. Then Gaia walked out with her sketch book pressed to her stomach and a sack dangling from her shoulder. Henry stepped behind her and called in a clear voice.

"Gaia."

She stopped, throwing a look meant for a complete stranger who could be of social importance, and then glanced around to make sure she was not alone yet.

"Gaia, you need to talk to me," Henry said with an urgency that clearly sounded of effort to suppress his desperation.

Gaia stood unfazed. "May I ask who I am talking to?" She said.

"You don't know me." Henry paused and managed a smile. Then he said, "That's only because you don't remember me. But that's beside the point."

Gaia seemed to suddenly recognize him; her hands around her art book tightened a little, and her posture stiffened. She took another look back, quicker this time.

"I know it looks very odd that I should go so far to give you this information," Henry continued, "but, I have thought it over at length, and have come to the decision that it is a very important thing that you should know."

"And what is this about?"

"It's about your mother."

"What about her? This is not actually about my aunt in the village, is it? Are you sure you aren't mistaking me for someone else?"

"Gaia, I don't have time to waste. I know what I am talking about. But it cannot be here. Why don't you meet me at the arcade tonight?"

Gaia didn't try to hide her disbelief and apprehension.

"You don't have to come alone," Henry said. "You can ask your fiancé to join us. He needs to know about this, anyway."

"I am not sure I want to do this. Besides, I don't want him to know anything about my mom. Even though I am not convinced there is any mystery about it."

"In that case, he can just come with you, and you can just talk to me. He does not have to take part."

Gaia listened without any apparent conviction.

"Why do you have to tell me this tomorrow night?" she said. "Can we do this later? I want to think about it."

"Gaia, I am leaving town tomorrow night. I have to. And more things are at stake than you can think of. I may not see you ever again. And there are things that need to be straightened out."

He paused and suddenly realized that his Gaia was standing right in front of him, confused and intimidated, and that he had exchanged many more words with her than he had planned for. Her beautiful eyes blinked in fear, her lips pursed, blobs of sweat forming below her nose. A few strands of hair flew helplessly around her neck. He was overwhelmed by an urge to take her into a hug. But that was only for a moment. Understanding the ease with which he could stir fear in her brought a cruel pity for her. And he did not have any doubt anymore that he would follow up with his plan.

"You take your time to think about it, Gaia. If you decide to see me, I will be there at the seventh nook. Two hours after the moon rises. If you decide not to come, I will wait there for half an hour, and then I will be on my way out of your life."

Gaia looked at him. Not a single muscle twitched.

Henry smiled. He advanced his hand a trifle toward her direction, paused and then turned and walked away.

* * *

When the ruthless smile of the waning crescent clambered over the trees and the motion of the leaves was stunned by the land and lagoon exchanging winds, two pairs of steps were heard approaching. A night bird whistled at a distance. As the footsteps neared, Henry couldn't recognize the sound of one of them—a heavy and long gait that followed Gaia's. Henry retreated further into the shadow of the seventh nook and waited until his guests appeared in front of him. Gaia was accompanied not by her fiancé, but by a very large man.

"You want to ask your companion to leave us for a moment?" Henry said as he stepped out of the shadow.

"It's okay," she said, a little startled. "Atlas can stay."

"Gaia, I trust your company, but this is something that I really need to talk to you about. Alone."

"That is not going to happen," Atlas interloped. "Either I stay here or we both leave."

Henry had to look up to get a good look at the man's face and found that it belied his ruthless voice, and his corpulent body. His face was surprisingly animated and imbued with reverence, love, and pity for Gaia. For Henry, in his tiny eyes, there was just a mote of intimidation.

Henry said with nonchalance, "Mister, could I talk to you for a moment?"

Atlas was affected by this change of events and brought his hands from behind his back. "What about? Go ahead. Speak."

"It's her safety that you are concerned about, correct?"

Atlas didn't seem to understand if that was a question or not. He nervously raised his right hand and scratched behind his ear.

"Come with me for a second," Henry said as he started walking in the direction they came from. "I have some information that may have a serious impact on Gaia's life."

Henry stopped to let Atlas go past him, then said, "It is very important that she alone decides whether she wants to keep it to herself or to divulge it."

Henry signaled Atlas to get behind a nook. It was dark on that side.

"Looking at you, I can tell you want the best for her," he said.

As he passed the column, Henry picked up a large knife resting in the dark.

"Still, it is up to you what you want to do."

Before Atlas could stop or turn around, Henry raised the knife high and brought it down into the back of his neck. It went through his throat and emerged from the front. Before the huge body buckled at the knees, Henry positioned himself to buffer it in order to soften the thud of the fall. Before Henry came out of the nook, he stood in the slanted light from the arcade and looked at his clothes to check for blood. His black garb concealed the thick red wetness. He wiped his face with the garb for good measure.

Gaia waited anxiously in the middle of the arcade. Her face filled with fear when she noticed that Henry was alone.

"Where is Atlas?"

"He has agreed to let us talk in private."

"What? Okay. But where is he?"

"Waiting in there."

"Atlas, are you there?" Gaia waited a couple of seconds, then started toward where Atlas had been. "Why is he not responding? I want to talk to him."

Henry stepped in her path and said, "Gaia, you don't want to see him now."

"What do you mean? Get out of my way!"

"You really don't want to see him, Gaia."

"What have you done to him? Have you killed him?"

"Gaia, you don't understand. There are lots of things that you just need to ignore now. You don't need to get worked up over every little thing. There are more important things hiding beyond the small things that you keep yourself busy with."

"Stop this nonsense. Let me go." She tried to pass Henry.

As Henry held her, Gaia scratched at his hands and cried, "Let me go! Let me go!"

"Stop it, will you?" Henry growled through clenched teeth and jerked her violently.

Puzzled, Gaia paused, and Henry held her in a tight embrace. Then he took her off her feet and moved beyond the wall in the dark and brought her down on the ground. Henry tried to soften the drop, but she was hurt and started flinging her arms and legs. Henry tried to tear her dress off, but the fabric proved to be too strong, and her gyrations didn't help.

"Stop it!" he growled. Grabbing her shoulders with both hands, Henry gave her another jerk. A thudding noise came from around her head, and she stopped moving. Henry grabbed the neckline of her dress and ripped it to her knees. He placed his hand under her knees and lifted her out of the dress. Then he got rid of her undergarments.

By the time Henry climbed onto Gaia's body, the crescent moon had reached above the truss over the arcade and framed their bodies inside a slanted square of soft moonlight. An owl on a nearby branch watched the blood trickle down Atlas's neck and heard Henry's breath getting faster. After a groan full of pitiful sobs, Henry let his own body drop onto Gaia's. He fondled her bare body with his tired hands. And he kissed her face. He combed through Gaia's hair with his fingers, and found the sticky, wet spot on her head. He jumped up. In the dark he couldn't recognize what was on his hand, but he wiped it off with her torn dress and ran. When he returned with a doctor, there was no body.

XIX

ECHO OF THE SILENCE

Penelope wears a golden gown. The diamonds stitched onto her chest sparkle with the slow heave of her breathing. Her hands, neck and ears are adorned with fine, elaborate jewelry in gold and diamond. Her frock sways gracefully with her elegant gait. Her eyes, fixed toward her destination, bear no sign of confusion, and neither do they glare with insolence. They are devoid of sadness but do not exude happiness. They are not burdened with cynicism, but they give no hint of modesty either; they don't burn with intensity, yet they don't languish.

Her neck is long. Her lips, colored in red, exude a softness that promises volubility, but at the same time their grace hints at prolonged silence. Her long fingers are clasped on her stomach, not too high to suggest urgency, and neither do they sag in lethargy. She doesn't walk fast, yet Henrique has to exert quite an effort to keep up. She does not have an entourage, but he cannot get any closer to her. Henrique feels weak, and he speaks out.

'Penelope. I am back to you. I have taken my revenge and made up for good. I have soiled myself. The most violent way you can imagine. I am not pure anymore. And now I am here to take you back. You don't believe me, do you? How can you not? You are my creation. You are not? Maybe. But why don't you believe what I say? You should know that much. Maybe it is me who doesn't know? That could be. It must be that. But what does it matter? I am saying that I have done it. I raped her. And I have taken her life. That is not good enough? What else do you ask for? You mean it wasn't a rape? Why? I imposed the task on my-self. Why don't you ask her what she thinks about it? It doesn't matter what she thinks of it? Of course it doesn't—it's me we are talking about. Not about her. So, could it be called rape? Maybe I cannot call it that. Because I loved her. I fell in love with her. But that happened because of you. You don't believe that? But you must believe this: Why else could I create you? And think about this—you waited for me, didn't you? You waited for me to come back to you. You did. And here I am. For the second time. I was the first one, wasn't I? But you did not take me. You said I was too pure. That you couldn't touch me because there was nothing to touch me about. Now I am back again. I have soiled myself. And you can touch me now.'

'You have soiled yourself, Henrique," Penelope said. "And I can touch you. I can. But why should I? What should I touch you for? You have nothing that I could want.'"

XX

❦

AN EPILOGUE FOR
HENRY APPELMAN

Henry Appelman pulls out the invitation letter, while the conference webpage loads on his laptop. The Internet connection strength moves between two and three bars. The router must be in the hotel office. When he chose his room, he asked for something at the back of the building, where the traffic noise was minimal. Now it appears that he sacrificed Wi-Fi strength for quiet. He can change the room tomorrow—the hotel is hardly full. Now he just wants to go over the list of speakers once more. As half of the banner image freezes at the top of the webpage, he unfolds the letter. Directions to the venue are given in detail—a little too much detail that only compounds his woes.

Henry is aware of this idiosyncrasy of his. He frequently gets distracted by the peripheral and tangential interpretations a new road may offer. And his strange predilection for unlikely alternatives sometimes lead him to pick a path that later turned out to be not so favorable. Its a trait he doesn't necessarily consider a vice. As it has different implications on different facets of his life, some of which turns out quite productive sometimes. His writing for instance. For him, writing have always been about exploring where a seed idea may lead him to. And a great many times some unlikely paths have taken his stories to unexpected but wonderful and satisfying destinations. Serendipity is not always that coincidental and intentionless. There is always an intent and willingness to chose uncustomary paths behind landing at exotic, flamboyant and novel harbors.

The conference is scheduled to start at nine-thirty in the morning. The letter promises a drive of less than fifteen minutes from the hotel. He plans an early start to allow the possibility of getting sidetracked, if it comes to that. The following morning that safety margin won't be necessary. Then again, there isn't always another morning.

The progress bar on the browser has moved, and the page displays half of the speakers at this moment. Sorted alphabetically by last name, his is at the top. "Henry Appelman"—a placeholder alias awaiting his photo. As he waits for the rest of the list to load, Henry tries to estimate the number of years that have passed since he last saw her. His sexagenarian memory toys with his mind, refusing to let him get more precise than 'four decades.' A few more seconds to load the list will not be the end of the world, but Henry is restless to the point of reassessing his earlier idea of deferring his room change until tomorrow.

"Penelope Nash," the screen interjects.

The names and the images of the speakers are framed in the quirky embellishments of an amateur web designer. They have used a five-year-old photo of him that he found unostentatiously youthful. He scrolls down. Penelope's photo reveals a total stranger with thick glasses and stern wrinkles, and a hairstyle and attire that kept up with the winds of fashion. Henry tries to see through those changes to mitigate the image that he has carried for about two thirds of his life. It doesn't quite come off. But something in that face, something quite inconspicuously familiar, hides beneath the indifference of the picture and impinges on his viewing.

Then it strikes him: that hint of a dimple on the right cheek of her slightly contrived pose. It offers him the thread of familiarity that he seeks. As he tugs at that thread like a loose end, the whole fabric of his oblivion comes undone. With that, starts a parade of memories from their shared youth.

The very first time he saw her was at a literature center. They participated in different study circles that occasionally overlapped. She smiled seldom, and her dimple didn't exist without her smile. Her eyes were always occupied in a strangely organized confusion from the handful of responsibilities she volunteered for. It was one year before their paths crossed, when they both joined the same critique group.

His reminiscing goes on like weaving a fabric that conjures a tapestry of images. That she might want to listen to what he had to say, and to dissolve her eyes in thoughts. That once in a while she would actually open her lips, whose sole purpose had seemed to be to maintain the grace of hiding away words of wisdom. That when she talked, she would let be known the secrets of a wonderful, melodious voice. That she could smile, even laugh. Laugh at *his* attempts at jokes, conjuring dimples that could safekeep memories for a lifetime.

Once their group went on an excursion to an island, where, even among all the others, the magic of her presence made him aware that the two of them were on an excursion of their own, separated on their own island, hidden away from the eyes of others, who were not privy to the sights that they had made their own. She wound him up at opportune times, for example, to take her hand under the pretext of helping her step down from a boat.

The day couldn't finish without the enchanting twilight by a pond cut right into the sea, where cypress trees lined up and sang like sirens in the magical evening wind. They talked of their fate—why, rather than how, they ended up there—and she offered him a look into his eyes that could build a bridge by which he alone could enter her castle, any time he wanted.

He never entered, and now he was not too sure why he didn't. Maybe because he knew that he could afford to step on that bridge at will, at a more auspicious time, whenever he wanted to. Only that he had no idea when that time would have come.

One day that bridge became enshrouded in a fog of confusion

resulting from an act that she committed. He turned and walked away. Unannounced.

Only months later did he realize that he had misconstrued her act. Or was it his predilection for adopting unlikely alternatives? Her act could have had many interpretations, but he ended up picking one that was, in hindsight, the most unlikely and detrimental to the trajectory of their relationship—essentially the doom of it. Oh, the enormity of penance for foibles so paltry! She had laughed with a friend of Henry—a laughter that Henry thought she reserved only for him. Henry was not jealous. But he deemed that the bridge he had thought was laid solely for him, maybe wasn't laid, after all, solely for him. Maybe everything that he thought had been special between the two of them were not special after all. It was but one interpretation of her one action, and an odd one for that matter. But it was the one he chose. And he walked away from her life.

The process of him realizing the falsity of that interpretation was long. It was no epiphany, but a process of comprehension that unfurled at such a slow pace that it warped the context along the way. By the time he realized that she had learned to laugh because of their shared merriment, that when she laughed with others it was only the reinforcement of that bridge, not the doom of it, he had strayed an awfully long way. Once he took that wrong path, there was no next morning.

Is there one now?

* * *

Henry follows the driving directions printed in the invitation letter to the dot, and ends up at the conference an early bird. He lurks with the anonymity of his facial hair and other small matters that come with four decades' hiatus.

Seating on a chair that gives a better view of the entry, Henry keeps an anxious eye on the door. A few minutes before time, other speakers start arriving. As the minute hand closes in to the hour, Henry feels increasingly restless. Then she enters. The glasses and the hairdo are unmistakable from the picture on the conference webpage. Her measured smile maintains a nonchalance—too conspicuous to be unaffected. She brushes a glance over Henry's face before catching him undecided on how to approach her. Or whether to approach her at all.

Her pronounced indifference leaves him by the door, to watch her trotting through the room from the full height of her grace. Before reaching the podium, she is swarmed by fellow speakers. Henry finds himself caught between spaces separated only by the question of whether crossing the threshold really matters. The dearth of an answer echoes in the monstrous weight of nothingness.

Milton Keynes UK
Ingram Content Group UK Ltd.
UKHW040632091123
432260UK00002B/124

9 798988 409410